THE WIDOW OF JERUSALEM

The Widow of Jerusalem

Alan Gordon

ST. MARTIN'S MINOTAUR ≈ NEW YORK

www.minotaurbooks.com

Library of Congress Cataloging-in-Publication Data

Gordon, Alan (Alan R.)
    Widow of Jerusalem / Alan Gordon.—1st. ed.
      p.   cm.
    ISBN 0-312-30089-1
    1. Feste (Fictitious character)—Fiction.   2. Crusades—Fourth, 1202-1204—Fiction.   3. Crusades—Third, 1189-1192—Fiction.   4. Fools and jesters—Fiction.   5. Tyre (Lebanon)—Fiction. I. Title.

PS3557.O649 W53 2003
813'.54—dc21

                                     2002024507

First Edition: March 2003

10 9 8 7 6 5 4 3 2 1

To my brother, Joshua Gordon,
for being there when I need him

ACKNOWLEDGMENTS

The author respectfully thanks Sir Steven Runciman, Kristian Molin, Maurice Chéhab, Merton James Hubert, Nina Jidejian, Wallace Fleming, J. E. Tyler, Peter V. Edbury, and the many contributors to *A History of the Crusades*, from the University of Wisconsin Press.

And Jesus sat over against the treasury, and beheld how the people cast money into the treasury: and many that were rich cast in much.

And there came a certain poor widow, and she threw in two mites, which make a farthing.

And he called unto him his disciples, and saith unto them, Verily I say unto you, That this poor widow hath cast more in, than all they which have cast into the treasury:

For all they did cast in of their abundance; but she of her want did cast in all that she had, even all her living.

—Mark 12:41–44

The Widow of Jerusalem

ONE

There once was a dwarf named Scarlet . . . well, that's a long tale, and best left to another day.

—*JESTER LEAPS IN*

Theophilos," intoned my wife as we rode along.

Portia looked up at her adoringly from inside the sling.

"Theeeeophilos," said Claudia again.

"Awooooo!" burbled the baby, dribbling for emphasis.

"Now, that was a very good try," I said encouragingly.

"It's a difficult name," sighed my wife. "It would have been easier if you stayed with Feste."

"Not much," I said. "She won't be using the *f* sound for at least a few more months. Besides, I'm back to being Theophilos for the near future, so stick with that. I think she's starting to get the hang of it. Perhaps she's inherited your knack for languages."

"Speaking of languages, we should pick one to use around her on a daily basis," said Claudia. "We've been changing with every country we've passed through. She'll never learn anything at this rate."

"Or she'll learn them all," I said. "But I see your point. Which one do you prefer?"

"Where do you think the Guild will send us?" she asked, trying to look unconcerned.

I shrugged. "Hopefully nowhere right away. We need to catch up on what everyone else has been up to. Tell you what. I'm Danish and you're Sicilian. What say we split the difference and speak Tuscan for now? It's the preferred dialect at the Guildhall, anyway."

"Tuscan it is, Signore," she replied, and we kept to that tongue for the duration of the journey.

We had left Constantinople the previous August. Fled with the permission and encouragement of the Imperial Treasurer, grateful that he let us leave on our own instead of at sword's point. Or in matching coffins. We traveled west to Thessaloniki, where our colleague, Fat Basil, awaited us. We tarried there for the winter rather than continue directly to the Guildhall because of Claudia's pregnancy. Portia was born on Twelfth Night, appropriately enough for a daughter of fools. In late March, Claudia felt sufficiently recovered to ride again.

We took the Via Egnatia across the mountains to Durazzo, where we added the mule to our company, then headed north. Passing through Orsino was a difficult business, as I was officially banned from the city for the crime of sneaking away with the young Duke's mother, who now rode beside me nursing his new half-sister. We solved it in part by removing our makeup and motley and donning the guises of a pair of returning pilgrims. We did have a clandestine meeting with the Duke in the dead of night. Mark had shot up a foot since we had last seen him, and it was clear that he was not far away from assuming his full title without the interference of a regent. Nevertheless, upon seeing us he became a boy who missed his mother, and tears were shed by all as the two embraced.

Yet she came with me once again, honoring the oath she made to the Fools' Guild when she became a jester and the one she made to me when she became my wife. Maybe someday, when Mark has full powers in Orsino, the two of us will be able to settle there in safety.

Then again, maybe we won't. A jester's life can take some odd turns.

From Orsino, we rode north along the Adriatic coast until we reached Capodistria, where we managed to find passage to Chioggia for two fools, a baby, two horses, and a mule. We made a brief foray into Venice proper to look up Domino, but I was saddened to find that the old fellow had made good on his threat to retire once his long-standing efforts to stall the Fourth Crusade from leaving came to their conclusion. His replacement as Chief Fool was quite amiable, but we struck out the next day for the Guildhall.

So it was that we found ourselves on the old familiar beaten path that wended its way several miles through the forest south of our little patch at the feet of the Dolomites. It was the middle of June, in the Year of Our Lord 1204, and the sunlight streamed through the leaves overhead to make its own motley patterns around us. Zeus, my arrant steed, must have sensed that we were coming home at last, for he pricked up his ears and nickered happily. Hera, who carried my wife and daughter, plodded on, one part of the world being just as good as any other in her opinion, while the mule, whom we named Hephaestos for his ugly mien and iron will, brought up the rear, laden with provisions, utensils, instruments, props, and costumes.

"I'm a bit daunted by the prospect of finally coming here," said Claudia. "I've been hearing stories about the Guild from you and Fat Basil and the rest of them for so long. It sounds like a fantastical place, all strange angles and hidden rooms."

"It is larger than life itself," I said. "But not that much to look at, if truth be told. The hall is high and deep, with wooden alcoves on both sides for classes. There's a simple stage at the rear and benches for the audience or for meals. Stables to the right and sleeping quarters in back. I had my own little room as a senior fool, but they'll have to come up with something a little larger now that there's three of us."

"I wonder what they'll think of me," she said.

"They will love you," I said. "As I do."

"Not as you do, I hope," she said. "One husband at a time is enough for me."

"Honored to be the current holder of the position, milady."

"But won't they resent my being made a jester without going through the formal Guild training? They all spent years at the Guildhall, most of them from childhood."

"You've had training," I said. "From me, and from Rico and Plossus in Constantinople. Combined with your own experiences and your abundant talent, that makes you as well-educated a fool as any in the Guild. And you're not the first to be certified as a jester without going directly through the Guildhall."

"I hope you're right," she sighed.

"Mind you, Father Gerald and Brother Timothy will probably want to put you through your paces," I said, a bit maliciously.

She smiled. "As for that . . ." she began, then stopped as a bird sang out off to the right somewhere. She looked at me warily.

I drew my sword, and she quickly dismounted and had her bow strung and an arrow notched, all the while shushing the baby.

"You know the countersignal," I said.

She nodded, pursed her lips, and made a chirping noise that would have passed as a bird for anyone who didn't know these woods.

The call we heard before was repeated, with two notes added. I sheathed my sword and dismounted.

"This way," I said, leading Zeus and the mule into the woods. She followed. When we had come about fifty feet in, I handed the reins to her, went back, and brushed away signs of our trail. I saw no one on the path in either direction.

When I rejoined my family, another fool was standing there. It was my old friend Niccolò, in woodsman's garb rather than motley and looking uncharacteristically grim. He touched a finger to his lips, reached for Zeus's reins, then realized what horse he was reaching for. He snatched his hand back quickly before Zeus could get any carnivorous ideas and took the mule instead.

We walked as quietly as we could into the heart of the forest until we came upon a small hut and stable in a clearing. A young man I didn't recognize stood in the doorway, bow and arrow at the ready. I spotted another high up in a tree.

"We can talk here," said Niccolò, then he grinned and pulled me into a bear hug. "Long time, Theo. It's good to have you back. And is this the legendary Lady Viola?"

"Claudia, if you please," she said, coming forward to shake his hand. "I use my Guild name here."

"Of course," he said. "Forgive me. This is Jean, and the fellow up in the branches is Hermann. Forgive the rude reception, but we have a bit of a problem."

"So I gathered," I said. "What's going on?"

"Jean, go watch the road," he ordered. The man in the doorway nodded and disappeared noiselessly into the woods. Niccolò beckoned us in. There were a couple of pallets laid against the walls. He motioned us to one and plopped down on the other.

"We can't risk a fire, unfortunately," he said. "By David's lyre, Theo, I never thought I would see you with a family. No offense, Mistress Claudia, but we've known this fool a long time. We knew he was mooning after someone all these years, but we never thought he'd catch up with her."

"Were you really?" she said, looking at me with a teasing smile.

"Of course," I said. "Everything this man will ever tell you is the truth. Now, Niccolò, what is going on? Why the lookout and diversion?"

He turned serious again. "The Guild's gone, Theo."

"What? What happened, a raid?"

[5]

"Well, a raid did happen. I'm sorry, I'm telling it badly. The Guild lives on, and everyone's safe. But they've fled the Guildhall."

"Why?"

"Rome, Theo," he said. "There's been pressure building up to quash the Guild. Our friends have been steadily losing their influence with Innocent, and what with the Feast of Fools and the troubadours associating with groups the Church has labeled heretical, it was only a matter of time. You heard this was a possibility when you were here last."

"But I hadn't heard about anything imminent," I said. "Why didn't we get word in Constantinople about all this?"

"I think Father Gerald thought you had enough to worry about," he replied. "There was nothing you could do there to help the Guild here."

"Does the Guildhall still stand?" I asked hesitantly.

He nodded. "We cleared out everything but left the building up. Just in case we ever come back. The village is still in the Guild's name. I made sure they took your belongings, Theo."

"Thanks," I said, then I smacked my forehead in chagrin. "I had an iron box buried back by the cemetery..."

"I packed that, too," he said, grinning.

"That was supposed to be a secret," I said sternly.

"Then you should have been better at keeping it one," he replied. "Like I said, we were thorough."

"What about the monastery?" I asked. "What happened to it?"

"It remains," he said. "We filled up the ends of the tunnel connecting it to the Guildhall. No one should be able to find it, not that that matters."

"Well, it will protect the monks from any connection. And Father Gerald?"

"Bundled safely and grumpily into an oxcart," he said. "Brother

Timothy, Brother Dennis, and Sister Agatha have gone with the Guild as well, so we should be able to start afresh without too much difficulty. You know where the haven is?"

"Yes," I said. "How much of a head start do they have?"

"About a week," he said. "But you should be able to catch up with them. They're traveling as a group of pilgrims returning from Rome, and most of them are on foot."

"Good," I said. "Thanks for keeping an eye out for me. How long are the three of you going to remain here?"

"Another fortnight," he said. "Until we've intercepted all of the troubadour routes and gotten the word out in every direction. There's only a couple of fools unaccounted for now that I've spoken to you."

"All right," I said. "We'll head out in the morning."

"How disappointing," said Claudia. "I'll never get to see the Guild-hall now."

"We may get it back someday," said Niccolò, but he sounded doubt-ful even as he said it.

"I wonder how the village will survive without us," I mused as I stretched out. "Paolo the barkeep will miss my patronage, I'm sure. Did you fetch my tankard from him?"

"Yes, Theo," said Niccolò, sounding weary.

"Good," I said. I turned to Claudia, who was looking at me quiz-zically. "The jesters keep personal tankards at the tavern. Those who are on missions leave them with a coin inside on a special shelf, so that no matter how badly things go, they'll have the price of a drink waiting for them when they return."

"Will I get my own tankard?" she asked.

"Of course," I said. "And once we get the new site set up, we'll—" I sat up suddenly. "What about the Scarlet Dwarf?" I asked.

"What?" said Niccolò in confusion. Then his face fell. "The Scarlet Dwarf," he muttered. "We forgot about that."

"What's the Scarlet Dwarf?" asked Claudia.

I scrambled to my feet. She looked at me with dawning suspicion. "Where do you think you're going?" she demanded.

"I'll be back," I promised. "And I'll be careful."

"Wait a second, I've heard that before," she protested. "And it's never good."

I walked out of the hut. She followed me. "We have a baby now," she reminded me.

"I know," I said. "You had better go and take care of her."

I left her standing there, fuming. Not the first time I've done that. Probably won't be the last, either. Part of the price for marrying someone like me.

I stayed in the woods, following the direction of the road. I came to the outer wall about a hundred feet from the gate and climbed a tree to survey the village. There was a guard at the gate but no patrols as far as I could see. That made sense. The village had no strategic importance to anyone who was not an angry pope, so there was no real need to make it into a sizable garrison. I suppose the Guild could have taken on the occupying forces with ease, had we chosen that course, but that would have done us more harm than good in the long run. We function better when no one pays us any attention.

The sun set while I perched there. A few torches were lit at the center of the village, mostly by the tavern. There were soldiers aplenty heading in that direction, of course. Our fickle barkeep needed to make up the business he lost from plying fools with ale. I waited until the noise of merrymaking was readily audible even from where I sat, then climbed along a limb overhanging the wall and swung down to the ground.

I took a deep breath, then dashed along the fields surrounding the town until I reached the back of the tavern. I pressed my back against the wall, and was about to make my next move when a pair of soldiers came out to relieve themselves. I ducked behind the rain barrel. Fortunately, they were more interested in the matter at hand than looking around. After a lot of ale passed through them, they reentered for a refill.

As soon as the door closed, I leapt on top of the rain barrel, then swung myself up to the roof. I crept quietly to the peak and peered down toward the front. No one was walking in the main street of the village.

I risked sitting up to get a look at the Guildhall. There were torches lit there, just enough to limn it against the mountains behind it. It gave me a pang to see the soldiers walking where only fools belonged.

"It is rather a grand thing, isn't it?" whispered Claudia in my ear.

I nearly fell off the roof.

"Just what are you doing?" I asked.

"Helping my husband," she replied simply. "You can't arouse both my ire and my curiosity without there being consequences. And someone has to watch your back."

"I can watch my own," I said.

"If that was true, then you would have seen me following you," she said. "Anyhow, I've seen the Guildhall, so let's get whatever we're supposed to be getting and get on with it."

"Well, since you're here, lend me your ankles," I said.

"Gladly, husband, but would you tell me why?"

"I need to hold on to them when I lower you off the roof."

"Ah. I knew there would be a logical explanation."

She stuck her feet in my lap. I grasped her ankles tightly, and she began to crawl down the roof. Then she looked back at me.

"Another question, husband?"

"Yes?"

"After you lower me from the roof, what is it that I am supposed to do?"

"Do you see the sign over the tavern door?"

She glanced down.

"I see it."

"Remove it."

"And then?"

"And then we go back to the hut."

She slithered back up toward me, her face a mask of anger and bewilderment.

"Do you mean to say that you are risking both of our deaths, or at the very least imprisonment and separation from our daughter, to steal a sign?" she hissed.

"Yes," I replied.

She smoldered for a moment, but thankfully did not catch fire.

"All right, lower away," she sighed, placing her feet back in my lap.

We inched carefully down the roof until we were at its edge. Some martial drinking song was being bellowed out by the customers inside. I dangled my wife headfirst over the entrance and lowered her, bracing my feet against the edge.

The sign was a broad, painted wooden plank suspended on a pair of hooks, which made it easy to remove. Claudia took it and tucked it under her arm. I was about to haul her back up when the door swung open and a particularly tall and extremely drunk soldier walked out and came face to face with her.

Of course, the face he faced was upside down and painted white. He blinked. She blew him a kiss with one hand, and with the other whacked him on top of his head with the sign. He stumbled back into the tavern. I pulled her back up, and we scrambled over the roof to the rear of the tavern.

We could hear a commotion inside, then the sound of the front door opening.

"It was a ghost, I tell you," shouted my wife's victim. "Floating in air right here."

"A ghost, eh?" said someone else. "What did it look like?"

"It was a woman," said the soldier. "She was upside down. But I think she was pretty. She tried to kiss me."

There was a roar of laughter at this.

"You see," I said as we ran through the fields. "You're in town only a couple of minutes, and already you've become a legend."

"You, on the other hand, may become a ghost if you don't come up with a good reason why we did this," she said. "I can't even see what's on the sign. There's no moon tonight."

"Give it a night's rest, my love," I implored her. "I'll tell you on the morrow."

We went over the fence and stumbled through the woods until we found the hut. Niccolò was inside, bouncing Portia on his knee. She looked at him with devotion.

"Thank Christ," he muttered when we came in. "This child does not want to sleep."

"Give her over," commanded Claudia, and soon the baby was fed and out.

"Did you get it?" asked Niccolò.

I held up the sign.

He shook his head. "You're insane," he muttered. "And she's crazy. It's a match made in heaven."

"You know why I can't leave it behind," I said.

"I know, I know," he replied. "I'm sorry we forgot about it. I should have known you would do something like this. But at least you got away with it. Now, get some sleep. You should be on the road at sunrise."

✻   ✻   ✻

The next morning, a merchant family emerged from the forest.

"Which way do we go now?" asked Claudia, as Portia began babbling at everything in sight.

"Back across the Adige river, then we follow the road north through the Alps until we reach Innsbruck."

"We're going to Austria?"

"Yes."

"Oh, dear," she sighed. "I suppose we'd better speak German to Portia."

"No, let's stick with Tuscan. We'll only use German when we need to. It's such an ugly language. I'd hate to hear it coming out of a baby."

We rode on. When the sun was a little higher, Claudia picked the sign out of her saddlebag and held it in front of her for examination. Portia immediately tried to grab it, pointing excitedly at the painting on it. It was of a little man, dressed in scarlet, juggling three tankards of beer and grinning merrily.

"So that's the Scarlet Dwarf," she observed. "Why is it so important to you?"

"It's a long story," I replied. "One with intrigue and ambition, love fulfilled and love unrequited, the ignominious deaths of the high and mighty as well as the low and forgotten, the reasons for which are known to but a few."

She put the sign back in her saddlebag.

"Nothing like a long ride for a long story," she said. "And you know how Portia loves to hear you talk."

"Very well then," I said. "It was in the summer of 1191, after the recapture of Acre by the Crusaders, that I first met a dwarf called Scarlet. It was a day filled with screams."

Ⓣwo

The reason that I'm here to-night
No one here can help but know,
Plain to all discerning sight:
Didn't grow.

           —WILL CARLETON, "THE
           FESTIVAL OF THE FREAKS:
           THE DWARF'S RESPONSE"

There was a tavern.

    There's always a tavern in your stories, remarked my wife.

There is always a tavern, a place where fools gather after dark, after their patrons have passed out in their palaces, exhausted from an evening of carousing and arousal, fueled by folly and doused by wine. When the normal people drift off, dreaming fitfully of the terrors that await them when they are once again sober, the fools slip away, pallid in the darkness, the moonlight reflecting off their white faces. Nodding familiarly at the night watch, they pad warily past the vagabonds settling down in the narrow alleys, seeking out the one tavern that never closes, with the tapster who welcomes any with a coin without asking how the coin was obtained, although not without assaying its true worth, inserting it between howsoever many teeth as are still available.

A tavern where God and the Devil, walking the cold earth in disguise, may meet by chance, see through each other's camouflage, and yet still sit down for a drink on neutral territory, eventually exchanging maudlin reminiscences about the old days before things all went so horribly wrong.

The tavern in this oft-conquered hellhole called Acre didn't even have a name. Tucked back in an unpromising dead end of an alleyway near the idle mill in the center of town, it had somehow kept going during the recent siege, running on a secret reserve of wine in the cellar while the populace slowly starved around it. The price of a drink there was at a fine balance between affordable and exorbitant, the tapster keenly attuned to the ever-shifting market. But on this mid-August day, I didn't care what I had to pay as I staggered across the baked earth outside the city walls.

I wanted a drink. I wanted one so badly that I would have paid with my own blood if that was the going rate.

I passed through what was left of the gate at what was left of the Turris Maledicta, both having taken the brunt of the French catapults and the English sappers during the recent siege. The wreck of the massive war machine that the troops had nicknamed Bad Neighbor was still there, a monument to its owners and a testament to the greater accuracy of Bad Kinsman, the Turkish counterpart that did it in. I headed west into the city until I found the entrance to the alley. Out past the seawalls, the sun was setting. As I came up to the tavern door, I heard music—singing and lutes, the sounds that would normally have me reaching for my own instrument without a second thought.

I entered the room and waited for my eyes to adjust. Only a single candle spat its light into the unreceptive gloom. The tapster, an ancient Syrian with a wine-stained beard down to his waist, stood in front of a shelf holding buckets of viscous liquid that he would ladle into earthenware cups that may have been washed once in their existence.

Off in the darkest corner of the room, I glimpsed a pair of faces, eyes closed and mouths open. Perfect harmony emerged, so beautiful that the rest of the imbibers sat in absolute silence, not daring even to breathe loudly while it persisted. "The Lay of Charlemagne," a song of noble warriors and conquest, sung by a troubadour and a jester.

I should say a troubadour and a jongleur. Ambroise was from Evreux, and insisted that *jongleur* was the proper term. He was about my age, but had been a fool much longer, having started training as a child of six. He had black, greasy hair that he plaited unevenly in back, and he generally smelled of yesterday's meal and last week's drunk. Yet, for all that, he had a good voice and a nice touch on the lute.

The troubadour was Blondel, a golden-haired youth so impressed with his beauty that he must have been surprised he didn't illuminate the room by himself. He had ingratiated his way into the Lionhearted's inner circle, perhaps even his bedchamber if rumors were to be believed. His conquests of both sexes were legendary for such a young life. Even now, he was turning his long lashes toward Ambroise so seductively that everyone in the room could not help but feel jealous of the greasy fool. But I knew it was part of the act, the twin poles of beauty and coarseness, the contrast making the harmony more miraculous as a result.

They finished, and the room burst into applause, which they acknowledged with noble nods. Gradually, the clapping died down, except for one pair of hands that kept on, slowly, methodically, ever louder. They looked at me in surprise as I walked toward their table, continuing the clapping until I sat across from them.

"Bravo, fellow fools," I said. "A beautiful performance. A breath of fresh air in a room that needs one badly."

"Hello, Theo," said Ambroise. "We were wondering when you would show up. Thought you'd be joining us for lunch."

"Something came up," I said. "A distraction."

"Well, still time to join us," said Blondel.

"Did you bring that report?" asked Ambroise.

I handed him a sheaf of papers from inside my tunic. He took it and squinted at it in the uncertain light.

"I suppose it will have to do," he muttered. "You could at least have put it into verse."

"Something for you to do on the voyage home," I said. "If you ever leave this place."

"As for that, we'll all be leaving soon, I should think," said Ambroise.

"Thanks to us," added Blondel. "Now that you're here, you can drink to our recent success."

"I'd love to," I said. "What success are you talking about?"

"The truce," replied Ambroise. "Don't be dense, Theo. You've been right in the thick of things. But we were the ones who prevailed upon Richard to make the deal with Saladin. It's all worked out beautifully. Richard received the first installment on the money yesterday. Just a few more weeks, and everything will settle down and we can all go home again."

"And he gave some to us!" chortled Blondel. "So, you'll be drinking on our coin tonight. Isn't it wonderful?"

"It certainly is," I said. "Congratulations. I would be happy to drink to your success. There's only one problem."

"What's that?" asked Ambroise.

"You haven't had any," I said.

They looked at each other, amused.

"Now, Theo," Ambroise admonished me. "We know that you've been in the middle of everything working your lute off while we've been languishing in the royal retinue, but we have done our share for the Guild. There's no need to be bitter."

"You've been in here all day, haven't you?" I said.

"Of course," answered Blondel. "A well-earned respite. It's work influencing a king as strong as the Lionhearted. Many long, hard nights." He nudged Ambroise, who chuckled.

"Listen," I said, holding up my hand.

They stopped, Ambroise tilting his head to the side.

"I don't hear anything," he said after a few seconds.

"Nor do I," said Blondel.

"I'm not surprised," I said. "There are too many walls around here to hear what's happening outside the city. And the noise has stopped, anyway."

"Noise? What noise?" asked Blondel.

"The screaming," I said.

"What screaming?" demanded Ambroise. "Was there an attack? I heard no alarum being raised."

"There was no alarum," I said. "But this treaty wasn't quite as solid as you said it was. The payment from Saladin wasn't enough for the Lionhearted. He had asked for the return of that chunk of wood that everyone thinks is the True Cross. He didn't get it. He was supposed to return the Saracen prisoners as part of this deal, wasn't he?"

"Yes," answered Blondel. "What about them?"

"That was the screaming," I said. "The prisoners. The English took them outside the walls where the other army could see them. Then they took them, row by row, and slaughtered them. Axes, mostly, but some swords and spears. They just cut them down where they stood and brought the next line in. Didn't waste any arrows. Good old English efficiency, but there were so many that it took the better part of the morning to kill all of the men."

"All of them?" gasped Blondel, turning pale.

"Well, I think they kept the wealthiest ones alive, the ones who might still bring a ransom. Always better to be rich, isn't it? So, they killed all the men first, broke for a quick meal, then started on the women. Same thing, only they raped a few of them first. The Turks attacked somewhere along all of this, but they were too few and were driven away. And then came the children. I couldn't help thinking what it would be like to be a child, to watch your father hewed down in front of you while his hands are tied behind his back, then your mother the same way, then to be dragged over to their corpses and see the monster whose language you can't understand raise his axe and even if you did try and plead for your life—"

"Stop it!" shouted Ambroise. "This couldn't be happening. Richard said—"

"He says a lot of things," I said. "He told his soldiers to kill them this morning. Sorry I wasn't in the inner circle. If I was, I might have tried to stop him. But thank goodness you're both part of it. How useful to the Guild you are! What were there, three thousand hostages?"

"Twenty-seven hundred," whispered Blondel.

"My error," I said. "Well, then I guess it wasn't as bad as I thought. Forgive me for interrupting your celebration. You didn't hear it. The screaming, I mean. Probably drowned it out yourselves, with all of that beautiful noise you made. I heard it. Couldn't do anything to stop it, of course. I'm just a fool. I think I might still hear it. There was this one high-pitched cry that—"

They rushed out the door, heading back to their lord and master.

Bad planning on my part, I thought. I should have at least waited for them to buy me a drink.

"I'll get some wine," said a voice below my right elbow.

I looked around uncertainly.

"Odd," I said to the air. "There's a voice inside my head that often says that exact phrase. But this voice isn't inside my head. And it's a different voice."

"Down here," said the voice. I looked, and saw a dwarf sitting on a three-legged stool by the table. I leaned down to peer at him but could not discern his features.

"*Stultorum numerus*," he muttered softly.

"*Infinitus est*," I responded, completing the password. I held out my hand. "Theophilos."

"Scarlet," he replied, grasping it. "I'm the Chief Fool of the Kingdom of Jerusalem."

"Which makes you the Chief Fool of nothing at the moment," I said.

"Which makes me the man you report to," he retorted. "Those two idiots think that with the Guild out of sight, they can do whatever they want. I'm hoping for better from you."

"You have it," I said. "I was told at the Guildhall that Scarlet was the Chief Fool of Beyond-the-Sea. But I thought you were based in Tyre."

"I am," he said. "But I have a particular mission to fulfill in Acre."

"What's that?"

"To get you as drunk as possible," he said. "Sounds like you need that right now."

He hopped off the stool and went to the bar. "A pitcher and two cups," he called up to the Syrian. He took a coin and tossed it high into the air. It landed in a cup by the barkeep's hand.

The Syrian handed him the pitcher, which made a comforting sloshing noise as the dwarf carried it back to the table. He placed a cup in front of me and poured, then sat back and waited.

"Aren't you going to have one?" I asked, pointing to his empty cup.

"I'm going to get drunk along with you," he said. "But I'm giving you a head start. You're a great, lumbering lummox of a man. It's going to take a few to have any effect. But I'm just a dwarf. If I have more than two, then I'll be dead to the world, and I'll wake to find myself having a game of catch with drunken soldiers. With me as the ball. So, drink up, brother Fool. I'll join you in oblivion soon."

I still couldn't make out his features. All I could see were his eyes, the pupils reflecting the candle. No, they shone of their own accord, I'm sure of it. And I might have wondered about that, but there was a cup of wine to be drunk, and another, and yet another after that. On the fifth cup, Scarlet poured one for himself and held it aloft.

"To forgetting," he said softly, and he drank.

And I can't remember the rest of that evening.

I woke in a small room with the sun shining directly into my face. I was lying on a pile of old straw, a blanket tucked around me. It was only when I saw the dwarf sitting cross-legged on a cushion by the opposite wall that I remembered some of the previous day.

Now that I could see him more clearly, I observed that he was clad from head to foot in no color but scarlet, down to his boots and up to his cap. He had a neatly trimmed beard and mustache, both black, and hair that was gathered in a single braid in back.

His eyes were deep blue, like the sea on a calm day. The flicker of the previous night was a mere twinkle now.

I couldn't guess his age, as is often the case with dwarves. He was, when we both stood up, about half my height. Less when I stretched, which I commenced doing immediately.

"Good old Guild training," he said, watching me with amusement.

"Get limber in the morning," I began.

"And you'll stay limber at night," he finished, and we had a brief mutual chuckle, remembering the motto of Brother Anthony, who had been the tumbling instructor at the Guildhall, a man who could still bend backward to touch his toes at sixty.

"When were you there?" I asked.

"As a child, and not for long," he said. "I've been out here since I was fourteen. Feel better?"

"Hung over," I said. "By which I mean, yes, a little better, thanks."

I looked around the room. It wasn't much larger than the two of us. My bag was at my feet, and a smaller one lay in the far corner. There was one large, shutterless window by where he was sitting.

"How did we get here?" I asked. "More to the point, how did you get me here? I'm guessing that you didn't carry me."

"No," he said. "I dragged you by the feet along several streets and up two flights of steps, taking special care to bang your thick skull on each one of them. What do you think, Fool? I paid someone to carry you. Not the first time I've done that for a colleague, I assure you."

"Thanks," I said. "How far into the day are we?"

"Midmorning," he said. "There's a nice view from here if you're interested."

I looked out the window. We were on the third story of a building that must have been in the eastern part of town, because I could see the bend in the outer wall at the Turris Maledicta.

On the other side of the wall, the bulk of Richard's army was bustling about, packing their gear, collecting spent bolts and arrows, repairing straps and saddles and disassembling some of the larger machines of war for easy transport. Even Mategriffon, the great wooden fort that Richard had brought in pieces from Sicily to be constructed anew before the walls of Acre, was being taken apart, its bolts and pins carefully packed into barrels.

"Where are they going?" I asked. "Aren't they going to finish rebuilding the walls here before they head home? This city is far from being defensible."

"Home?" he snorted. "Do you really think that they would come all this way and lose all those men just for Acre?"

"Acre, and Cyprus, and Sicily," I said. "Not a bad haul for one crusade. King Philip already went back to France. I was hoping maybe Richard would want to get back to his territories before Philip started moving on them."

"A smart king would do that," said Scarlet. "A rational king, one who cared about his subjects, would do that. But Richard's bloodlust

[21]

is up. Twenty-seven hundred hostages was a mere snack, something to whet the appetite. He won't be satisfied until he has Saladin's head on a pike, the True Cross in his saddlebag, and possession of Jerusalem."

"Madness," I exclaimed. "There're miles of bad road between here and the Holy City, and Saladin's men behind every rock."

"Nevertheless, he leaves tomorrow. Which is where we come in."

I looked down at him. He hadn't moved from the cushion, hadn't even looked out the window since I woke up.

"Have you slept at all since last night?" I asked.

"Slept?" he laughed. "I'll sleep when I get back to Tyre. After I deposited you here, I went everywhere, pumping my sources for whatever information they had and eavesdropping to get the rest. One of the great advantages of being small, by the way, is that big people with big plans tend not to notice you when you're listening to them talk about the big plans with their big voices. Now, I have a modest little plan of my own, but I will need your assistance, and possibly Blondel's, if we can tear him away from the nearest looking-glass long enough. But mostly you. I've been hearing quite a lot about you, Brother Theo, and if even half the stories are true, you're one of the most reckless, adventurous, near-suicidal and, I'll say it, foolhardy fellows the Guild has ever produced."

I bowed in reply. He stood up, grinning.

"I can use someone like that," he said.

"Use away," I said. "What are we going to do?"

He hopped up on the windowsill and leaned out, looking north.

"There's a supply ship that landed up the coast a ways," he said. "They'll be unloading onto wagons tomorrow. Enough food and weapons to last the Crusaders all the way to the Holy City."

"Where did you hear this?" I asked, impressed.

"They sent a rider down to inform the troops," he said. "A very thirsty lad who's been at sea too long. I persuaded him that the urgency of his message was not as important as the urgent needs of a lively wench of my acquaintance, especially as the King wished not to be disturbed at night. He agreed with the logic of my assertion, and allowed me to be his guide to these earthly pleasures. He should wake up in a few days."

"So, the Crusaders leave tomorrow, and they don't know about the supplies yet."

"Exactly."

"But they'll learn of them soon enough, won't they?"

"No," said Scarlet. "They won't."

"Why won't they?"

"Because we are going to steal them," he said, and the grin grew even wider.

ℭHREE

His fool ... was not only a fool, however. His value was trebled in the eyes of the king, by the fact of his being a dwarf ...
　　　　　　　　　　　　—EDGAR ALLAN POE, "HOP-FROG"

H ave you got any rope?" I asked.
　　"As a matter of fact, I have," he said. "Why?"

"Because if I'm going to be hanged, I'd rather do it myself," I said. "I want to make sure the job's done right. Why are we going to steal the Crusaders' supplies?"

"Grab your gear and come walk with me," he replied.

We descended the stairs and emerged into an inn that was deserted at the moment, the working people having gone off to scavenge what they could from the corpses outside the walls. Scarlet raided a cupboard for some bread and water, which we proceeded to divide unevenly between us.

"The odd thing about this part of the world," he said with his cheeks stuffed with food, "is that everyone more or less gets along fine in spite of their religious beliefs, at least until the Pope gets involved. There're always some local squabbles, especially when someone in charge dies and there are too many relatives fighting over too little inheritance, but that's normal. The current mess started when Reginald of Karak got greedy and started attacking Saladin's caravans. Saladin responded, and suddenly everyone was slaughtering each other while invoking Christ and Allah. Jerusalem could have stayed in Christian hands for a reasonable tribute; instead, the citizens got all high and mighty, which kept them going for about twelve days before they surrendered. And even then, everything could have been worked out, but once the folks back west hear *Jerusalem*, it's cross-sewing time, and now everyone's honor is at stake."

"And there's nothing like a full-scale holy war with the promise of plenary indulgences to send the honorable soldiers to their honorable slaughter," I said.

"Exactly," he replied. "Now, the only way we can restore peace is to end the Crusade. I thought we were there when you persuaded King Philip to go home—"

"What makes you think that was me?" I interrupted.

He grinned. "It sure wasn't those two, and you're the only fool who's connected with the French. Even if it wasn't you, you might as well take credit for it. That will get you the price of a drink at the Guildhall. Anyhow, with the French gone, and Richard looking for a truce, I thought we were looking at the end of the war. But now it's back in business. Which brings me back to my job."

We finished eating and walked out into the city.

"Jerusalem cannot be won by what's left of the Crusaders," he said softly. "It's sixty miles to the city, and Saladin will block every well between here and the city walls. Even if the Lionhearted does make it to Jerusalem, he cannot hold it. It's in the middle of nowhere. I always thought God must be one of the Fools' Guild to make somewhere so remote so holy."

"So, if we divert the supplies, then Richard won't attempt it?" I asked.

"Right," he said. "Hopefully, we'll accomplish two tasks. We'll discourage the attempt, which means he'll keep to the coast, which is where most of the Frankish settlements are. Saladin can live with that. His troops want to go home, too. And if we can get the supplies sent to Tyre instead, then we'll help a place that has practical strategic value, unlike Jerusalem. Tyre anchors the entire coast, and it was the only city to resist Saladin successfully."

"How did they manage that?" I wondered.

"You'll understand when you see it," he said.

"Wait a second," I protested. "I have to go to Tyre?"

"Well, it's less likely that you'll be hanged there than here," he replied impishly. "Especially once we take the supply convoy."

"So, you and I come charging out of the hills, waving our swords, and frighten the whole group north?" I asked.

"I do have a plan, you know," he said, looking wounded.

"Let's hear it," I said.

"You will pretend to be a captain under Richard's command," he said. "You will meet the convoy, suitably attired, and present them with a document in Richard's hand instructing them to send the supplies to Conrad of Montferrat, the current commander in Tyre."

"To pull that off, we are going to need the Lionhearted's seal on the orders," I said.

"Precisely," said Scarlet. "So, the first step is to steal the seal."

I looked at him.

"Do you have a plan for how we're going to do that, too?" I asked.

"Of course," he said. "Find Blondel, and meet me back at the tavern by noon. Oh, and make some excuse to your lord. You'll be away for some time."

My patron at the time was a smallish king from a smallish kingdom tucked away in a section of the Alps that no one particularly wanted. He was good-natured enough for royalty, but when called he came crusading with all due seriousness. He was a vassal of France, and when Philip left Acre, he gravitated toward the Duke of Burgundy, the highest-ranking Frenchman remaining. His name was Denis, and he was nineteen years old.

"You want to do what?" he exclaimed when I informed him of my plans.

"Sire, I have encountered an old friend who is but lately come from Tyre," I said. "I know that you are going forth to attack the Holy City. It will mean nothing but fighting the entire way, and I will be only a distraction to you."

"But the whole point of having a fool is for the distraction," he pointed out.

"True, milord, which is why, as a Christian and your loyal servant, I cannot let my profession be a hindrance to your divine task."

That straightened his shoulders a bit.

"Very well, Fool," he said. "God only knows I owe you this favor. You've saved my life twice since we started on this campaign."

Three times, I thought, but he would never know about the other one.

What was that all about? asked Claudia.

Another story. Let me finish this one.

I found Blondel in the Pisan quarter, strumming to an admiring throng of merchants who were trying to reestablish their pre-Crusade trading relationships before the Venetians and the Genoese did. I caught his eye, and he quickly came to a triumphant conclusion, accepting compliments with grace and coins with a flourish of his plumed hat. Then he came over to me.

"Not comforting your king?" I said.

"Enough, Theo, you've made your point," he said. "Richard is making preparations to leave the city, and he has no need of me until later."

"What's later?"

"There's a triumphal feast at the castellum tonight. They'll be needing plenty of entertainment. Want to come?"

"Want to and need to. What about Ambroise?"

"Ambroise is holed up with a bottle and a whore somewhere. I haven't seen him since last night."

"Well, it's you I wanted to talk to."

"What's up?"

"Where does Richard keep his signet ring?"

He frowned.

"That's the sort of question that invariably leads me to regret giving the answer," he said. "Why do you want to know?"

"Scarlet has a scheme," I said. "Where's the ring?"

"What makes you think I would know?" he said.

"Don't be coy. This is Guild business we're doing."

"In a locked bronze coffer by his bedside," he said. "The key is on a ribbon around his neck and under his tunic. He's kept it like that ever since his signet-bearer went overboard at Cyprus."

"I remember you mentioning that. I figured that the fellow was helped into the sea by someone."

"By me, actually. It turned out that the signet-bearer was working for the Cult of the Assassins. Anyhow, since that incident Richard hasn't trusted anyone with the seal but himself."

"Is the lock pickable?"

"Yes," he said. "I've picked it once or twice for practice. The problem isn't the lock. It's the room."

"Why? Which room did he take?"

He turned to face the castellum, which rose over the city like a mountain. It was set against the center of the north wall. It had a central tower that had to have been sixty feet tall and flanking towers only slightly shorter.

"He sleeps in a room in the middle tower," he said, pointing to a window that was halfway up. "He likes the view. He impresses himself with how far he has risen since he arrived in Acre."

"The stairs to the tower are guarded?"

"Of course. And another guard is outside his room at all hours."

"That ruins the direct approach," I mused, looking up at the center tower. Its sandstone blocks were too smoothly joined to permit scaling from the outside.

"Did that little bastard tell you why he needed us?" asked Blondel.

"He says he has a plan. Want to know it?"

"I have a feeling that I don't," sighed Blondel. "Let's go."

Scarlet was already waiting for us at the tavern, three cups, a pitcher of wine, and a small repast on the table before him. He waved us to a pair of stools, and we sat meekly before him like schoolchildren.

Blondel filled him in on the signet ring and its protectors.

"That's about what I figured," said Scarlet. "Getting the ring will be hard enough, but returning it before anyone discovers the theft is the part that may be truly impossible."

"May be," I said. "But not definitely, I take it."

"The way I see it, there are three levels and three of us. One in the tower, one on the roof of the castellum, and one on the ground."

"To do what?" asked Blondel.

Scarlet reached into his cloak.

"You asked me about rope earlier," he said to me. "I, of course, prefer smaller things." He pulled out two balls of twine and handed one to each of us.

"You told me yesterday that you could have Richard anytime you wanted," said Scarlet.

"I may have been exaggerating," Blondel said quickly.

"Let's find out," said Scarlet. "Get into his room. Get him drunk enough to fall asleep, then lower the casket from the window to the roof. Theo, you'll take it from there."

"The roof is patrolled," I pointed out.

"But not heavily," said Scarlet. "Not with the bulk of the army still camped outside the walls. So, you get the casket from Blondel, carry it over to the side overlooking the wall, and lower it down to me. There's a trench where a sapper's tunnel caved in just to the left of the center tower. That will give me enough cover to have a candle lit and still be hidden from anyone on the ground. I'll pick the lock, use the seal, then send it back up to you, Theo."

"And I tie it back on the string," I continued. "Then Blondel brings it back up, and goes to sleep."

"Fat chance of that happening," he said. "I'll be a disaster in the morning."

"We only need you to be beautiful tonight," said Scarlet. "In the morning, the two of us will be long gone."

"A pity you'll miss my beheading," sighed Blondel. "I can think of a hundred ways this can go wrong."

"And I can think of twenty-seven hundred reasons why you have to do this," I said.

"Yes," he said, looking down. "So can I. Look, we can keep this simple. Give me the document, and let me do the sealing in the room. Then I can just give it to you in the morning."

"There are two reasons that won't work," said Scarlet. "First, we need to be out of the city and at the supply ship before dawn breaks. Second, if you're caught tinkering with the casket, that will be awkward, but if you're caught tinkering with the basket and have the document as well, that would be fatal. I don't want Richard to know what we're doing."

"But you'll have both," objected Blondel.

"Yes," replied Scarlet. "So I'll be the one taking the brunt of the punishment. In fact, if they catch me, the two of you should have enough warning to get out."

"Oh, good," said Blondel. "On the run in hostile territory with

Theophilos. A dream come true. Well. See you at the party."

He stood, swallowed his wine in a gulp, and left.

"Do we trust him?" asked Scarlet.

"He's still one of us," I said. "He's young. The Guild training is still fresh in him, so he's game for anything. You have to survive to my advanced age to become disillusioned."

"And yet, aged one, you persist," he observed, smiling. "Why?"

I shrugged.

"Survive a little longer, and you get past the disillusionment," I said.

"How old a man are you?" he asked. "I would have guessed around thirty."

"Old enough to be a fool. Lucky enough to be this old. I should have died any number of times."

"Cheer up," he said. "Maybe you'll get your chance tonight."

The feast was one of those sad exercises in forced frivolity. The women of the town, having lived on a siege diet for so long, were thin to the point of emaciation, and desperate enough to do what they had to do for food and money. They decked themselves in silken finery and dug up what jewelry they were able to secrete when the siege began. They painted on their smiles and danced bewitchingly enough to entice the soldiers, whose desperation was of a different type entirely. Wine was produced, probably from the King's own stock, and that erased any last vestige of discrimination from the soldiers, who vied feverishly for the attentions of these scrawny hens. Fights broke out, and were broken up and resumed in fits and starts. It was all a grotesque parody of that thing some call chivalry.

In all this time, you never had a woman?

Not in Acre, my sweet. I see too much desperation and deception in my life to settle for the semblance of love. I try and hold out for the thing itself.

[31]

Noble, but impractical. I don't believe it for a moment.

Then believe this. A fool appeared less desirable to those who would do it for money. The soldiers got all the ones worth having.

The great hall of the castellum had also been tarted up for the occasion. When the town finally surrendered to the Crusaders, those fortunate enough to be allowed to leave had to abandon their belongings, so there was ample silk to drape the walls and dangle from the balconies. The hall was enormous, capable of holding five hundred people comfortably. I think twice as many crammed inside on this night, flowing in and out as the increasingly drunken men followed first this woman, then that barrel of wine, then some tray of sweetmeats. The musicians were up in a balcony, and Blondel and I glided through the room, singing the praises of those gathered and telling amusing stories at the expense of the equally gallant soldiers of Saladin.

This was one of the rare occasions in which I saw the Lionhearted unarmored, his mane of auburn hair towering over the sea of pates before it. He cut a mean caper himself, leaping about with a gold goblet that seemed never to be empty, bellowing along with the song of the moment.

The French in attendance remained uncharacteristically sober, choosing to watch their counterparts act like idiots. I knew that they were much less enthusiastic about venturing forth to Jerusalem—they would have been content to remain in Acre until the walls were repaired and then to follow the example of their King and return home.

The Duke of Burgundy held forth on one side of the raised platform at the rear of the hall. A cousin to the French king, he had been the intermediary on all of the missions calling for diplomacy. Now, he had been left behind in command of the French troops, but under Richard's command and dependent on the English for funds. He was careful now to laugh at the Lionhearted's attempts at humor.

With him was Henry of Champagne, the nephew of both kings. He was just beyond a boy, with a pale, young beauty that was due in part to the illness that had beset him when he first arrived. Indeed, illness probably wiped out more of this army than any Saracen blade, but they were all guaranteed places in Heaven, so who cared how they went?

Henry was talking to a man I had never seen before, who wore Frankish garments as far as I could tell. He was about my height, with thick, black curls cascading greasily over his collar. At one point, I saw the other man burst into laughter at something. Henry only smiled a bit wanly. I had never actually seen Champagne laugh, which I regarded as both a character defect and a personal challenge. I decided to take him on.

I attempted to cut through the reveling throng to get closer to the higher commanders, trying to catch any useful information, but the mass of bodies was too thick. By the time I reached the rear, Richard was standing with his arm draped about Burgundy's shoulders, spilling wine on the Frenchman, who pretended not to notice.

Henry of Champagne was standing by himself now, watching his uncle's revels. I forced my way to a spot next to him, sweating heavily by the time I was there. I gasped loudly which drew his attention. He looked displeased upon seeing me.

"Why do you draw breath so suddenly, Fool?" he demanded.

"Sir, there is no air left in this room anymore," I replied. "I thought there would be a more rarefied atmosphere in the vicinity of great ones such as yourself, and came only but to sample."

"I would think that a fool like you would enjoy crowds," he said.

"I do love a crowd," I agreed. "But it all depends on where they are standing. If a thousand men have their backs turned when I am performing, then that will do me less good than ten watching me."

"A worthy point," he said. "It's like having an army under your command, but too far away to be of any use."

"How far is Jerusalem?" I asked.

[33]

"Too far," he muttered, but then caught himself. "A tune, Fool. Something to lighten my heart."

"An air in this airless room? A brilliant idea, milord. But why are you so glum? There is pleasure to be had but a few steps away. I would think that someone like you could have the pick of the ladies."

"Perhaps," he said. "The trouble is these ladies have been picked many times before. I didn't take the Cross and sail the seas so that I could sample the local whores."

"Indulge, sir, indulge. When a plenary indulgence awaits, a secular indulgence should be taken."

He looked across the sea of revelry with an expression of disgust.

"I should not condemn them, I suppose," he said. "We all may be marching to our doom. Yet I would rather go to Heaven with a pure soul than have to rely upon a papal bribe for the privilege."

"But these men have fought long and hard—"

"And I have not!" he barked. "I have not earned the right to dance with whores and drink strange wine. I have lain abed while arrows and stones flew and lesser men died in my place. I have earned nothing, and shall partake of nothing until I deserve better."

I plucked a goblet from a tray passing by and handed it to him.

"If you partake of nothing, than you shall be ill once again," I said. "Avoid women by all means, but wine and song shall sustain you on this mission of God."

I sang to him, an old song from Champagne, and he sipped the thick red wine as he listened. I don't know if it was the wine or the music that brought the color to his cheeks, but when I was done, he nodded slightly, his eyes glistening.

"I thank you for that, Fool," he said softly. "I have thought of home ever since I left it."

"And you shall see it again, I hope," I said.

"Somehow, I think not," he said. "But I made my vows in Cham-

[34]

pagne, and I will not come home until I have completed my appointed task."

"And if it cannot be done, milord?" I asked gently.

He turned his light blue eyes on me.

"Then I die here," he said.

The lad needs a woman, I thought to myself. If he had one, he wouldn't be so certain about everything.

I heard another voice raised in song nearby and looked to see Blondel strumming his lute. But he was not the singer. It was Richard himself, and he was not half bad, I must say. Blondel joined him in the choruses, and when they were through, the soldiers in their vicinity applauded heartily. Richard bowed, and Blondel smiled at him. I was near enough to overhear as the troubadour leaned toward his monarch.

"There's a moon out tonight, sire," he purred. "And I have heard that a man can see Jerusalem from the top of your tower. Will you show me?"

By God, I would have jumped him myself if he had pointed those eyes and words in my direction, and I knew he was pretending. Richard had a skin of wine inside him, and needed no further persuasion.

"This way, my canary," he rumbled. "Let us sing across the hills so that Saladin himself will hear it."

They left that hall arm in arm, the troubadour supporting the king when he stumbled.

That was my cue. I played on for another twenty minutes, then purloined a wineskin and headed for the roof.

ʄOUR

"Wit, an't be thy will, put me into good fooling."
—WILLIAM SHAKESPEARE,
TWELFTH NIGHT, I.v

The roof between the towers gave a good view of the Crusader encampment to the north. A hundred fires dotted the landscape, with the largest forming a perimeter a hundred feet past the camp, preventing any suicidal Saracen from getting too close unobserved.

With the security geared toward the perimeter, the castellum roof was relatively unguarded. But it was not deserted. A few glum Normans were scattered about, calling the watch every few minutes.

I didn't want to be cut in half before they could figure out who I was, so I strummed a few chords to announce myself. I was met at a somewhat leisurely pace by a fat guard in an ill-fitting breastplate.

"You're not supposed to be up here," he barked.

"Yes, I know," I said. "I'm not supposed to be up here, and I'm not supposed to be carrying this wineskin, either."

He looked at me, then began to smile.

"What else aren't you supposed to be doing?" he asked.

"I'm not supposed to be giving any wine to the brave men who sacrificed their chance at festivity so that their fellows could sacrifice their chance at virtue."

"Well, when you put it like that," he said. I handed over the wineskin, and he upended it for a long count of ten before coming up for air.

"Who sent you?" he asked.

"Some count of something," I said. " 'Take this up to the boys on the roof,' he said, 'and tell them it came from me.' Had I not partaken of so much earlier, I'd be able to tell you his name."

"Bet it was Clarence," he said after another pull at the wineskin. "Always remembers his men, no matter how drunk he is."

"I'm supposed to bring it around to the rest of the watch," I said, reaching for it.

"One moment," he said, taking a last swig. Then he stiffened.

"What is it?" I asked.

He turned, staring in toward the central tower. "I thought I heard something."

"Where?" I asked.

"From up high," he said.

"Do the Turks attack from the skies?" I scoffed.

"I heard something," he insisted. "A scraping sound."

I had placed a few rocks in my pouch for this very occasion. I quietly removed one and tossed it behind us. It skidded along the roof stones. The guard whirled.

"It's over there, now," he whispered.

"But I don't see anything," I said. I took a few steps that way, then started and stomped my foot. "Ugh, come look."

He tiptoed over and looked down at my feet. A rat lay dead, apparently crushed by my quick attack.

"There's your Turk," I laughed.

He grimaced and kicked it over the side into the darkness.

"They go everywhere, don't they?" he observed, relieved.

You had a dead rat in your pouch? asked Claudia.

I had a dead rat in my pouch.

She tickled Portia, who squealed.

See what you have to look forward to? Claudia said to our daughter.

I wandered about the roof, chatting with the guards and offering them libations. As I passed by the central tower, I saw the strong box resting at its base. I quickly slashed the twine above it and hid the box under my cloak. I walked along the edge of the roof that joined the outer wall and looked down. Forty feet below, the ground was broken and rutted from the months of siege. A small flame flickered from one of them. I could have sworn I could see Scarlet's eyes as well, but from that distance it was probably just a trick of my imagination.

I took the ball of twine and tied one end around the box, then cast it over the edge. The twine played out until there was a thud below. I prayed that it was the box hitting the ground, and that I hadn't manage to brain the little fellow. A second later, a tug from the other end reassured me. I sat down, my legs dangling over the edge, as if I were on some wall by a river, waiting for a fish to bite.

But I had to wait for a while, and the guards were beginning to look in my direction.

"Hey, Fool!" one called. "You're not hogging all that wine for yourself, are you? Bring it over."

The problem was the twine. I couldn't drag it with me, because Scarlet needed to find it again. But there was nothing nearby to which I could tie it, and if I lost my end, we'd never get the strong box back up.

"Fool!" cried the guard, starting in my direction.

"Anon, good sir," I called back. I took one of the stones from my pouch and wrapped my end of the twine around it, then placed it carefully on the roof stones, five feet from the edge, which was all the length I had left to work with. I quickly ran over with the wineskin before the guard could get too close.

However, this drew the attention of the fat guard who first met me. Like a pesky pigeon pursuing the last crust of stale bread thrown, he waddled along the northern edge of the roof toward me, which put him on a direct route to my precariously anchored twine. The guards I was with were still sharing the skin. I watched out of the corner of my eye the fat man's progress.

"Enough, good fellows," I said when he was within ten paces of the stone. I snatched back the skin and ran back to the fat man. To my horror, I saw his right boot strike the rock, sending it skittering toward the edge. My last step was a leap, and I landed with my left foot on the roof's edge, directly on top of the end of the twine.

"Your wine, sir," I said, handing the skin to him. I heard the other guards protesting behind me, but the fat man growled good-naturedly in their direction, and they laughed and withdrew.

He tilted his head back and drained the skin, tapping it until not a drop remained. Then he wiped his mouth with his sleeve and handed it back.

"Many thanks, Fool," he said. "Now, you'd best be going before the next watch comes up and finds you empty-handed."

"My pleasure, good soldier," I said. "Let me just relieve myself before I go."

"Be my guest," he said.

I stood at the edge of the roof, then glanced back.

"Do you mind?" I said. "It's a bit finicky about being stared at."

He shrugged and walked away. I reached down and grabbed the twine, then quickly hauled the box back up.

I walked casually over to the main tower and trailed my fingers along the smooth stones until I grasped the end of Blondel's twine. I tied the box to it and tugged twice. Blondel began pulling it up. I waved, even though I couldn't see him, and began walking away.

Then I heard the box scrape against the stones above me. The fat guard started in my direction.

"I heard it again," he said, showing no effects of the wine he had consumed. "That was no rat, Fool. There's something funny going on around here, and it isn't you."

"Sir, I assure you that I haven't seen anything untoward since I've been up here," I said.

"It's not your job to see things, it's mine," he said, staring up at the tower. "There's something up there."

"A bat?" I guessed. "Or an owl?"

"No," he said. "I thought I saw—"

"Hallo!" came a shout from the ground below. "Help, for the love of Christ!"

The fat guard dashed over, soon joined by the rest of the guards and myself.

The ground patrols outside the wall rapidly converged on the source of the shouting. Their torches revealed Scarlet trying to scrabble up the side of a six-foot hole, then falling back repeatedly. As his attempts grew more frantic, his failures became more comical, and the soldiers, both on the ground and on the roof, were soon guffawing helplessly.

"It's a fine thing for the guardians of Christ to be laughing at a poor dwarf's misfortunes," grumbled Scarlet. "Here I am in this pit, this chasm, near death, and you laugh."

"Chasm?" said one of the patrol. "It's just a small hole in the ground."

"To you, a small hole," said Scarlet. "To me, it's the gateway to Hell, the Stygian depths, the bottomless pit of Revelation, and I wonder if one of you will help me out before I run out of metaphors?"

A soldier reached down and grabbed the dwarf's hand, then hoisted him easily to the surface.

"How came you to this pass, little one?" asked a soldier.

"I'm not rightly sure, and that's God's truth," said Scarlet, his speech slightly slurred. "I was drinking with a group of Burgundians, and one of them was wondering if I weighed as much as a catapult stone, and another said, 'Let's find out,' and before I knew it, they were boosting me into one of those infernal machines. I jumped out and took to my heels without looking where I was going, and, fulfilling the ancient prophesy that he that fleeth from the fear shall fall into the pit, the next thing I knew, I was staring up at the moon from six feet under. I cannot tell you how relieved I am to find out that I'm not actually dead."

I had eased my way to the back of the pack by this point and managed then to slip away to the steps down. I noted with relief that the box was no longer in view. I blessed Blondel for the risk he took and cursed him for carrying out his task so clumsily.

When I reached Scarlet's room, a hauberk, ganbisson, and surcoat lay ready for me, along with some gauntlets, chauces de fer for my legs, and espalieres for my shoulders. I've rarely worn armor in my life, and then only for disguise. The idea of going into combat with that kind of weight hindering my movements confounded me, but so did the idea of going into combat, period. A jester does his best work away from the battlefield. If a battle actually commences, that means he has failed in his principal mission. It also means he should stay the hell out of it if he wants to survive.

A rule you knew then, but forgot later, commented Claudia.

I always knew that rule, I replied. *I just break it every now and then.*

Scarlet came in as I finished packing.

"At your service, Captain," he said, bowing and handing me the sealed scroll.

"Horses?" I asked.

"Procured and saddled," he replied, picking up his gear. "Let's go."

I stuffed my foolish noggin into the chain mail coif, topped the whole mess off with a pot helm, and staggered noisily down the steps.

Two reliable-looking steeds awaited us in the stables. I was surprised to see a second horse instead of a donkey, but the dwarf took a running start and vaulted up without assistance. I actually had more difficulty mounting with the extra sixty pounds of metal on my body, but I managed eventually.

"Where did you get the armor?" I said.

"Scavenged from a battlefield by someone who sold it to me at a reasonable price," he said. "There's a sword in the scabbard in case you need it."

"Norman colors," I observed. "Where's the fatal hole?"

"It's a little dented near the back of the helm," he said. "Poor fellow must have fallen and broken his neck."

"Well, his loss is our gain. It should lend us some authenticity. How long have you been preparing this little escapade?"

"I have armor from several nations stashed away for these occasions," he said. "I obtained the horses two days ago."

"Obtained," I said. "Not necessarily bought."

"They won't be missed," he said. "For a while, at least."

We rode north. When the sun finally put in an appearance, we were about six miles from Acre, well past the outer limits of the patrols. We kept to the coastal road, traveling slowly in case of ambush from any quarter. I was sweating like a pig in the armor, frustrated by the limited visibility, spooked by the unfriendly surroundings, and irritated by the absolute complacency of my companion.

"A thought," I said.

"About time," he replied.

"If I am some Norman captain carrying out an important assignment from King Richard, shouldn't I have some kind of escort accompanying me?"

"Are you saying that I'm not impressive enough to be your escort?" he replied plaintively.

"Well, yes. It's not your size, mind you . . ."

"No, of course not."

"But your numbers—which, to put no small point on it, are one. If that."

"So little respect from one's minions," he sighed. "When one's heart is pure, one's arm is greater than all the armies of the enemy."

"Is your heart that pure?"

"Probably not. I take your point. In fact, I took it a few days before you made it."

"Meaning?"

"Meaning let's turn off the road at that well over there."

I hadn't even spied the well, but the horses were quite happy to see it. We dismounted and watered the beasts, then Scarlet lifted a bucket to his lips.

"Have to wet my whistle before I whistle," he remarked. Then he pursed his lips and pierced the air with a noise that could have attracted every hawk in the kingdom.

A minute later, I heard hooves galloping in our direction. I placed my hand on the hilt of my sword.

"No need," said Scarlet.

Six horsemen in Norman armor rounded the bend, kicking up the dust, followed by several boys divided among some wains. They came to a halt in formation, and their leader saluted me.

"My lord," he said with a trace of a Syrian accent.

"Hail, fellows," I said, then I turned to the dwarf. "Who are these fine men?"

"Your escort," he replied.

"Which you conjured out of the air by that whistle?"

He smiled. "You think you're the only fool working for me?"

"Are they Guildmembers?"

"Not yet," he said, pulling himself onto his horse. "But the ones in armor have been apprenticing to me, and the extra boys are refugees that I hire for special occasions. Normally, the apprentices are scattered around the kingdom, checking on what's going on, but I summoned them to Tyre when Acre fell. Friends, this is Theophilos of the Fools' Guild, my brother in motley. Treat him better than you treat me, and he may reward you with a few tricks I don't know about."

"I'm beginning to think there's nothing I can do that you don't already know," I said, mounting my horse. "Gentlemen, fall in behind me."

I spotted the ship about ten minutes later. A Pisan merchantman, anchored about fifty feet out. We rode up to the shore and hailed them. A boat was lowered over the side, and the sailing master came to us, his crew heavily armed. The rest stood in the bow, bows at the ready.

"It's about time you got here," he said in heavily accented langue d'oc.

"We met up with a little trouble," I replied. "A Saracen patrol. We killed two and spent some time chasing the others. Why haven't you started unloading the supplies?"

"How do I know you're the right man?" he asked.

I pulled the scroll from my pouch and handed it to him. He examined the seal, then broke it and handed it to another man who read it to him. They looked again at the second seal inside.

"Tyre?" said the sailing master. "We could have gone straight there."

"The decision was made only last night," I said. "Start unloading."

"I don't like it," he said.

I shrugged. "It does not concern me what your likes and dislikes are."

"But my orders were—"

"Do you see that little fellow?" I interrupted him, pointing to Scarlet. The sailing master looked over at the dwarf, who was reclining in his saddle and thumbing his nose at the crew.

"What about him?" said the sailing master.

"His job is to make me laugh," I said, shifting to Pisan dialect to drive the point home. "Laughing keeps me from flying into murderous rages at a moment's notice. But right now I am talking to you, and I don't find you the least bit amusing."

Scarlet's fake soldiers maintained a properly menacing mien behind me. I sat on the horse, drumming my fingers on my sword's hilt. The sound drew his glance toward the sword, then he looked up at my face. I smiled. He turned and waved a yellow handkerchief at the boat. The crew scrambled to hoist the anchor, and the oars came out to bring the ship in closer.

They were a good crew and had the supplies unloaded in less than an hour, including two more wagons and a quartet of donkeys to draw them. The two extra boys on the wains took over the wagons, and we were soon ready to leave.

"What about my payment?" said the sailing master.

I whirled, sword in hand.

"Do you take me for a fool?" I shouted. "You were paid before you ever left Pisa. Now, get out of here before I add your swindling head to my trophies."

The small boat took off so fast that it nearly rammed the merchantman, and the sails were raised in a trice.

"North, men," I ordered, and our group trundled forward, the horsemen falling into place neatly beside the wagons. Soon, we were beyond the sight of the Pisans, and I couldn't say which group was happier to see the back of the other.

"What made you so sure he had been paid in advance?" asked Scarlet.

"He was no gambler," I said. "Some of these suppliers may be

[45]

speculating that there will be a market when they arrive, but this fellow wasn't the sort to be taking any chances."

"Unlike us," said Scarlet. "Brother Theophilos, you and Blondel have exceeded my expectations. Although the blond one needs some practice lowering strongboxes from towers without hitting the sides."

"The next time the situation comes up, I'm certain he'll do better," I said. "That was a most timely intervention on your part, by the way."

"I heard the guard react after the box hit the tower going back up. I figured a distraction was in order. Well, Captain, since I am to amuse you during this journey, how about a little music while we ride?"

"It would be a pleasure," I said. "Especially since I can't play my lute with these gauntlets on."

He pulled an instrument from a case shoved into his saddlebag. It was a guitar, one of those Arab instruments, only scaled down to a child's size.

"I haven't heard one of those in years," I said as he tuned it. "Do you prefer it to the lute?"

"Definitely," he said. "It has more character. It's louder, and you can bend the tones more readily. Listen."

His fingers danced along the strings, and some melody that might have come from a mullah's throat sang out.

"It suits this world," he said, looking out at the harsh landscape, the small patches of green fighting for existence in the sandy soil. "A lute is for artificial prettiness inside walls, but a guitar sounds a man's soul in the wilderness."

He leaned back in his saddle and played and sang. His singing voice was sweeter than his speaking voice, and at an unearthly high range. He sang in langue d'oc, Greek, Syrian, and Arabic, covering the range of nationalities among the apprentices behind him. But everyone knew some of the songs, and some of us knew all of them, so it was quite the talented armed choir traveling up the searoad.

*   *   *

It was a two-day journey. We broke for camp at a deserted stone chapel that was fairly defensible. Scarlet organized the watches and had a fire going in no time. I hauled water with one of the boys. I say boys, because with their helms off, it was clear that none of them was more than sixteen.

It was another clear night, and we sat outside as the fire died down, looking up at the stars. Scarlet and I talked about many things, and his fingers on the guitar strings never rested, providing a soft, subtle counterpoint to the conversation.

"What do you know about Tyre?" he asked me at one point.

"I've never been there," I said. "I know what everyone knows, I guess. It's on an island connected by a causeway. It's an old city, mentioned in the Bible a few times."

"Humph, the Bible," he said.

"What have you got against the Good Book?" I asked.

"Do you know how many times dwarves are mentioned in it?" he asked indignantly. "Once! And we're lumped together with crookbacks, blind men, and the generally blemished, as if we were something to be passed over."

"Being passed over isn't always a bad thing. I think the Old Testament mentions that at some point. And I've known a crookback or two who was quite decent. What was the question again?"

"Tyre. Your knowledge thereof."

"Um, conquered and reconquered over the years. Last bastion of Outremer remaining after Saladin went on his little rampage. And I gather that the succession is in dispute?"

"That's putting it mildly," said Scarlet, the guitar twanging a discordant agreement. "I'll give you the brief version. No, that's impossible, there is no brief version. All right, the last undisputed king of Jerusalem was Baldwin the Fourth, who was a leper without issue. His sister,

Sybil, married Guy de Lusignan. She had a son and, lacking much in the way of imagination, named him Baldwin. The Fourth named his nephew as his successor and stepped down. The boy was only five, so Raymond of Tripoli became regent."

"What number was he?"

"Raymond? He was Raymond the Third."

"So, the Fourth abdicates, leaving the Fifth with the Third."

"You've got it," smiled Scarlet. "Now, in 1185, six years ago, the Fourth dies, and the Fifth dies a month later. There is no named heir, but by all rights the kingdom should go to Sybil. Guy claimed it as her husband, but Raymond claimed it as the regent. The dispute goes on for a couple of years, then is rendered somewhat moot by Saladin's victory at the Horns of Hattin. Raymond fled, Guy was captured, Jerusalem fell, as did Acre, Ascalon, and everywhere else. Everywhere but Tyre.

"Tyre held because one day Conrad of Montferrat showed up. There was a rumor that he was fleeing from Constantinople, but his arrival was opportune nevertheless. The defenses were disorganized, the city was flooded with refugees, and the plains were filled with infidels. Conrad took charge but insisted he be given absolute power in Tyre. The people went along with that. He made his first point by not just banishing Saladin's envoys but having them thrown into the fosse at the base of the landwalls. He then organized the army and rebuilt the fortifications.

"Saladin showed up with his armies and one person he thought would be useful: Conrad's father, William the Old, who had been taken at Hattin. Saladin paraded the old man before the walls of Tyre and promised to trade him for the city."

"How did Conrad react to this challenge to his filial piety?"

"He picked up a crossbow and took a shot at his father. Barely missed him. He shouted that he'd rather kill the old man himself than surrender a single stone of the city. I think he impressed Tyre more than he frightened Saladin, but the Turks withdrew rather than attempt the walls. Conrad became the people's champion."

"But how did that play into the succession?"

"Because Sybil had no surviving children," replied Scarlet. "Saladin let Guy de Lusignan go, either because of a ransom paid, or because Saladin thought Guy and Sybil would cause more havoc inside the walls of Tyre than he could outside. But when they showed up, Conrad refused to let them in."

"A fine way to treat a putative king."

"Putative, but not crowned. And then Sybil died, and with her any claim Guy had to the throne of Jerusalem. Not that that's stopping him, but lacking support and legality, it's a long shot at best. The next in line in succession was little sister Isabelle of Jerusalem. She was married to a decent enough man named Humphrey of Toron."

"I've seen him about. He speaks fluent Arabic, so Richard uses him as an envoy a lot. He struck me as being rather effeminate. Never thought he'd be the marrying type."

"It was a political match. He was of influence. She was eleven."

"Poor girl."

"Actually, she adored him. He was uncommonly beautiful, immaculately groomed, well-mannered, every girl's dream of what a husband should look like. And, fortunately and unfortunately, he had no interest in women."

"Fortunately and unfortunately?"

"Fortunately, because she was eleven, and did not have to be subjected to any indecencies. Unfortunately, because when she was old enough . . ."

He trailed off, and the music gave a dying fall.

He was silent for a while, watching the embers burn down.

"It's hard enough to learn about love from a husband in an arranged marriage," he continued finally. "Her mother, Maria Comnena, was a Byzantine, and knew all too well the fine art of gaining power through alliances. Mama saw the future in Conrad and sought an annulment on the grounds of Humphrey's effeminacy and Isabelle's age at marriage. Since everyone knew about that when the marriage was first arranged, it didn't carry much weight. But the Archbishop died, and Maria seduced the Papal Legate, who then approved the annulment. They gave this beautiful young woman to this ambitious, battle-scarred old man, and all of Tyre cheered. Humphrey was bought off with the promise of some land, and Conrad reigns in Tyre. But he hasn't been coronated yet. Richard still favors Guy, Philip favors Conrad, the Pisans favor Guy, the Genoans favor Conrad, the Venetians just want their piece of the city, and it's an ungodly mess in the Holy Land."

He started playing again.

"Whose fool are you in all of this?" I asked, starting to drift off.

A mournful, romantic melody rose into the night sky.

"I belong to the Queen of Jerusalem," he said. "I was a wedding gift."

ƒIVE

"Tyre is a town that is like a fortress."
—IBN DJOBEIR, 1185

We met the first patrol out of Tyre at the springs at Ras el-'Ain, a few miles south of the city. Aqueducts carried the water north. We were watering our horses for the final push when the riders hailed us.

I walked up to meet them, but their captain ignored me and proceeded straight to Scarlet.

"We've been waiting for you for two days," he said.

"It was a complicated matter," replied the dwarf. "But successful, as you can see."

"Good," said the captain. "We'll take them from here. Your lord wants to see you."

"In good time, Captain. We will refresh ourselves and see him when we are ready."

The captain scowled but did not argue.

"Oh, Captain?" called Scarlet as the latter turned to take over the supply train.

"What, Fool?"

"I know the contents of those wains down to the last speck of flour. Make sure they travel these last three miles without loss."

We passed through fields of sugar cane, then spotted the tents outside the city a mile later. The road took us through the middle of them as thousands of refugees went about the daily business of survival, waiting patiently at cisterns with buckets, stripping the countryside of anything they could burn for cooking fires, and carrying on lively debates in several languages.

"And these are the lucky ones," pointed out Scarlet. "Saladin made a fortune ransoming them. Ten bezants a man, five per woman, one per child, all for the privilege of abandoning everything they ever owned to him. There are over twenty thousand people living in these tents, and Tyre's been feeding them as well as it can for years."

"The city is that wealthy?" I asked.

"The city depends on sugar, glass, and a mollusk the size of your thumb," he said. "They supply purple dye made from it to Constantinople and beyond. If purple ever falls out of fashion, that will be the end of Tyre."

"Thank Christ for royal vanity," I said. "I'm surprised Saladin didn't make more of an effort to take the city."

"The effort would be extreme," he said. "Take a look and tell me how it would be done."

Ahead of us, a broad causeway jutted out from the coastline. The aqueduct ran down one side of it, plunging through a hole in a massive curtain wall that traversed the end of the causeway. The fosse lay before it, dry at the moment but with locks at both ends that would allow it to be flooded at a moment's notice. A single drawbridge crossed the center of the fosse. The ramparts of the wall were heavily patrolled.

Beyond the wall was a higher wall. Beyond that was an even higher one.

"How would you press the attack?" asked Scarlet. "Each wall can be defended by the one behind it, and all of them give the archers a clear shot at the causeway."

"By sea?" I suggested. He simply pointed in reply.

The harbor was enclosed by towers built on small artificial islands. A pair of walls stretched into the water, curving toward each other to form a seagate for the inner harbor.

"At dusk, they close the inner harbor and raise heavy chains from tower to tower," said Scarlet. "If you get close enough to a chain to try and ram it, you'll also be close enough to catch a cauldron of Greek fire."

"Impressive," I said.

"When an army comes by, usually Tyre will wave a flag of truce and invite the commander in for a tour of the defenses, just so he knows what lies in store if he attacks. Most of them will see that it's a waste of men and move on. As I said, Saladin tried the hostage approach, but he had the wrong opponent for that tactic. Oh, you had better take this."

He handed me a document with the seal of Richard the Lionhearted on it.

"That will get a Norman captain into the city," he said.

"But once I revert to foolery, won't I need something else?"

"I'll take care of that."

We rode up the causeway, over the drawbridge, and through three sets of gates. The latter were staggered to prevent an easier line of assault, so the process took a bit of time, but finally, we emerged.

"Welcome to the play," said Scarlet.

The layout was haphazard, as though people had tossed pebbles into the air and set up shop where they fell. Then they built, and when they needed more room, there was none around them. So, they built up, and up again. Everything was six or seven stories high, and sometimes the higher stories matched the architecture of the lower ones, and sometimes it was as if an entirely different building had been plopped down on the top of an older one. Stones had been taken from whatever structures had collapsed or been torn down before, so there was a mixture of materials—sandstone, granite, marble, and what have you.

"It's like a motley in rock," I marveled. "I've never seen anything like it."

"It is a place that a fool could call his natural environs, certainly," laughed Scarlet. "I've only been here a few years, but I've grown quite fond of it. I think the height of the buildings has the same effect on normal people that normal people have on me: at first, you become dizzy and overwhelmed by the madness of your surroundings, a Tower of Babel at every step. But gradually you get used to it, and soon you take everything you see in stride. I prefer it to Jerusalem. Everything there is so sacred that you have to walk on tiptoe to avoid offending anyone, and God forbid you disturb a single stone trying to improve things. Here's where I live. We'll take the horses around back and you can ditch the armor in the stables for now."

I cannot say how happy I was to be back in motley. The aches and pains of the journey dissipated with each clunk of a piece of armor falling to the floor. I stretched in every direction, then did a standing back flip, just to make sure that I still could.

"I was always grateful that no one ever expected me to do one of those," commented Scarlet as I landed. "Another advantage to being a dwarf: one's appearance is sometimes all that is needed."

"Do you juggle?" I asked as I collected my gear.

"Of course," he said. "Brother Timothy didn't slack off on anyone at the Guild. He always said if I didn't master juggling, he would start juggling me along with a couple of axes. He was a great one for in-centive."

"We'll have to work on some two-man routines," I said. "Now that I'm staying for a while."

"Let's go," said Scarlet. "It's a bit of a climb."

It was seven flights of stairs. No, it was six flights of stairs, and just when my legs were starting to scream, we arrived at a rickety ladder on the seventh floor leading to a hole in the roof. Scarlet scampered up with no sign of weariness. I sucked in my complaints and followed him.

On the roof of this large building, he had a small one of his own, a two-room cottage that had been slapped together by an untalented mason. But it was just high enough to give us a panoramic view, the sea to the west, the plains to the east, and the coastline stretching out to either side.

"Spectacular," I said.

"I'm glad you like it," he replied. "It's not necessarily the most convenient location, but only a truly determined thief would bother with the climb. I also keep a coop for my carrier pigeons on top. And at night I can draw the ladder up for safety. But I think it's worth it for the vista alone. I've spent so much of my life with my view of the world blocked that I find it truly liberates the spirit to have it all on display."

We unloaded our gear. I put together my working kit and, with a sigh, followed my leader back down to the street.

"A question, my liege," I said.

"Speak, minion," he replied.

"How much does Conrad know about the Guild?"

"He knows nothing," he said. "He's an untrustworthy, deceitful, scheming, and occasionally vicious despot. At least, until you get to know him better."

"Oh," I said. "Then how did you end up running errands for him?"

"It suited my purposes," he said. "In his eyes, I'm not only a fool but a truly talented thief."

"Can't understand where he got that idea," I said, laughing. "So, am I to be your brother in larceny as well as motley?"

"As far as he is concerned, yes," he said. "I'm also going to be using you as my eyes, ears, and much longer legs in town and in the tents.

Conrad is everything I said he is, but he's also smart enough to know that the only way he'll maintain control of Tyre is to make peace with Saladin. That makes him the best candidate for the throne as far as the Guild is concerned. So, I want to make sure he stays on top, no matter how much I distrust the bastard. Guy de Lusignan still has supporters here, and there are plenty of other sources of trouble. We'll keep busy."

"What about when my crusading patron returns?"

"We'll worry about that when it happens."

If it happens, was the unstated thought in both of our minds.

The castellum was back near the northern end of the innermost wall, allowing it to defend both the wall as well as the approach from the north by sea. Towers of recent construction stretched above everything, and the guards swarmed about the entrances. Yet Scarlet passed through unchallenged, greeting many of the soldiers by name and introducing me to the various captains and sergeants.

"Well?" he said as we entered through the kitchens, where an array of cooks boiled fish into stew.

I rattled off the names and descriptions of every man we had met.

"Good," he said.

We entered the great hall and marched past a line of petitioners. At the far end, a grizzled, bearded man in his late fifties sat on the throne, scribbling with a small quill on documents as they were handed to him.

It was not the first time that I had seen Conrad of Montferrat, but it was the first time I had seen him close up and sans armor. He had made periodic appearances at Acre, mostly staying by the side of the King of France, murmuring advice and occasionally directing the distribution of supplies. In retrospect, I imagine that he had directed some of them north to Tyre. He was lean but powerfully built, a scrapper's body with immense forearms. They said he could wield a sword proficiently with either hand, and he favored a hauberk made of many folds of linen stiffened with brine instead of a coat of mail, preferring the lighter weight and mobility.

"Not possible," he was saying to a priest as we approached.

"But the church," protested the priest, a walking corpse of a man whose bony hands emerged from his robes to clasp in skeletal supplication.

"The church will be a mosque inside of a year if I shift even one repair crew away from the defenses," interrupted Conrad of Montferrat. "Put some of those fat deacons to work. It will be good for them. They can get into shape and ennoble their spirits at the same time."

"That's Philip, Bishop of Beauvais," muttered Scarlet. "A righteous man in the ways of greed and ambition. I'll tell you more about him later."

Conrad shoved the document back into the priest's hands, and the latter slunk away.

"Next!" shouted Conrad.

"If it please you, sir," said Scarlet. "I wish to rule in your place."

A broad grin split the almost-monarch's face as he beheld the dwarf.

"Be careful what you wish for, little friend," he chortled, stepping down. He picked up Scarlet and set him on the throne, then looked at him critically. "It suits you," he said.

"Well, of course it does," replied the dwarf regally. Then he looked up and gasped. "No," he cried. "The weight of responsibility! The burdens of rulership! Aiieee!" He shoved his arms into the air as if he were Atlas trying to support the world and slowly collapsed. "Take it back, Conrad," he said, his voice muffled. "It's too much for me."

Conrad threw his head back and roared.

"Come here, you scamp," he shouted, and the little fellow jumped into his arms.

"Greetings, liege," said Scarlet. "I return heavily laden."

"So I hear, so I hear," replied Conrad. "Well done. You've made good on your boasts, and then some. And I see you've brought a companion."

"This is Droignon, a fellow fool," said Scarlet by way of introduction.

Droignon? exclaimed my wife. You called yourself Droignon then? How many names have you had in your life?

So many that even I cannot remember all of them.

She looked at Portia. Forget about Theophilos, she said to our daughter. You had better stick to Mama and Papa until you're old enough to make sense of all of this.

"So, Droignon, you've come to seek your fortune here?" asked Conrad.

"Mine, or someone else's," I said, winking at him.

He looked at Scarlet knowingly.

"I take it that this fool shares some of your talents," he said.

"He does," replied Scarlet. "We were quite the entertaining team in Acre, although I cannot say that we left them laughing."

"As it turned out, the joke was on Richard," I added.

"Then, Monsieur Droignon, I am in your debt as well," pronounced Conrad.

"Twenty bezants," I said.

"What?"

"Your debt to me. Twenty bezants. That's what I was promised for risking my neck. And there were expenses."

Conrad looked at Scarlet, who shrugged.

"The price of leadership," sighed Conrad, handing me some coins. I bowed.

"And I'll be needing papers for the city," I said. "I burned quite a few bridges behind me. If Richard finds out that we were involved, he's likely to send someone to seek recompense, and not necessarily the monetary kind."

"Why should he find out?" inquired Conrad. "Didn't you conceal your identity?"

"I did," I said. "But the captain of your patrol who met us knew what we were up to. So, I should guess, do many others around here. I'm sure that Richard will have word from his spies within the week. So, I need papers. I plan to lie low here for a while."

Conrad snapped his fingers, and a clerk drew up the document. The marquis added his signature and seal. He held it toward me, then snatched it back as I reached for it.

"Ten bezants," he said, grinning.

"What?" I exclaimed.

"Your original price did not include any documents," he said. "The price of occupancy inside the walls is at a premium right now."

Scarlet began to laugh, and after a bit of feigned chagrin, I joined him.

"Here, milord," I said, handing him half of my new fortune. "I hope to be of service to you again."

"You are most welcome in Tyre, Droignon," said Conrad. "Pray, leave me with my little friend so that I might catch up on the latest news from Acre."

I retreated to the front of the hall and made myself useful by entertaining the stalled line of petitioners as well as the guards. Scarlet was perched on the arm of the throne, having a hushed conversation with Conrad. Finally, the marquis let my colleague go.

"I had to bring him up to date on the negotiations with Saladin," he said as he rejoined me. "Not to mention as much gossip as I could gather while I was in Acre."

"Doesn't he have other people with Saladin? I never saw you when I was there."

"No, you didn't," he said. "But I saw you. Where did you learn your Arabic, by the way? It's excellent."

[59]

"In Alexandria when I was younger," I said. "How come you never contacted me before Acre?"

"I couldn't risk being seen with a secret envoy from King Philip when I was an equally secret envoy from Conrad. Even two fools working toward the same goal can end up at cross-purposes."

"I wonder whom Saladin will make the deal with. If he decides to deal at all."

"I think he will," said Scarlet. "The war has gone on too long, and his troops don't want to fight year round. For now, he'll play Richard and Conrad against each other while he consolidates his gains. Maybe we'll have a truce by winter. Or maybe Richard will give up and go back to his kingdom before he loses control of it."

"In the meantime, what are we doing right now?"

"I am going to give you the tour of the castellum and an introduction to the key people around here. You met Conrad and you saw the Bishop of Beauvais. I cannot believe you pulled that stunt over the money."

"I thought it would be in character. Besides, I made ten bezants. Tell me about the bishop."

"He's been around a few years," said Scarlet as we left the hall and walked a series of corridors and staircases. "He was an active participant in persuading the Papal Legate to annul Isabelle's first marriage, practically procuring for Maria Comnena. When Conrad married Isabelle, Beauvais performed the ceremony, blessing the hypocrisy with everything he had."

"Was he a friend of Conrad's before this?"

"Not to my knowledge. I think he saw an opportunity for power and influence in an ever-decreasing sphere. He's been away from Beauvais a long time, and he's wondering now what he's going to get to show for it."

"It doesn't sound like he's getting much from Conrad today."

"He should get a little more. I put a word in for him."

"You did?" I exclaimed. "Since when do we help out the Church?"

"Beauvais is at least a neutral party as far as the various splits between England and France and between Pisa and Genoa. We need him on Conrad's side, because Conrad has no natural constituency of his own, just a lot of sycophants and soldiers of fortune."

"And the Queen of Jerusalem."

"And the Queen," he agreed.

He stopped outside a massive oaken double door.

"I am taking you in to see her," he said, suddenly stern. "You are to behave in a proper manner. No coarse ribaldries or suggestive puns, and none of your rustic capers. Think of her as the Queen of the Courts of Love, a place where chivalry actually exists. Sing in your sweetest voice, and only romances and ballads. Make your courtesies with elaborate flourishes, and speak only when she speaks to you."

"Will that be all?" I asked.

"I'm serious, Theophilos," he said. "She is a rare creature and not to be subjected to any insult, intentional or accidental."

"I understand," I said. "Come, let us greet this paragon."

He rapped softly three times on the doors, then two times more. There was a rustle of silk on the other side, then the two doors were opened by a maidservant who giggled the moment she saw Scarlet.

"He's here, milady," she called.

We walked in, and I thought I had stumbled into Paradise. The room was draped in silks of different hues, and statues of marble and porphyry gazed benignly from niches in the walls. The furniture was ornate, with elaborate carvings on the arms and legs, and birds sang from gilded cages suspended from the ceiling. Yet in the midst of all this splendor, the most splendid of all was the lady with the alabaster skin, the golden tresses, and the dancing eyes who reclined on a divan in the center. She was about twenty, but there was still something of the little girl in her.

"My sweet Scarlet!" she cried, rising to her feet and rushing to him. She knelt and clasped him to her bosom, covering his face with kisses until he blushed more deeply than his name. "You've returned at last. I've been simply miserable without you."

"Then let me be scourged for bringing the slightest hint of misery to your chamber," laughed the dwarf. "Surely you've managed to keep yourself entertained in my absence."

"Entertained?" she scoffed. "How shall I be entertained when the prince of performers has abandoned me? Did you find some other lady with flashing eyes and exquisite boredom while you were in Acre?"

"Never even saw another woman while I was away from you," said Scarlet. "Some wretched things were paraded by me that I was told were beautiful maids, but how could I believe that when I have beheld you? My Queen, there can be no other woman for me."

My, he could lay it on thick, I thought. Do women really appreciate that sort of thing?

You could try it on me once in a while, my wife said acidly.

"And you've brought a friend," she said, casting a smile in my direction that almost blinded me.

"My Queen, allow me to present my friend and colleague, Droignon," said Scarlet.

I bowed so low that my bells tickled my toes.

"You are welcome, Droignon," said Isabelle, extending her hand. "A friend of Scarlet's will always be welcome in my court."

"A benefit of his friendship beyond price, milady," I said, grazing her hand with my lips. I looked sideways at my colleague, who was nodding approval. "Scarlet, I admit that I was wrong."

"About what, friend Droignon?" he asked.

"You had said during our journey that there could be no lady fairer than the one that you served, and I had dismissed your words as mere hyperbole. But now that I have seen her, I will brook no comparison with any other woman in the world."

"Now, sit and tell me all about Tyre," she commanded, motioning him to a scarlet pillow by her divan and me to an overcushioned chair nearby.

"Accompany me, if you please, Droignon," said Scarlet.

I pulled out my lute and began to play softly.

"Tell me the news, my pet," said the Queen. "Is that nice Cecille still there?"

"Aye, lady, but much worn with cares."

"Is she? Alas, poor dear. That will doubtless have ill effect upon her complexion. What is the fashion amongst the ladies of the town?"

"Slender," said the dwarf.

"Really?" said Isabelle in horror, glancing at her own figure.

"They haven't had much to eat," explained the dwarf gently. "It was a long siege. Now that things have settled down, they should be getting back to where they should be."

"Well, that's good," she said.

"And they are getting plenty of exercise," I added.

"Are they?" she said, frowning slightly.

"Promenading in the streets and entertaining the soldiers," I said.

"Yes, as good Christian ladies should when good Christian soldiers are present," said Scarlet hurriedly.

"Oh, I see," said Isabelle. "Then it is charity on their parts."

The going rate was a loaf of bread, I had heard, but Scarlet's expression stopped me from uttering that thought.

Scarlet gossiped on as if he had never diverted a single bit of flour or crossed an enemy line during his sojourn, and she laughed and asked nonsensical questions about clothes and jewels.

"And how does the Marquis treat you?" inquired Scarlet.

"Oh, you know how it is," she said, her cheeks turning crimson. "I am trying my very best to be the sort of wife he likes, but he would rather sit up all night with his friends, drinking and dicing. When he does come to my chambers, he's usually drunk. But he can be quite kind and charming when he's sober."

She sighed. "I had a young, beautiful husband who didn't want me. Now, I have an old, ugly husband who wants me occasionally but seldom can do anything about it. It's not at all the life I expected when I became queen. I thought there would be more parties, and state occasions, and cheering crowds."

"There will be, milady," said Scarlet. "And in the meantime, there is me, back to be your own personal state occasion and cheering crowd."

"Oh, Scarlet, I've missed you so much," she said, with another fit of dwarf-clasping. I began to worry that he might suffocate from her attentions. "Don't ever leave me again. At least, not for such a long time."

"I will do my best," he promised. "But your lord sometimes needs me for these little errands of his."

"Can't he send one of his men instead?" she protested.

"Send a large man for such a little errand?" he responded. "No, lady, a little errand requires a little man. There are too few soldiers to waste around here. Having no fighting ability, I must make myself useful in other ways."

"Well, I don't want you to do it anymore," she said. "I'll talk to Conrad at the dinner tomorrow."

"There's a dinner tomorrow?" asked Scarlet.

"Yes, and I want the two of you there to entertain," she said. "Do a good job of it, sweet Scarlet, so that Conrad will see that you're more valuable here amusing us than out on those silly missions of his. Now, sing to me."

We sang, and eventually she fell asleep. We tiptoed out.

"I find myself in a professional quandary," he said as we walked back to his place. "The entertainer in me wants to knock them dead tomorrow, while the practical side wants to be able to still be available for Conrad, which means I shouldn't perform well. But that would displease Isabelle."

"You've forgotten something," I said.

"What's that?"

"You now have a second fool on the premises. You no longer have to be two fools at once. Make your queen happy, my friend, and I'll do the dirty work for a while."

He smiled. "Fair enough. Shall we rehearse some two-man work?"

"By all means."

And, having spent the morning riding and the afternoon getting acquainted, I juggled my way into the evening on the roof of a dwarf's cottage, with all the world spread out before me.

𝕾IX

"*Tyre is a beautiful city.*"
—BENJAMIN OF
TUDELA, CIRCA 1167

I awoke midmorning and did my stretches on the roof, using the vantage to get the shape of Tyre in my head before I ventured forth. Scarlet had already left; a note on his pallet said that he was attending his queen. I had noticed by this time that he subsisted on little sleep, even now that we were safely back in Tyre, yet he seemed ever alert, his gleaming eyes always watchful.

I spent the rest of the morning walking about the city, frequently getting lost despite my aerial reconnaissance. The streets were laid out in a haphazard manner due to the constant tearing down and rebuilding. Despite the many wars and sieges it had been through, or perhaps because of them, Tyre appeared to be a city of vast wealth. I would turn one corner and come across a square with a huge, sculptured fountain, water spewing from the ewers of marble maidens. Another turn would lead me to a slave auction, with recently captured Saracens up for sale. The fish market was at peak activity, the boats docked in the inner harbor while their crew flung their catch to the waiting hordes of servants and cooks.

The usage of space ranged from economical to insane. I constantly had the illusion that the towers were leaning over me, ready to topple, yet they seemed to stay put, and the other pedestrians didn't even look up. The town hall was an immense building, so large that the land itself could not hold it. It was over a hundred yards long, at least a third of it extending onto bitumed wooden posts driven into the harbor floor.

I saw the cathedral, which looked in decent enough shape despite the Bishop of Beauvais's public anguish. Perhaps he was hoping to add another wing to it. There was another grand church with granite columns that was reserved for the use of the Crusaders. The Emperor Frederick Barbarossa was entombed there, his body carried in state all the way from the Calycadnus river in which he had drowned. They had filled his coffin with vinegar in an effort to preserve his body until it reached the Holy Land, but by the time they reached Tyre there was nothing left but pickled bones. At least he got a decent tomb. There were plenty of Crusaders whose bones were being picked clean by buzzards on Syrian plains.

There were mosques in abundance, and even a Jewish temple by a small but active street of artisans working in glass, making delicately hued vessels with long necks. All the citizens—Christian, Saracen, and Jew alike—walked about the city with a sense of purpose, unmolested by their fellows, just as if their brethren weren't bent on slaughtering each other just a few days' ride south. Yet for all that bustle, the streets were immaculate. The respite from the war allowed the use of water for the luxury of washing the grime from the paving stones and the buildings, and the baths were thriving. I noticed that the cisterns and wells were in good repair and filled to the brim.

All in all, I was most impressed with how this rogue from Montferrat was managing the city.

I was wandering along the northern wall when Scarlet hailed me.

"I've been looking everywhere for you," he said, puffing a bit as he joined me.

"That's where I've been," I replied. "I'm surprised you didn't see me there."

"Well, since we're here, let me show you something interesting," he said. "Give me a hand up."

I lifted him up to the top of the wall, then pulled myself up next to him.

"When the weather's been good for a few days, you can see them," he said, looking down at the water.

"What?" I asked.

"Just look," he said.

I gazed down at the waves below. They were crossing our field of vision, racing toward the beach north of the causeway. It was getting toward low tide. I was about to ask him again when there was a momentary stillness in the waters, and I gasped with amazement.

Pure white marble gleamed up from the sea's depths. I saw columns, steps leading to nothing, flagstones laying out roads for undersea charioteers.

"What fabulous place was this?" I asked.

"Tyre," he said. "Tyre that was in the time of Alexander the Great. Remnants of a mighty warrior and a mighty civilization. He's dust, and those are the bones of a city that thrived long before Christ came to redeem this world."

"Amazing," I said.

He hopped down.

"I like to look at that every now and then," he said as we walked to the castellum. "Sometimes it depresses me. Sometimes it gives me hope."

"How?"

"It depresses me during those times when I think that all of our efforts will amount to nothing in the long run and that the impact of the Guild will matter as much to the future world as Alexander's does to us."

"And the hope?"

"The hope comes from realizing that even the most powerful tyrants cannot last, and that with faith and patience, we may yet find our way to the city of God."

"Meaning Jerusalem?"

He shrugged.

"And are you hopeful or depressed right now?"

He shrugged again.

"What's the occasion for the feast?" I asked, changing the subject.

"There's food," he replied.

"But isn't there generally—?" I stopped, grabbed him by the shoulders and spun him to face me. "Tell me that this feast isn't the food we stole!"

"Take your hands off me," he said calmly.

"Or you'll do what?" I said.

He thought for a moment, then brightened. "Please take your hands off me," he said.

"I want an explanation why—" I started, and then I found myself flat on my back with Scarlet sitting cross-legged on my chest.

"I did say, 'Please,' " he reminded me.

"How did you do that?" I asked. "Professional curiosity."

"By letting people underestimate my abilities," he said. "Would you like me to get up?"

"Please."

He stood and offered me a hand. I'm not the sort of man to refuse the hand of a smaller man who has just bested him. I took it, and he hauled me to my feet.

"Most of the food has been distributed to the tent people," he explained as we walked to the palace. "But Conrad has to entertain his supporters every now and then, just to show that he can, and to let them know he hasn't forgotten them. So, yes, some of the food we diverted from the Crusaders is going into the stomachs of the rich and powerful in Tyre. That is the price of charity. I wish things were done a little more equitably, but that wouldn't be the world, would it?"

"No," I said. "But I don't like knowing that I joined this venture so that lords might stuff themselves."

"If you feel that strongly about it, then don't partake once we're there," said Scarlet. "Of course, you might offend Conrad, and then you'll be back to being a street fool, moping around the tents until your patron comes back from the wars."

The tables were already set up in the great hall when we entered, and Conrad's throne had been placed at the center of the main table, a smaller throne for Isabelle to his left. We set up a pair of stools on a raised platform in the rear corner, which allowed us a view of the entire room as well as the entrance through which the guests arrived.

We began playing, he on guitar and me on lute. The only listeners were servants, who were just finishing setting up the tables and sideboards, but a fool cares not about the rank of his audience, just that he has one.

The guests trickled in, with Scarlet providing a constant commentary in low tones. Most of them were officers who took their places at the ends of the tables closest to the entrance.

"Quite a variety," I commented, observing the different coats of arms.

"Some came from Constantinople with Conrad. A couple have been with him ever since he left Montferrat, and the rest have all fled from different parts of Outremer, staying one step ahead of the Saracen lances. Not many Crusading types in Tyre—they've all had enough of that nonsense. These men will fight first for survival and second if the money's right. They might become more dangerous if a treaty's struck, because they'll all go looking to reclaim what they once had."

"Or claim somewhere else to replace it."

"That, too." He suddenly struck up a lively, welcoming march, smiling broadly. A hale warrior with pure white hair and beard was making his way through the hall, stopping to greet every man present. Regardless of nationality, they stood to salute him respectfully.

"Balian d'Ibelin," whispered Scarlet. "The best man in Tyre, for my money. He's the second husband of Maria Comnena, which makes him Conrad's stepfather-in-law. But he's Conrad's closest adviser as well, and that's on merit, not connection. He's been the main strategist on the negotiations with Saladin."

Was he married to Maria when she seduced the Papal Legate? asked Claudia.

I think so. I always wondered how much her husband knew. Or cared. Some men don't mind being cuckolded if it leads them closer to power.

She shuddered. I am fortunate that you're not one of them, she said.

And I am equally fortunate that you're not one of them, *I replied.*

The Bishop of Beauvais entered and quietly took his place opposite Balian. Then a brace of raucous young men came in, slapping their fellows on whatever piece of armor made the most noise. The older one was also the larger, boasting a fine head of long blond hair tied back and legs that were slightly bowed, as if he had spent more of his life on horseback than on foot. The younger had brown hair, as well as a mustache and short pointed beard that bespoke an hour of preparation before the glass prior to their public appearance.

"Two of the brothers Falconberg," said Scarlet. "Hugh and Ralph. There are two more, William and Otto. They are the stepsons of Raymond of Tiberias and have the dubious honor of being the first to lead their men into battle against Saladin at the Horns of Hattin."

"Which means that they became the first to flee?" I guessed.

"You've got it," he said. "Like all good fleers, they ended up here, but they've made up for their early failure by being quite competent in assisting Conrad. Hugh, in particular, has become his right-hand man, and rode by his side whenever Conrad led a sortie out of the city gates. He's married to Margaret d'Ibelin, the daughter of Balian and Maria Comnena."

My head was swimming. "That makes him Isabelle's half-brother-in-law?"

"Correct. You're doing well."

"My God, I'm going to have to make up a chart with all these interconnections."

"I have one in my room. Feel free to study it."

There was a flurry of activity outside the entrance, then a steward entered.

"All hail Isabelle, Queen of Jerusalem," he cried as attendees rose to their feet. "All hail Conrad, Marquis of Montferrat."

"He doesn't call himself king," I noted.

"Not yet," said Scarlet. "But he will."

We bowed as the half-royal couple entered arm in arm. Isabelle was radiant as one rough warrior after another paid his respects to her, while Conrad beamed at her as if watching a talented child recite verses at school.

They took their places at the table, and the Queen lifted a golden goblet.

"Good friends," she said. "Welcome to our home. Our shelter, our bastion. For the defense that you have given us, we thank you. For the love that you have shown us, we bless you. Please, share our table with us and grace us with your company."

The assembly pounded the tables with their fists in approval, and the feast began.

Even with the provisions we had brought, there was little fresh food other than what came from the sea. Bowls of dried figs and dates were interspersed among the tables, along with the inevitable fish stews. But the main course was delicious, at least that portion of it that was sent over to the two of us by the Queen herself. Gobbets of lamprey in a thick wine syrup dotted with ginger, baked into a pie.

I was hungry. I partook.

Hypocrite, muttered Claudia.

"Play something lively," commanded Scarlet when the main course was over.

I struck up a jig on my flute, keeping the beat by tapping my foot on a tambourine. Scarlet took a running leap onto the table, skidding amongst the dishes, and commenced a silly, skillful dance that sent his feet flying around the crockery without disturbing a single piece. From a number of small pockets concealed in his motley he produced a variety of small instruments—castanets, bells, whistles—which he would play one after the other before handing them to the diners. He could get the most fearsome military specimen up and dancing with the most ludicrous noisemaker, and those who spurned his offerings quickly received the brunt of his ridicule.

Balian d'Ibelin needed no coaxing. The Nestor of the room was up and capering with a small drum that Scarlet produced from a bag at his belt. The dwarf started singing in a nonsensical tongue of his own devising, and had the room repeating each string of syllables giddily within a minute. When Hugh Falconberg missed a syllable, Scarlet motioned the rest of the room to be silent, and sternly took the man through an improvised language lesson that had his brother in hysterics by the end. Scarlet then turned his attention to Ralph, and it was Hugh's turn to laugh when the younger man did even worse.

By the end of the performance, all were weak with laughter, and the room seemed brighter than it had been. Scarlet finished with a bow to the Queen and the Marquis, and the applause lasted for several minutes. I joined in wholeheartedly.

Cakes dusted with sugar and cardamom were passed around, then Conrad stood to address the room.

"We give thanks for our food," he said. "And to those benefactors who provided it."

The only one who glanced in our direction at this was Balian, I noticed.

"I was hoping to have some news to share with you," continued Conrad. "But, alas, my emissary has not yet returned—"

"He's here," came a cry at the door, and a man strode into the room, greeted by shouts from the Falconberg brothers. The French garments had been replaced by a more local garb, but his height and the black curls immediately identified him as the man I had seen at the Lionhearted's revels.

"Another Falconberg?" I guessed from his reception.

"That's William, the youngest," replied Scarlet.

"I saw him in Acre," I said.

"Not surprising," said Scarlet. "Conrad uses all of the brothers as his emissaries."

"You are most welcome, my friend," said Conrad as a bowl of stew and a goblet of wine were shoved in front of William. "How does King Richard?"

"He has departed Acre," said William.

"He's returned to England?" exclaimed Conrad. "Without any warning to us?"

"Wrong direction," said William. "He's gone south and east."

There was a sudden silence in the room, broken only by the youngest Falconberg digging into his cold stew. He sopped up the dregs with a piece of bread, then looked up to see everyone staring at him.

"He's going after Jerusalem?" said Conrad.

"Well, it's not as if I could stop him," William said.

"No," said Conrad slowly. "I suppose that nobody could."

I could sense Scarlet wince at that.

"We thought that he might be inadequately supplied to make such an attempt," said Balian.

"He is," said William. "The men are terrified. The French are bringing up the rear, just so they can make a break for it if they have to. But Richard leads onward. They still haven't finished refortifying Acre."

"If Saladin cuts around to the north, he could take the city again," mused Conrad. "I wonder if he knows that?"

"Please, must we speak of this dreadful business?" said the Queen.

"My dear, this is your kingdom that is being fought over," said Conrad, patting her hand. "Every mile conquered is yours, and every mile lost is your loss as well."

"And this is my dinner as well, and you're spoiling it," she said petulantly. "I want my Scarlet to perform again."

"Then so he shall," said Conrad, a bit wearily. "My Lord Dwarf, would you be kind enough?"

"One can never be kind enough, milord," said Scarlet. "There can never be a limit on kindness. Well, Monsieur Droignon, what shall we play?"

"How about the Puppeteer?" I suggested sotto voce.

He grimaced. "I always end up playing the puppet. Can't we do something else?"

"Yes. The Puppeteer with me as the puppet."

It was the first time that I had actually surprised him.

"I've never been the Puppeteer before," he said in delight. "Let's go."

He had to use a high stool to pretend to maneuver my invisible strings, but it went over splendidly, maybe even more than usual given the role reversal and the contrasts between our heights.

"Wonderful!" cried the Queen, clapping her hands at the end. "You were marvelous, Scarlet. And you, too, Monsieur Droignon."

We bowed.

"My friends, this will conclude our feast," said Conrad when the applause died down. "I will ask our spiritual leader to give us a blessing."

The Bishop stood, his hands raised.

"In the name of the Father, the Son, and the Holy Spirit, we give thanks for this food with which we have been blessed," he began.

"You're welcome," muttered Scarlet.

"Grant us the restoration of the lands walked upon by Your Son," he continued. "And in Thy mercy and wisdom, inflict failure upon our enemy."

"Amen!" shouted the brothers Falconberg to this last, and the rest of the room joined in, stomping on the floor until it shook.

"He didn't specify the enemy," I pointed out.

"I wonder if he meant Richard," replied Scarlet.

"Now, good friends, go with our thanks," said Conrad. "I ask that those at my table remain for some discussion."

The room cleared, and the servants came in to take away the emptied dishes, grumbling about the scant leavings. The two of us continued playing softly in our corner.

"I want to talk to you about Acre," said Conrad. "I'm not happy about the position in which Richard left it."

"My husband, must we always talk about war and strategy?" complained the Queen. "Talk instead of peace and happier things."

"I wish that I could, my sweet," said Conrad, patting her tenderly. "And I pray that the time comes soon when we will. But though it makes us men fierce and warlike in your eyes, never forget that we do this for your honor and safety."

"I know, I know," said Isabelle sadly. "I just wish for once … My lord, forgive me. I am weary of this talk, and there is nothing my voice can add to the discussion. Good gentlemen, I beg your indulgence."

We rose as she exited. She turned just before the entrance to the hall.

"I will await you, Conrad," she said, and then she left. Two servants closed the doors behind her.

Conrad stood looking at the doors for some moments, then resumed his seat.

"Where was I?" he said.

"Acre," prompted Balian.

"Yes, Acre," he said, rubbing his chin. "Should we be reinforcing it?"

"Milord," said the Bishop, pointing to us. "Shouldn't you be sending the fools out of the room?"

"Them?" laughed Conrad. "Let them stay. The music will help the discussion along. Now, if Richard took the Crusaders toward Jerusalem, then they most likely will not be returning. Saladin knows the territory better than they do. How many did he leave behind to guard the city?"

"Those who were wounded and a few token squadrons," replied William. "But there are supposed to be Pisan and Genoan ships coming in soon with supplies and men."

"Which means that Acre will soon become a battleground for the Pisans and Genoans," said Balian. "They'll be at each other inside a fortnight."

"How close is the city to being defensible?" asked Conrad.

"The walls and gates will take another week of repairing," said William.

"You're Saladin, what would you do?" demanded Conrad of the room.

"I'd go after the Crusaders," said Hugh.

"Let them get in too deep, intercept the supply lines when it's stretched too thin," agreed Ralph.

"And harass the rearguard into taking flight," finished William.

"You're Richard, what would you do?" asked Conrad.

"Go home," called out Scarlet, and the table burst into laughter.

"If only he would," said Balian. "I would stick to the coast, where it's more fertile, and raid the area for food while hoping a supply ship or two straggles in. Maybe try for more of the coastal cities first."

"That would be smart," said Conrad. "But that wouldn't necessarily be Richard. I think he's going to strike out to Jerusalem while he still has enough loyal troops, and look to take Saladin's head on the way. The coast is no good to him. Haifa's been destroyed, Caesaria's not worth the effort, and Ascalon is too far. He wants Jerusalem and nothing else, and only Jerusalem can still inspire the men. They haven't come all this way just to take the coast."

"Then what do we do?" asked Balian.

"We wait," answered Conrad.

"We're getting to be good at that," muttered William.

Conrad stood, strode angrily over to him, grabbed him by his hair, and shoved his face into his bowl.

"There will be no insubordination in this room," said Conrad, looking around the table. "Not if we're going to pull this off."

"You're not the king yet," spluttered William.

"And what is the word on that?" demanded Conrad, still clutching the youngest Falconberg's head.

"Richard still supports Guy de Lusignan," said William quickly, then he flinched as he felt Conrad's grip tighten. He continued quickly, "But the French barons are solidly for you. If it came to a vote now, you would be king."

Conrad released him.

"Then why hasn't it come to a vote?" he asked quietly.

"Because Richard is moving so quickly," replied William, wiping his face with a cloth. "The succession is not of the moment."

"Well," said Conrad, walking back to his seat. He folded his hands before him. "Let us pray that the expedition be resolved successfully." He looked around the table. "For the French," he finished, smiling.

"Amen," said the Bishop of Beauvais piously, casting his eyes toward Heaven.

The room emptied, leaving only the Bishop, Conrad, and the two of us. The Bishop knelt before the table.

"What is it, Philip?" asked Conrad wearily.

"Milord, I am leaving Tyre to rejoin the Crusaders," said the Bishop.

"Are you?" exclaimed Conrad. He studied the Bishop's face, looking for any sign of guile. "Well. Keep an eye on them for me, will you?"

"Of course," said the Bishop. He stood, turned to leave, then looked back over his shoulder. "We've come so far and endured so much. I truly would like to see Jerusalem before the end." He left.

Conrad rested his head on his hands, looked over at Scarlet, and smiled.

"I shall stay here," he said.

"No sense in rushing into anything," said Scarlet.

"That's what I think," said Conrad. "If we reinforce Acre without being asked, we will be seen as seeking it for ourselves."

"Which you are, of course," said Scarlet.

"Of course," said Conrad. "But why waste the men? If Saladin wins, then we'll get it by truce. If the Crusaders win, they'll hand it to us on a silver platter. Either way, Acre is ours."

He stood and stretched, groaning under the weight of his armor.

"Affairs of state," he sighed.

"Milord?" Scarlet piped up.

"Yes, little Fool?" replied Conrad.

"The Queen awaits," said the dwarf, winking.

Conrad trudged toward the door, shaking his head.

"That's what I said," he muttered. "Affairs of state."

Too old for her, I guessed. Too weary to make a young wife happy, yet dependent on her position for his own ambitions. He should try harder, or other men might want his place both on his throne and in his bedchamber, I thought.

For I had seen Ralph Falconberg looking after her like a hungry wolf as she left the room.

$\mathcal{S}$EVEN

Tyre was frequently the refuge of people in revolt or in disgrace.
—MAURICE CHÉHAB, *TYR À L'ÉPOQUE DES CROISADES*

A few days later, we were playing in that same corner of the great hall while Conrad was conferring with Balian d'Ibelin. A servant came in and whispered something to the Marquis. He frowned for a moment, then waved his hand in assent. As the servant left, the Marquis turned to us.

"There's an envoy from Richard," he said quietly.

"Should we make ourselves scarce?" I asked. "Just in case we are suspected."

"Quite the opposite," said Scarlet. "We are known to be the fools in Tyre. If we hide from the envoy, he will suspect us all the more. Put faith in God and in your whiteface, Brother Droignon. We shall brazen this one out."

The envoy was Clarence d'Anjou, a toady of Richard's who volunteered to be an envoy whenever a battle was looming. Invariably, his missions took him in the opposite direction, hence his appearance in Tyre. His armor gleamed, his surcoat was glorious, and a peacock feather was stuck in the helm that he carried in the crook of his arm.

"My lord Marquis, the King sends his greetings," he said as he strode into the room.

"My thanks for them, and for your troubles," replied Conrad courteously. "I trust that your journey was uneventful."

"Sir, thanks to the Lionhearted, this road is safe for Christian travelers once again," said Clarence.

"How does the King?" asked Conrad. "We hear that he intends to take Jerusalem next. We wish him well."

"He will be glad to hear it," said Clarence, then he paused for effect. "And he will be even more glad to hear it in person."

"Then, when we see him again, we shall wish it to his face," replied Conrad smoothly.

Clarence smiled. "The king asks that you join him, bringing sixty knights and as many sergeants, foot soldiers, archers, and crossbowmen as you can safely muster."

"I can safely muster none," said Conrad. "We have only enough to defend these walls and those refugees outside who are under our protection. We cannot abandon them to the mercies of the Saracens. It would be dishonorable. Indeed, it would be un-Christian."

"Then the king requests that you release to him the hostages that were entrusted to you by King Philip so that he may ransom them and use the funds for this expedition."

Conrad raised an eyebrow at this. "I am astounded by this request, my friend," he said. "Those hostages were given me to use as I see fit for the reinforcement of Tyre, nothing else. I swore an oath to that king that I would not sell them for personal gain, an oath of which Richard is well aware. Surely he cannot have expended all that he has gained from selling the hostages he had in Acre?"

There was a long pause during which Conrad sat smiling slightly and Clarence stood with his mouth agape.

"Unfortunately," began the envoy, then he switched topics. "There is another matter."

"Out with it," said Conrad encouragingly.

"Certain supplies were expected at Acre," said Clarence. "They did not arrive, and we have reason to believe that they came to Tyre instead."

"Did they?" said Conrad, tearing off a piece of a freshly baked loaf of bread on the table and munching on it.

"Our information was that they arrived in this city in a convoy, escorted by a dwarf. This same dwarf, your dwarf, had been seen nosing around Acre. A messenger from the supply ship was found drunk and in questionable company. He blames your dwarf for leading him astray."

"I am not his dwarf," said Scarlet sharply.

The envoy looked at a spot over his head and sniffed.

"Did you speak?" he said haughtily.

"Did you hear?" retorted the dwarf. "I am used to being overlooked, milord. Not to mentioned kicked, bumped into, trampled and, worst of all, going entirely unnoticed even when I make some noise. But to make insinuations about me when I am in the room while pretending I'm not even here is the height of rudeness. However, I will say it again, for I have a soft spot for the hard of hearing." He jumped onto a stool and shouted, "I am not his dwarf!"

"Whoever's dwarf you are, you're a thief," said the envoy. "We demand the return of our supplies."

Conrad picked up the remainder of the loaf and tossed it into the envoy's helm.

"Take that to your king," he said. "That is all he shall have of me or of Tyre. Remind him that I am not a Crusader. I care not a whit about Jerusalem or any place that may only be won by throwing away men's lives."

"You're a coward," said Clarence. "Your king—"

"He is as much my king as Scarlet is my dwarf," said Conrad. "I know all about the loyalty of kings. I sat at the right hand of the Emperor of Byzantium, threw myself into the thick of battle to destroy his enemies, and was rewarded by the joyous privilege of having to flee for my life from Constantinople. I learned a few things from that. One is that the word of a king is only smoke that vanishes on the slightest change in the wind. Another is that the whole point of having good walls is staying inside them. You call me a coward, milord? If I was, I would call you out just to prove I am not. But I have an entire city thankful that I came here to save them. My duty is to Tyre, not Richard."

"Then I shall leave you to hide," said Clarence. "Guy de Lusignan—King Guy—is by Richard's side, fighting bravely and earning the respect of all. When Jerusalem is restored, perhaps he shall be as well. My lord Marquis, I bid you adieu."

He left.

"That may have been a bit precipitous," commented Balian.

"I want someone in Acre," said Conrad. "Who should we send?"

"How about Ralph Falconberg?" suggested Balian. "He's the sharpest of the brothers."

"Good. Do it," said the Marquis. Balian left to give the word, and Conrad turned to us. "I hope you appreciate what I've done for you," he said.

"I'm sure you'll find some way for us to repay your loyalty," said Scarlet.

"Oh, yes," said Conrad, grinning evilly. "I will."

We left the castellum on that note.

"I am glad he sent Ralph out of Tyre," I commented as we walked toward the gates to the causeway. "There's something about him that I don't like."

"Really?" said Scarlet. "He's a smart man. Generally considered one of the best legal minds in the kingdom."

"Then that's another reason. But at the feast the other day, he gave your queen such a lascivious stare that I'm surprised it didn't shred her gown."

"Oh, well, he is a lecherous beast," Scarlet acknowledged. "But he knows his limits. And God knows he wouldn't be the first to look at her like that."

"She is a rare beauty," I conceded. "It is surprising that the Marquis does not respond as eagerly as one would think."

"He grows old," said Scarlet. "I think he tires of the lifelong striving for fortune. He probably thought he would be comfortably set up long before now, rather than the warrior-king of an overcrowded, besieged city."

"Yet he stood up to Richard today," I said. "Was that greed or nobility speaking? Perhaps he has grown into leadership during his time here. He never took the cross to come here. He could leave at a moment's notice, taking whatever treasure he has stashed away. But he doesn't."

"No," said Scarlet. "He's a rare bird. Many kings become thieves, but for a thief to become a king and then play the role to the hilt—well, now you can see a little of why I support his cause. In the meantime, keep your eyes peeled for Richard's men. The Lionhearted won't be happy with Conrad."

"Or with us," I added. "Where are we going, by the way?"

"I have something to show you," he said as we emerged from the last gate into the world outside the city.

We walked through the tent city. Thousands of people with nowhere to go and nothing to do. The men sat around, discussing, planning, forming unofficial councils with much debating and no deciding. The women glumly stood with buckets in lines by cisterns and mobbed wains loaded with foodstuffs, not even thanking the people who brought them.

Yet the children still played, streaking barefooted over the caked earth, chasing each other around the tents, pretending they were soldiers and pirates as do children everywhere. They greeted Scarlet with shouts and shrieks, and he waved and patted, tousled and tickled, sending his merriment amongst them.

I did the same, of course, but I was new to them, and a terrifying giant next to the comforting child-sized Scarlet. An artfully placed pratfall or two cut me down to the right size, however. I have often found that height is less intimidating to children when they see it stumble.

We came out the other side of the camp and passed into a group of low hills. Within a few paces we were completely shielded from view. Scarlet directed me around to the right. There was a small stand of trees, and a clearing inside them about the size of the great hall we had left earlier.

In the clearing were about two dozen children, ranging in age from about five to sixteen. Among the older ones I recognized our recent escort from the supply ship. They were divided into two groups, each of which was engaged in a familiar routine of stretches and tumbles.

"Welcome to the eastern branch of the Fools' Guild," said Scarlet. "When things are calm, I'm out here on Thursdays, training these children. I am now making you a guest lecturer."

He clapped his hands, and the children quickly formed two lines.

"Good morning, boys and girls," he said. "This monstrous large man to my right is Monsieur Droignon, my brother from the Fools' Guild."

"Are you really brothers?" asked a small girl, looking back and forth at the two of us.

"I got the height, and he got the looks," I replied.

Scarlet bowed to me.

"All right," he continued. "Younger children with me for language.

Monsieur Droignon, take the older ones through some advanced tumbling techniques."

"I would be delighted," I said.

The smaller children scooted over to the edge of the clearing, clambering over each other to sit as close as possible to Scarlet.

"What were we speaking last time?" he asked them.

"Greek," they called out.

"Very well. Today, it shall be Tuscan."

I turned to my charges, who were looking at me curiously, having only seen me in borrowed armor previously. I pointed to one lanky youth, and said, "Back flip, then dive into two forward somersaults, ending on a handspring."

He did it perfectly. I had each of them do the same, then picked up a branch and handed it to the first boy.

"Repeat it," I said. "But hold the branch this time in your right hand. If it breaks while you are doing that routine, you lose."

"Why?" he asked.

"My pupils, both Scarlet and I trained under a group of aging fools who had us do what we regarded as the most absurd, ridiculous tasks," I said. "Every single one of them has helped me at some point in my career, and a few of them saved my life on various occasions. If you are lucky enough to survive the journey, maybe you will travel to the Guildhall and come under the wrathful glare of that doddering Irish priest who runs it. But for now, let's see if you can tumble without breaking that branch."

"Is he truly as old as they say?" asked another boy.

"His first student was Methuselah," I replied. "Tumble!"

Hesitantly, he began his routine, holding the branch out awkwardly. At the second somersault, it came under his body and snapped. The others laughed nervously.

"Good for a first try," I said encouragingly. "Now, everyone get a branch. First to complete the routine without breaking it gets a penny."

They scrambled around the tree trunks, collecting branches. Then they began, flipping and rolling, occasionally colliding. There were shouts of glee as the branches broke right and left, but soon they got the hang of it, and finally one flipped from a one-arm handstand to his feet and held an unbroken branch aloft in triumph.

"Excellent," I said, tossing him his reward. "What's your name?"

"Ibrahim," he replied.

"Well then, Ibrahim, let me show you why this matters," I said, pulling my dagger from my sleeve. "Stand over there with your feet apart."

He did, eyeing my weapon with trepidation.

I took a breath, gathered myself, and flipped into a series of rolls, turns, somersaults, and leaps, the dagger out and slashing the air in every direction. I finished with a front flip, throwing the blade. It stuck in the ground between my target's feet. The children looked at me in awe.

"If you can do it without breaking a stick, then you can do it with a knife and not cut yourself," I said, retrieving the dagger. "Fools don't wear armor, so we have to compensate with speed and surprise when we fight. Master this technique, and you'll—"

"Droignon, cease!" shouted Scarlet, enraged. He strode up to me. "Just what do you think you are teaching them?"

"Guild fighting techniques," I said. "Isn't that what you wanted?"

"I wanted advanced tumbling, not advanced killing," he said. "These children are survivors. They have no families and have had to scrap for everything ever since they escaped the Saracens. I want them to get out of here and become jesters across the seas. They already knew how to fight. I am trying to teach them how to live."

"It helps to know both," I objected.

[88]

"How many men have you killed?" he demanded.

"I don't think that's—"

"How many?"

"A few," I said.

He looked at me sadly. "How many? And don't tell me that you don't know the exact number."

I folded my arms in front of me and looked down at him. "Five," I said.

"And when you close your eyes at night, how many of them do you see?" he asked softly.

I didn't respond.

"How many?" he repeated.

"All of them," I answered reluctantly.

He turned to the students, who were watching us wide-eyed.

"There may come a time in your lives when you think it is necessary to kill," he said. "You may think it is justified, even holy. And if you don't think about it any further, you will think that you can struggle through it."

He paused, looking at each of them.

"It is easy to kill, that's the truth of it," he said. "You've seen it all of your young lives. Some of you have seen it happen to your own families while you hid in cellars or in bushes. You can treat your enemies as animals and slaughter them in the name of whatever cause you are fighting for. And then you drown the horrors in as much wine as you can, like Brother Droignon here, because otherwise you would go mad.

"The difficult task is not killing, especially when it seems like there is no other course, that it is his life or yours. I have been on this earth as long as Droignon. I have seen as much danger and been in as many precarious predicaments, and I have managed to get myself out alive every time. And I have not killed a single person doing it. Now, I have shown you ways of fighting that allow you to disarm your opponents and render them helpless. Use them when you have to, but the best way to avoid killing someone is to make sure the fight never happens in the first place."

"Easier said than done," I muttered.

"I never said it was easy," said Scarlet. "But it can be done. Brother Droignon, switch to repertoire for a while. Teach them some new routines."

Well, I was chagrined and shamed by it all, but he was the chief, so I took it like a fool and moved on.

You still see them at night, don't you? asked Claudia.

Sometimes. Much less since we've been together. But it's a lot more than five now.

She looked out toward the mountains looming before us.

I see the ones I've killed, too, she said. I thought I would forget in time. But you never do, do you?

I don't know, I said.

When our tutoring for the day had ended, we walked back through the tent city. The sun was beginning to set, and cooking fires were springing up all around us.

A pair of men stood as we passed their tent and followed us. We stopped to let them catch up. I made sure my dagger was loose in my sleeve, Scarlet or no Scarlet. I still feared the wrath of the Lionhearted.

They were Syrians as far as I could tell, the wooden crosses dangling from their necks and the woolen girdles with their belted tunics being the traditional garb of the Syrian church. Both appeared to be in their late twenties and boasted fine black beards that were trimmed about two inches below their chins. I thought at first that they might be brothers, but closer examination belied that. The first man had a broad face, his eyes set unusually far apart. One of them bulged slightly. The second one was leaner, with a large, long nose that wouldn't have been out of place on a hawk.

"Good afternoon, friends," said Scarlet, nodding courteously.

"Christ be with you," said the first one. "We wish to ask a favor of you."

"Ask if you wish, but be prepared to be disappointed by the answer," laughed Scarlet. "I am but a lowly fool."

"They say that you are King Conrad's dwarf," said the second man.

"Then they are wrong on two counts," said Scarlet. "Conrad is not a king, and I am not his dwarf."

They looked at each other in confusion.

"But do you not perform for him?" asked the first man.

"For him, for the Queen, for whoever happens to be in the room at the time," replied Scarlet. "Also for the people in the streets, the soldiers on the walls, and the children here. Toss me a coin and I'll sing for you right now."

"Do you have the ear of Conrad?" persisted the first.

"When I sing, he listens," said Scarlet. "That's all we do. Get to the point. What is it that you seek, gentlemen?"

"We have families," said the second man. "They are not safe in these tents. I have a daughter. She is twelve. The men are looking at her in ways that I do not like. Our wives live in fear, and we cannot be constantly protecting them. We seek work."

"We wish to live in Tyre," added the first. "Even the humblest hovel inside the walls is better than the most gracious tent here."

"I sympathize," said Scarlet. "But I do not have the power to help you. I suggest that you petition either the Marquis directly, or perhaps one of his advisors. Balian d'Ibelin is a good, sympathetic man, and he frequently visits these tents."

"Thank you," said the first. He hesitated, then spoke again. "Would it help if we were to convert to your church? We were brought up with the Greek rites, and it seems that the Franks favor their own."

"It matters not to me," said Scarlet. "But you may be correct. If your safety means more to you than your religion, then by all means, convert. Good luck to you and your families. What are your names, friends?"

"I am Balthazar," said the first man. "My friend is named Leo. We used to farm near Margat."

"Maybe you will again someday," said Scarlet. "Good day."

"Is that unusual?" I asked as we walked back to Tyre.

"Not at all," said Scarlet. "I wish I could bring everyone inside, but it's impossible. I would have to judge who is worthy and who isn't, and who am I to make those decisions?"

We passed through the last gate.

"I'm sorry I came down on you so hard," he said.

"Could you kill someone if you had to?" I asked suddenly.

"I cannot think of a situation where that would be the only way," he said.

"But what if there was?" I said. "What if—"

"What ifs don't interest me," he said. "I've already said that I am not worthy of judging who comes into the city. How could I judge who should live and who should die?"

"Sometimes they judge themselves first," I said.

"And you become their executioner," said Scarlet. "No offense, Theo. I prefer my way, and I have no trouble sleeping."

"You rarely sleep," I pointed out.

The month of August passed without further incident. We continued with our classes, and the novitiates took quite well to my particular style of pratfall. I noticed as we returned one time that Balian d'Ibelin was deep in conversation with Balthazar and Leo. I hoped for their families' sakes that they would prevail. I worried about their fates if they continued outside the walls. The economy of the tent city included a lively section devoted to prostitution, I discovered.

How did you discover it?

Just by passing through it, my dove.

There was also music out there. A friendly discussion about instruments led to an invitation by a pair of guitarists to join them for dinner. Scarlet had to pay attention to the Queen, so I made the journey alone. There was a clearing in the middle of a group of tents, and many precious logs were piled into a good-sized bonfire. The meagerness of the food was made up for by the after-dinner entertainment. I contributed my share of fooling, but kept it to a minimum as the main event was the music.

Here, where Greeks, Italians, Franks, and all manner of Saracens had collided and intermingled, the music had done the same. None of our sedate tunes from the same modes handed down unchanged from the ancient Greeks. The rhythms here were complex, sent galloping around the bonfire before being reined in at the last second, while men and women sang from within their throats and improvised ornamentations that I could never imitate. I gave up trying to use my lute, fell behind with the flute, and was reduced to beating on my tabor. When I did pick up the rhythms at last, I felt the music surge through me, transporting me into an ecstatic state. Women were picking up tambourines and dancing barefoot about the clearing, whirling until their skirts were almost parallel to the ground, in constant danger of catching fire.

I lost track of time, but was brought back to earth when I heard a pair of horses gallop up. It was Hugh and William Falconberg, their empty wineskins bearing witness to their revels of the evening. They watched the women with undisguised desire, then they leapt from their steeds and started capering about in crude imitation of the dancers.

The men of the tents watched them with hostility, but feared to challenge them. William grabbed one woman, a striking beauty with strange designs in henna on her face as well as her otherwise bare arms and legs, and writhed against her, pawing at her tunic. I looked to see if anyone dared to intervene, and wondered whether I should do something about it myself.

But the evening was interrupted before I could decide. There was a tumult in the distance, which grew louder and louder. From its midst, a single rider crashed through the tents, screaming at the top of his lungs, waving his sword around his head until it whistled.

"My brothers, our armies are victorious!" cried Ralph Falconberg as he reached the clearing. "Saladin has been defeated on the plains of Arsuf!"

He jumped from his horse in midgallop, the leap carrying him over the fire while the horse rampaged unguided through the tents. He was met by Hugh and William, and the three of them grappled each other, roaring into the night skies. Without letting go, they capered clumsily around the fire, sending up howls that echoed into the distant hills, while the refugees watched them warily. The brothers Falconberg danced into the night, though the music had stopped long before.

€IGHT

It is an honour for a man to cease from strife: but every fool will be meddling. —PROVERBS 20:3

The news of the victory at Arsuf reached Tyre in the middle of September, and it energized the refugees like nothing else could. Many were ready to head back to their homes in the interior without even waiting to hear whether it was safe or not. Fortunately, wiser heads prevailed, and most settled for waiting until the spring. Still, having lived for so long with the invincible procession of the Saracens, it was miraculous to learn that Saladin could actually be defeated. The stories of the battle spread and multiplied without depending on any actual basis in fact, and many purported witnesses dined out on their accounts of what happened, dwelling in particular on the heroism of King Richard.

A week after Ralph returned to Tyre, I was shaken awake by Scarlet.

"Grab your gear," he said. "Something's up."

I slapped my makeup on quickly and grabbed my bag and weapons. He was waiting for me outside his rooftop cottage, staring out to the east.

"Look out there," he said, pointing to them. "Do you see that bit of scarlet cloth fluttering on a pole in the rear of the tent city?"

I squinted, shading my eyes from the midmorning sun with my hands until I saw it.

"You have sharper eyes than mine, my master," I said.

"That's because I know where to look," he replied. "Check that location every morning. The scarlet cloth is a signal from the novitiates that there is some emergency."

"Let's find out what it is," I said, and we rushed down the steps and out of the city.

Ibrahim was waiting for us by the pole, leaning against it casually. He was a promising pupil—one would never have known from his demeanor that anything was amiss. He snatched the cloth from the pole when he saw us approach, and walked away from the tents. We followed him at a distance.

The novitiates were waiting for us at the clearing where we held our classes. Instead of exercising, however, they were fanned out around the perimeter, keeping watch.

"This way," said Ibrahim. He led us to the far end of the clearing, where a path curved into the woods. He kept to the side of the path and pointed down.

Something had been dragged along, though the dead leaves covering the ground kept the marks from being distinct enough to figure out what. About fifty paces in, the trail left the path and went right. Another ten steps brought us to a slight declivity. At the bottom of it was the body of a woman.

She was young and of Bedouin stock. At least, that was my guess. A convert, however, for she had a cross on a cord around her neck. The neck may have been a pretty one before her throat was slit.

We squatted by her and looked at the body for a while. There was no purse, no pockets with belongings or coins, nothing that told us anything about her. The blood that had drenched the shoulders of her blouse was dry to the touch. Black flies swarmed busily over it.

"Did everyone see her?" asked Scarlet quietly, as if he feared waking her.

"Yes," said Ibrahim. "No one knew her. Magdalena thinks she saw her once recently. She may have been newly arrived."

"Poor creature," said Scarlet. He straightened up. "Well, it is good that you alerted me, but unfortunately I don't think that this is any of our concern. She must have been accosted by someone who then did away with her afterward and dumped the body here."

"That's not what happened," I said.

"Why do you think that?" asked Scarlet.

"As you pointed out, I have a lot more experience with killing than you do," I said. "There are no signs that she struggled. Her nails aren't broken, nor is there any blood under them. And the cut to the throat was done with a single, swift motion. If she had been killed during a struggle, then there would be more cuts, or more of a jagged one. It came from behind, and went left to right, so our man is right-handed and knows what he's doing with a knife. He dragged her while she still bled, which is why the blood is mostly on her shoulders, and not down the front of her blouse."

Scarlet looked at me, then back at the woman.

"Well, experience counts for something," he said. "Still, it's not our business. We'll report it to the captain of the guard. Who found her?"

"I did," said Ibrahim. "I was looking for mushrooms at dawn before exercises started. When I found her, I waited in the clearing for the rest of the novitiates and organized everything."

"Well done," I said.

"All right, send them back," said Scarlet. "Let's find that captain, Droignon."

Ibrahim ran ahead, and by the time we reached the clearing, it was deserted.

"Good lad," I said. "We should get him back to the Guildhall."

"We should get them all there," he said. "Or at least away from here."

We found the captain of the squadron responsible for the safety of the refugees eating inside a large tent. He was oblivious to our entrance, looking up only when Scarlet sat next to him on the bench.

"What do you want?" the captain barked.

"There's a dead woman," said Scarlet. "One of the children found her in the woods with her throat slit."

"Which child?" demanded the captain.

Scarlet shrugged.

"A small one," he said. "I couldn't possibly remember which. There are so many."

The captain groaned and stood, wiping his hands on his thighs.

"Show me," he said.

A couple of his men fell into line behind him as we led him past the tents.

"Don't know what I'm expected to do," said the captain as we walked. "We can't be watching everyone at once. They're a bad lot. Animals, most of them. We get a body turning up every week or so."

"It must be very difficult for you," I commented.

"You have no idea," he said.

We took them into the woods. The soldiers drew their weapons, possibly fearing the trees. When we came to the spot, they stood around the woman, staring for a while.

"Any idea who she is?" asked Scarlet.

"Probably some whore," said the captain. "Picked the wrong client this time, got her throat slit for her trouble." He looked at her for a while. "Too bad. I wouldn't have minded a romp with her myself. You two, pick her up and take her to the cemetery. I'll roust that Greek priest to do the praying. She doesn't look like she belonged to Rome."

One of the soldiers threw a blanket over her, and then a second helped him pick her up and lug her away. The captain left without saying anything, leaving the two of us standing there.

"At least she'll be buried," commented Scarlet.

"And the man who killed her?" I asked.

"He'll die someday," said Scarlet.

The next day, the Bishop of Beauvais returned with the news that Jaffa had been captured. Conrad called his council in. Once again, he decided to have musical accompaniment.

"What are their plans?" he demanded. "Will they go straight to Jerusalem?"

"The King wants to," said the Bishop. "The French are less eager. They caught the brunt of the losses during this last campaign, and they would be just as happy to go back to Tyre. But I think they will be equally happy in Jaffa."

"Why is that?" asked Conrad.

"Because when I rode from Jaffa to Tyre, I was passed by a contingent of loose women going in the other direction," laughed the Bishop. "None of the Franks will want to trade the comforts of the coast for the dangers of the interior."

"Jaffa," muttered Conrad. "That's a pilgrim's port. The city's worthless if the pilgrims can't get to Jerusalem. We'll never get a single bezant from them. What about Ascalon?"

"It's a concern," said the Bishop. "The scouts report that Saladin is destroying the walls. Richard is thinking of trying to take the city before they're finished, just so he doesn't have to rebuild them. But many of his men would rather head straight for Jerusalem."

"If they take Jerusalem now, it could be disastrous," commented Balian.

"Why?" asked Conrad.

"Because, according to the oaths taken by the Crusaders, once they retake Jerusalem, they are freed of their obligations to the Crusade," said Balian.

"And they can all go home," finished Conrad. "Leaving us stranded with Saladin and no truce. I don't like that idea one bit."

He stood and strode about the room while we watched.

"We need a truce," he said. "But we need more to bargain with. Ascalon would give us most of the coast, and Saladin has virtually no navy left. The winter approaches, which means no one will be marching anywhere for a while."

"Another season here, and Richard will be running low on money to pay the mercenaries," commented Balian.

"He's running low now," said Conrad. "He sent to me for funds."

"A man must be desperate indeed if he thinks he can get money out of you," called out Scarlet, provoking a bark of laughter from the Marquis and knowing grins from the rest of the room.

"So, if he loses the mercenaries and the French don't want to leave the coast, he won't be able to control the interior," said Hugh Falconberg.

"And he'll want to be getting back to his own kingdom before King Philip starts moving on it," added Ralph.

"Not to mention he left his brother Prince John in charge, and John cannot be trusted," finished William.

"No younger brother can be trusted," laughed Hugh, cuffing William affectionately. The youngest Falconberg gave him a goofy smile.

"Then we are agreed," said Conrad. "We're better off if they stay on the coast. It makes it more likely that he'll negotiate a truce instead of trying to conquer everything." He turned to Beauvais. "My lord Bishop, may I prevail upon you to return to your flock and give them guidance? Suggest to the King that Ascalon is the key to the coastal defenses and must be secured before any attempt is made on Jerusalem."

"I will do so, milord," said the Bishop.

"It occurs to me that that would put their armies even further away from us," mused Conrad. "Perhaps we should extend our help to Acre while Richard is so engaged. Well, something to be considered. End of meeting, my friends. Let's eat."

Food was brought in.

"Milord, if we are done with the present business, there is a small matter I wish to bring up," said Balian.

"There are no small matters with you," laughed Conrad. "Speak, old friend."

"It amounts to a request," said Balian. "An appeal was made to my sense of Christian charity."

"Money?" asked Conrad irritably.

"No, milord," replied Balian. "Shelter. There were two men from the tents, Balthazar and Leo. They are concerned about the safety, indeed the very honor, of their families. They were also concerned about their souls. They wish to convert to the Roman rite, and find safety somewhere in the city."

"It's crowded enough," muttered Conrad.

"Yet people come and go even now," urged Balian. "Surely, the addition of two small families in a corner of a room somewhere would not overburden the resources of the city."

"Everyone inside these walls works," said Conrad. "The people outside in the tents are useless. They only sit around complaining about how things used to be, and how they are going to get back at everyone who put them there as soon as they get back on their feet."

"Which is why they are harmless," I said. "Revenge and indolence are an ineffective combination."

"True enough," agreed Conrad, a bit surprised that I spoke. But not displeased.

"If it's a concern, milord, I'm certain that I can find them employment," said Balian.

"Milord, let me join in your good father-in-law's suit."

The table collectively turned and stared at William, who had spoken up.

"Well, friend William, what have you to say about these fine fellows?" asked Conrad.

"I met them," said William. "They seemed decent folks. And one of them has a very pretty wife."

The table burst into laughter, the other Falconberg brothers pounding him on the back.

"No higher recommendation is needed," roared Conrad, wiping tears from his eyes. "Very well, my friends. Let them come to Tyre, the men for the Church, and the women for the Falconbergs."

As had happened before, all the advisors left after the meal, leaving Conrad alone with us. He motioned us to keep playing, so we did while he sagged back in his chair, idly scratching himself.

"It was good of you to let them into the city," commented Scarlet.

"Seems like they should manage to cram in somewhere," said Conrad. "And I cannot deny Balian anything. He has done so much for me already. He's like the father I never ransomed."

"And William?" I asked.

"I have to throw the boys a bone every now and then," replied Conrad. "That's what leadership does. If I become king, my charity will know no bounds."

"Remember the little people," chirped Scarlet.

We left him to visit Queen Isabelle. Scarlet saw her on a daily basis, but it had been a week or so since I had had the pleasure. She was dining in a room with a large window overlooking the city. I had a feeling that she had been given rooms facing away from the tent city to shield her from any possible hint of unpleasantness.

Or, suggested Claudia, to shield her from any possible missile in case of siege. I don't see any problem in keeping the women on the safe side of the castellum.

"Monsieur Droignon, it is so nice to see you," she said graciously as we entered. I bowed in reply.

"And me, milady?" asked Scarlet, looking wounded. "Isn't it nice to see me?"

"But I saw you only this morning," she said, smiling.

"And you had enough of me," he sighed. "Familiarity breeds contempt. I've lost my charm after all these years."

"Nonsense, my own little one," she said. "My day is incomplete until I have seen you. Is it true that the Lionhearted has retaken Jaffa?"

"It is, milady," he replied. "And Ascalon may be next."

"Ascalon," she mused. "We used to visit there when I was little. Mother would take us to the shore and let us splash in the sea. I missed the sea when we were in Jerusalem. And now that we're in Tyre, there is almost nothing but the sea, yet I cannot bathe in it."

"Why not, milady?" I asked.

"They won't let me," she said simply. "The Queen may not bathe because it is not safe. The Queen must stay inside the walls of the city. Nay, inside the walls of the castellum."

"Would you walk amongst the rabble?" asked Scarlet. "I'm sure the streets of Tyre would be of no danger to you. Especially with me protecting you."

"Well, I have more reason to take care of myself now," she said, and I suddenly was aware of how the sunlight trailing in from the west suffused her skin. No, she was glowing of her own accord, and the sun was merely celebrating with her.

"I am with child," she whispered furtively, then she glanced quickly around the room, even though only the three of us were present.

"Are you sure?" exclaimed Scarlet delightedly.

She nodded happily.

"A baby for Isabelle at last," said Scarlet in wonderment.

"Congratulations, milady," I said.

She stood by the window, resting her hand lightly on the sill, watching the sun begin to set.

"An heir for Conrad," she said softly. "He'll have to stay, now. Won't he?"

"Of course, he will," said Scarlet, running over to give her a gentle hug. "There was never any doubt of that."

She looked down at him and ran both hands through his hair, smoothing it back in a familiar way.

"He'll love me now, won't he?" she said.

"There was never any doubt of that, either," said Scarlet, yet I felt the hesitation in his voice as he said it. It was unintentional, no doubt, but I think that Isabelle felt it as well.

"How did he take the news?" I asked.

She blushed. "I haven't told him yet."

Scarlet looked at her in surprise. "You mean to say that you told us before you told your husband?"

She knelt down and hugged him.

"Oh, my sweet Scarlet," she cried. "My oldest friend, how could I not tell you first? You came to see me, and I have never had any secrets from you. Let my husband visit me as much and he shall know as much."

"Isabelle, you must go to him straightaway," said Scarlet firmly. "Otherwise, he will be offended."

"Must I?" she said, sighing. "Yes, I suppose I must. I will see you tomorrow, Scarlet. Good day, Monsieur Droignon."

She left, calling for her servants.

"She told me first," said Scarlet, shaking his head in amazement.

"How old were you when you became her fool?" I asked.

"Fourteen," he said. "Fresh out of the Guildhall. My first time out of the country. You should have heard the locals laughing at my attempts to speak Arabic."

"I don't think that there's any surprise about her telling you first," I said. "You're her friend. Conrad's merely her husband. How do you think he'll take it?"

"He'll be pleased," said Scarlet. "After all, having an heir gives him a leg up over Guy de Lusignan, whose only claim to the throne is through his dead, childless wife. Now, Conrad is the father of the next King of Jerusalem. And having a child might make him a more loving man to my Queen."

"I hope that it does," I said. "She deserves to be loved."

"She is loved," he said.

Conrad was more than pleased to hear the news and wasted no time in proclaiming it to the city, the tents, and the nearby villages. William Falconberg was sent galloping after the Bishop of Beauvais so that the people of Acre and Jaffa could share in the general joy. Isabelle was embraced publicly by her husband and displayed on an ornate chariot as the two rode through Tyre, the citizens rushing from their markets and warehouses to cheer as they passed. She waved adoringly to her people, and they basked in her radiance.

In private, he did pay her more attention.

"But is it love, or merely the counterfeit?" grumbled Scarlet.

"What does she believe it to be?" I asked.

"She wants to believe it, so she does," he said.

"Then let her," I said. "Why disillusion her?"

Disillusionment, however, would find its way into the castellum from another source a few days later.

I was in a tavern—

I was waiting for a tavern!

—near the inner harbor, one favored by the sailors who came and went on the merchant ships. I was on my own, as Scarlet disliked the roughness of the patrons. But it was a fine place to catch up on the gossip of the rest of the world, as well as a likely one to receive the occasional message from the Guild. None had arrived since I had come to Tyre, but I am ever vigilant when it comes to my duties.

Especially when you can drink while performing them, teased Claudia.

But of course.

I usually managed to avoid spending my own money. Sailors are usually flush and in need of entertainment, so it was an ideal situation for me, along with the various ladies who cater to sailors.

On the occasion of this particular evening, the crew coming in to celebrate were from Constantinople. The sailing master was in the service of the Byzantine Emperor, coming to claim a cargo of glass beads and purple dye. He was a hairy fellow with only a few teeth, which he displayed constantly, throwing his head back and guffawing at the slightest provocation. I decided to become the slight provoker, and we had a fine old time.

About halfway into the night and at least two-thirds of the way into drunkenness, he turned to the local tidings.

"What was all the commotion in the streets this afternoon?" he asked. "Seemed like a parade of one woman. People were jumping over each other trying to get a glimpse. Pretty little piece, but how was she worth all the havoc?"

"Must have been the Queen," I said. "People are still celebrating the news."

"Which is what?" asked the sailing master.

"I told you earlier, Matthias," said the tapster, refilling our cups. "Our Queen is expecting."

"Happy day," said the sailing master, raising his cup in salute. "Wait a second." He started laughing, harder and harder. "Oh, that is rich. They'll love this back home."

"What's the joke?" asked a Pisan sitting next to him.

"She married that Conrad fellow, the one who used to be kaisar to Emperor Isaakios, right?"

"She did," said the tapster. "What of it?"

"So, when he was in Constantinople, he was married to the Emperor's sister, Theodora," said the sailing master. "Practically part of the imperial family. Did some good things for the city, I have to say. Got Isaakios to sit up and take notice of the world, especially when parts of it were rebelling. Conrad led the troops against that Branas fellow."

"They say he defeated him in battle personally," said the Pisan.

"True enough," Matthias agreed readily. "Branas was pleading for his life, and Conrad told him not to worry, he'd do nothing more unpleasant than take his head off. And he did!"

This got a laugh from the collected sailors in the room. I noted that for future use.

Thief, muttered my wife.

"So, he figures he's in but good, but the Emperor won't give him any more power or praise. Conrad figures he's doing all the dirty work while Isaakios takes the credit, so he ups and leaves, comes here, and ends up marrying your queen. And that's the joke."

"I don't get it," said the Pisan.

"Theodora was still alive when he married your queen," said Matthias, practically choking back the guffaws. "The new royal pup is going to be a bastard."

He could restrain himself no further. The laughter erupted from him, spewing over a suddenly silent room.

$\mathfrak{N}$INE

An instructer of the foolish, a teacher of babes . . .
—ROMANS 2:20

I raced back to Scarlet's rooftop. When I got to the top of the ladder from the last floor, I found him awake, sitting cross-legged on the roof of his cottage, strumming his guitar.

"What's wrong?" he asked upon seeing my expression.

I told him the sailor's story. Even in the moonlight I could see him turn ashen.

"That can't be true," he said. "He wouldn't have done that."

"Are you sure?"

"No," he said reluctantly. "How many people heard about this?"

"Too many. And telling that particular tapster is as good as hiring a herald with trumpets."

"Then it will be all through the town by midday," he said. "Well, since we can't quash it, we'll just have to ride it out."

"I hope the Queen is strong enough," I said.

"She's strong," he said. "Conrad is about to learn just how strong."

We decided in the morning to let the news play out naturally. We couldn't warn Conrad without betraying Isabelle, and Scarlet felt that it was not his place to tell her.

"It is just a rumor so far," he said. "She shouldn't hear gossip like that from me."

But one of her ladies-in-waiting lacked his reticence. As we entered the great hall, we heard a commotion from outside. Then the doors burst open behind us and Isabelle stormed into the room.

"Tell me it isn't true!" she shouted as she charged her husband.

Conrad sat on his throne, staring in shock at the sight of his wife in full rage.

"What on earth are you talking about?" he asked.

"You were still married?" she cried. "When you took your vows before God? You were still married when you swore eternal faithfulness to me? When you came to my bed?"

"It isn't true," he protested.

"Liar!" she spat. "It's all over Tyre. You've disgraced me and our unborn child. You've made the heir to Jerusalem a bastard."

"My Queen, where did you hear this arrant nonsense?" he demanded.

"One who came from Constantinople, who knows full well your ambition and your treachery, lifted the veil from our eyes," she said.

"Who?"

"A sailing master to the Emperor. They say his name is Matthias."

"Matthias, Matthias," he muttered, scratching his head. "I remember him. He gained his position with the Emperor by the worst kind of toadying and rumor mongering. He was one of the faction that wanted me out of the city because I was doing too good a job of cutting into their graft. If he is in Tyre and telling stories about me, you can depend on them for being lies."

She stood before him, digging her nails into her palms. He stepped down from the throne and tried to embrace her, but she stiffened and lurched back.

"Isabelle," he pleaded. "I swear by all that is holy that I was a widower when I came to Tyre. I took the oath of marriage before God with a pure heart. Our child, the next king, is legitimate."

She said nothing. She looked at him for what seemed like hours, though it could not have been more than a few seconds, then turned and strode out of the room.

"I don't think she believes me," observed Conrad.

"Isn't that strange?" said Scarlet. "Normally, ambitious schemers are the first people one would trust."

He was standing in front of the throne, looking up at Conrad in undisguised fury.

"*Et tu*, Scarlet?" replied the Marquis. "What has gotten into everyone today? One vile story from a questionable source, and suddenly I am the scourge of Tyre."

"Look me in the eye and tell me the truth," said Scarlet.

"Who are you to question me?" roared Conrad, turning crimson. He leapt from the throne and picked up the dwarf. He was on the verge of heaving him across the room when Scarlet spoke again.

"Since you're already looking me in the eye," he said calmly, "you might as well level with me."

Conrad stared at him, then took a deep breath.

"I saw her put into a grave," he said. "If she wasn't dead when we buried her, she certainly was soon after. Satisfied, Dwarf?"

Scarlet looked at him, then nodded. Conrad released him abruptly, and the dwarf landed lightly on his feet.

"But I am not the one who must be satisfied," he said. "Be honest with her for once."

Conrad walked to the door, then turned to face him.

"It's a good thing for you that you're a fool and not a knight," he said. "Otherwise, I'd be suspicious of your intentions toward my Queen."

"It's a good thing for you that I'm a fool and not a knight," retorted Scarlet. "Otherwise, you'd be seeking a surgeon."

Conrad made a disgruntled snort of a laugh and left.

"Good comeback," I remarked. "It's fortunate that he knows you were joking. Otherwise, he might revoke your license."

"I wasn't joking," said Scarlet.

The next day, Scarlet was summoned for a private audience with the Marquis. I accompanied him to the castellum, then paced outside for an hour until he reemerged. He was fuming.

"What's the punishment?" I inquired.

"A mission," he said. "An appeal to my better nature, the worst kind of seduction. He's sending an envoy to Saladin to restart the negotiations. He wants me to go along to renew my own contacts and see what we can get through the back door. Think he wants to get rid of me?"

"For a while, anyway," I said. "It might not be the worst thing. Every time he sees you now, he's reminded of what you said. Give it time and come back with good news, and you'll be back in his good graces again."

"You're making sense," grumbled Scarlet. "I don't need sense from a fool right now."

"What advice would you give to someone in your position?" I asked. "Especially when it involves a mission of peace?"

"I know, I know," he sighed. "Come with me while I pack."

He showed me what I needed to do to care for the carrier pigeons, then selected two and placed them in a small, wicker cage.

"I'll send one when I arrive, and the other when I'm about to leave," he said.

"I'll watch for them," I promised.

"Keep an eye on the Queen," he said.

"I'll visit her every afternoon," I said.

"And don't forget the novitiates' training," he said.

"I won't."

"But no teaching them how to kill while I'm away," he warned.

"They're in safe hands, my Chief," I said, grinning. "Trust me."

"I do," he said, sighing. "It's the rest of the world that frightens me." He headed down the ladder.

"Scarlet," I called.

He poked his head back up.

"What if this turns out to be some treachery on Conrad's part?" I asked.

"I've considered that," he said.

"And?"

"I've concluded that it's a distinct possibility," he said. "See you when I see you." And he vanished.

Well. Temporarily on my own. Unsupervised.

How delightful!

The novitiates were a bit surprised to see me without their master. I led them through their stretches, then showed the older ones some group acrobatic techniques. I left them under the supervision of Ibrahim after designating him my assistant in a grand mock ceremony that I made up on the spot, and worked with the younger ones on langue d'oc. By the end of the lesson, they had gleefully memorized a number of bawdy troubadour songs.

"That should get you in good with your friends," I said as I reassembled the two groups. "Now, everyone sit down." They did.

"The other day, you saw a dead woman in the woods," I began. They all nodded. "You come from different parts of the kingdom and now live in different parts of the tent city. You've had several days to learn more about her. What have you found out?"

"Scarlet said it wasn't our problem," said one of the older boys.

"Maybe not," I said. "But it is still a curious event. How is it that no one knew of her? You all keep your eyes open as to what happens here. It's a basic survival skill. Yet you've heard and seen nothing?"

"She may have just gotten here," said Ibrahim.

"Then why would someone be so quick to kill her if she's a stranger?" I countered. "I don't think that this was merely a simple instance of someone killing a prostitute. I have seen that kind of lovely behavior before, and it's usually much more brutal. This was a quick, efficient throat-slitting, and that intrigues me."

"But what can we do?" asked a girl named Sara.

"You've learned tumbling, juggling, music, and all manner of comic routines," I said. "But you've never been trained in one of the most useful tools for fools, the one that will keep you employed long after your physical skills have rusted."

They leaned toward me as if I had just told them I would share the secret of the philosopher's stone. I let the pause draw out for effect, then uttered a single word: "Gossiping."

There was a groan of disappointment.

"Gossiping is for silly women," said one of the smaller boys, and his mates echoed their agreement.

"Not always," I said. "Silly men do it just as much, though they may call it something else. Besides, it's the silly women who are in charge of the great households, especially when the silly men are off fighting their silly wars. If you wish to make a good living as a jester, you might want to attach yourself to such a household, and it will be the women, whether it's the lady of the house or the head of the household servants, who you will need to please. You can't be spending the entire time tumbling and jesting—that gets old quickly. But good talk about the everchanging state of the world or who Lady So-and-so is seeing on the sly will always be fresh and valuable. Let me demonstrate. Sara, come sit by me."

She scampered up and plopped down on the ground beside me. She was a lithe gamine of twelve with unruly brown hair and a face that I had never seen clean.

I leaned over to her and said, "Did you hear about Ibrahim?"

"What about him?" she asked.

"He says he got up at dawn to pick mushrooms," I said. "But I think he lies."

"Really?" she exclaimed. "Why?"

"Because I saw a flower sticking out of his pouch," I replied. "I think what he really was doing was picking flowers for someone."

There were some knowing giggles from the rest of the girls, and Ibrahim turned beet red.

"And I bet you know who it was," I continued.

"How did you know I knew that?" she protested.

"You told me just now," I said.

Her mouth dropped open. "You tricked me!" she accused.

"Rather easily," I said. "So, who is the object of his affections?"

"I promised I wouldn't tell anyone," she said miserably.

"It's all right," I said. "I already know. I can see Magdalena's blushes from here."

There were hoots of laughter from the rest of the children. I held up my hand to quell them.

"Now, all I had to go on was one guess based on the flower I saw," I said. "But in the space of a minute, I teased out the rest of the story. That gives me information about several of you that I didn't know before. Perfectly harmless information under the present circumstances, but if I did the same in a noble household, I might learn about a romantic dalliance that could have political repercussions. Depending on what they were, it may be Guild policy to either encourage the

[114]

romance or discourage it. If there were no repercussions, it might still be the sort of thing you could introduce in a conversation with someone. They may then tell you a bit of news that is actually something you could use. I generally recommend that you start with the cooks. They always seem to hear everything, probably because they stay in one place while the other servants come to them."

I stood and slapped the dirt off my motley.

"Your assignment for your next lesson is to find out everything you can about that poor woman," I said. "It may not be our concern, but it is still an event worth looking into, even if it's only for the gossip. Listen for word of anyone in mourning, or who's concerned about someone who either went missing or never arrived in the first place. The soldiers carried her body through the tents. It must have drawn someone's attention. Listen everywhere—you'll find that the paths taken by gossip are easily traveled and have many branchings. Lesson learned?"

"Lesson learned," they chorused.

"Then class dismissed," I said, and they ran back to the tents. Magdalena dawdled behind, waiting for Ibrahim, but he flew by her at full speed without even glancing in her direction. She gave me a nasty look and walked away.

I hope that you had enough conscience to feel guilty about that.

I did, actually.

I went to pay my respects to the Queen in the afternoon. As I was coming up to her door, it opened and Ralph Falconberg came out. He smirked when he saw the surprise on my face.

"Come to amuse the Queen, Fool?" he said.

"That is my purpose," I answered.

"Then you're too late," he said. "I've already done that." He walked away, chuckling.

[115]

I entered to find her standing by her window. I have mentioned how pale she normally was. On this day, her cheeks were full of color, and she started when I greeted her.

I know of several ways in which a man can change a woman's complexion. I wondered which one Ralph Falconberg took.

"Monsieur Droignon," she said. "Forgive me, but I am not in the mood for entertainment just now."

"I am not here on your behalf, milady," I said.

"For what, then?" she snapped.

"I am here at the behest of your faithful servant, Scarlet," I said. "He made me promise that I would visit you daily."

She looked away, her eyes brimming with tears. "I wish he was here," she said softly.

"He is in spirit, milady," I said. "Think of me as his proxy, and use me as you will. What would he usually do about now?"

"He would tell me something to distract me," she said, wiping her eyes with a kerchief. "But I am not in the mood for gossip today. I think the only gossip in Tyre right now is about me."

"Then it is fortunate that I am here, milady," I said.

"Why is that, Monsieur Droignon?"

"For my powers of gossip are not limited by the walls of this town. I can give you gossip from the tents, from Acre, and from points south, if you like."

"Has anyone else been scandalized as I have?" she asked.

"When the rank is great, the scandal must be commensurate with the rank," I said. "But the scandal to the lowest person will still be great to her."

"In other words, you're saying that my problems are insignificant?" she said, turning on me.

"No, milady, but they shall pass in time," I said. "In my experience, things either get better, get worse, or stay pretty much the same, and that's God's truth."

She laughed in spite of herself. A bit ruefully, it's true, but a laugh none the less. She sat down and motioned me to do the same.

"Scarlet used to say the same thing when I was little," she said.

"Does he say it anymore?"

"No," she replied. "I guess that he thought that I knew it by now. Tell me, Monsieur Droignon, what trouble do other women have right now? Start with the tents."

"There is a sad story, but I do not wish to burden you any further."

She sat up straight in her chair.

"I am the Queen," she said. "I don't want to be shielded from the cares of my people."

"This one is beyond care," I said, and I told her of the dead woman.

"And she has no one?" she asked when I was done.

"I don't know," I said. "But I am trying to find out."

"Are you?" she said, a bit surprised. "What was she to you?"

"I never saw her before," I said. "I'm just naturally curious."

"So am I," she said. "Please, Monsieur Droignon, find out more about her. And tell me when you do."

"I will, milady."

"That will be all for today," she said. "Thank you for the distraction, Monsieur Droignon."

I stood, bowed and left.

When I arrived at the novitiates' clearing the next morning, the boys and girls were buzzing with news, sitting in a large circle and tossing the rumors back and forth to each other. I sat and listened.

"Her name was Rachel," said a boy. "She was from Tortosa."

"Not from Tortosa," corrected a girl. "From a farm near Tortosa. Her family was killed by the Saracens."

"No, they died before Saladin came."

"Except for—"

"Except for—"

"There was a sister!" shouted Sara triumphantly. "An older sister, who had been married off and went to live with her husband."

"And where is she?" I asked.

"She's here," said Magdalena. "She lives in the tents. I heard some women talking about the one who was weeping in her tent just after Rachel's body was taken through. Her name is Mary."

"But she's not here anymore," Ibrahim said.

"Where did she go?" I asked.

They looked around at each other, waiting to see which one had that vital piece of information. After a minute, a collective sigh rose from the circle.

"Well, that was excellent work for one day," I said encouragingly. "Now, if we find out where Mary went—"

"You saw her, you know," said Peter, one of the smaller boys.

"I did?" I said. "When?"

"She was one of the women who danced when you came to play with the musicians," he said. "I sneaked out to listen. I always sneak out when there's music. I'm a good sneak."

"A worthy attribute for an aspiring fool," I laughed. "There were several women dancing. Can you describe her?"

"She was the one with the henna designs on her face and arms," he said.

"A pretty maid and a good dancer," I recalled. "She should be easy enough to find. Let's get to our regular exercises. Continue your gossiping assignment when you go back to the tents."

I called to Ibrahim when they finished and gave him some extra instruction after the class.

✳   ✳   ✳

Some excessive cooing woke me a few mornings later. I looked out to find that one of Scarlet's pigeons had returned and was being greeted by its colleagues, no doubt catching up on their own gossip. The note tied to the bird's leg said tersely, "Arrived safely. Back unstabbed. So far."

The Bishop of Beauvais returned on the same day as the pigeon, bringing the news that Richard had indeed settled for seizing the recently abandoned Ascalon and rebuilding its walls. He blamed the oncoming winter for his reluctance to take on the Holy City. Privately, he had been advised by the Templars about the effect that the conquest of Jerusalem would have on his troops' obligations, and he had come to the same cautious conclusion that Conrad had before. I heard much later that Blondel and Ambroise also had some part in influencing him, but I don't know the whole story.

With the fighting season over, negotiations began anew. Richard sent an envoy to speak with Saladin and was still awaiting the results when the Bishop left for Tyre.

The Bishop's arrival created an opportunity for one noticeable public ceremony: a baptism of many new converts, including Balthazar and Leo, who were now Balian's protégés. It took place in early November on a beautiful cloudless Sunday, with the sea breezes cooling the air to a deliciously comfortable level.

A good portion of the Christian population turned out for the ceremony, pouring between the granite columns into St. Mary's. I came in ordinary garb, sans makeup. Although I generally wear whiteface and motley in church, this was my first time in this particular house of worship, so I thought I would blend in until my position in the town was more established. No one recognized me this way.

It was a grand cathedral inside, three aisles stretching nearly three hundred feet to the triple apse at the end, the ceiling a barrel vault sixty feet above us. The narrow, arched windows were unshuttered, letting in enough light to warm us up and enough air to cool us back down.

The Queen and her husband were seated together at the front, along with Balian d'Ibelin, the Falconbergs, and their families. I was in the back with the rest of the servants, trying to get a glimpse of the proceedings. Fortunately, the sound carried well, and Beauvais turned out to be quite the public celebrant, his voice booming across the congregation like the Herald of God.

After praying at the altar, he marched up the aisle to the front doors, flanked by a pair of priests. As these were adults being baptized, he wore a flowing white cope embroidered with gold threads over his regular vestments, and as he passed by each window, the incoming sunbeams reflected off the garment and dazzled all who beheld it.

The priests each stood by a door and, upon the Bishop's signal, flung them open. Outside stood the catechumens, each dressed in white. They were taken in one at a time, exorcised, crossed, blessed, and salted, ready to make their plunge into Roman ritual.

The various sponsors beamed as they stood to join the ceremonies. The catechumens prostrated themselves before the altar, recited the prayers together, and stood by the font.

When it was Leo's turn, Balian d'Ibelin himself stood as sponsor, placing his hands on the younger man's shoulders.

"What error do you now renounce before God?" inquired the Bishop.

"I renounce the error of the Syrian rite," replied Leo.

Balian braced him, and the Bishop bent him back until his head was in the font.

"Leo, I baptize thee in the name of the Father, the Son, and the Holy Ghost," cried the Bishop. Leo came back up, looking a bit dazed, and the Bishop anointed him with chrism.

That left only Balthazar. I had supposed that Balian would sponsor him as well, but there was a sudden burst of murmuring that formed at the front and spilled through the cathedral.

Conrad had taken his place behind Balthazar. He stood calmly before the gathering storm, and answered the Bishop's questions with ease.

"Sinner!" someone shouted off to my right. The Bishop stopped in midquestion and looked furiously in that direction. Someone booed from behind me and was joined in by first a few, then practically the entire congregation.

"Adulterer!"

"Bigamist!"

"How dare he stand before God and renounce Satan? He is the Devil!"

Conrad's face grew dark, but he continued his responses to the catechism. Then Balthazar stepped forward.

"I renounce the error of the Syrian rite," he said, and he was baptized, Conrad keeping his hands on his shoulders the entire time. When the Bishop finished anointing him, Balthazar took his place with the other converts. Conrad stepped to the center of the apse and held up his hands.

"Look at them," he cried. "They are clean, washed in Holy Water, consecrated with this newest member of our church. I came to Tyre with clean hands, and they remain so. I swear by every icon, relic, and artifact in this church that I am neither adulterer nor bigamist but a poor widower who found new happiness in this city. Have you forgotten, my friends, everything that I have done for Tyre? What I was willing to sacrifice?"

He held out his hands in supplication toward Isabelle.

"Will you not believe me, my Queen?" he implored her. "Take these hands, as they once took yours, and denounce those who would libel us for their own petty purposes. I am your husband and no one else's. I am the father of the future King of Jerusalem. I have no other ambition than to be reconciled to your bosom. Before God, will you not take my hands again?"

Slowly, she stood and approached him. Without a word, she took his hand and turned to face the congregation.

The boos and catcalls stopped. Then there was a cheer, and another. Slowly, each congregant joined in, and the Bishop himself stood behind the couple and blessed them.

Yet her eyes remained dull, her tongue mute. She smiled, but I knew that it was forced. The whole thing had been stage-managed beautifully.

After the service, the converts were escorted from the cathedral by their sponsors.

"For your part in this, you shall find a place in my service," said Conrad to Balthazar as they passed by me.

"Bless you, milord," cried Balthazar fervently.

Outside, the converts lined up to receive the congratulations of the congregation. Three women joined Balthazar and Leo. The former's wife and the latter's wife and daughter, I guessed. Balian went over to them and embraced each of the men heartily. The brothers Falconberg followed. I noticed that William extended his embrace to the women, an especially enthusiastic one to Balthazar's wife.

I stood in line and congratulated the two men.

"You must thank your friend," said Leo. "His guidance proved worthwhile. We cannot thank you enough for directing us to Balian."

"I am glad that you were successful," I said. I smiled at his daughter, who peeked out shyly from her cloak. "This one is certainly worth protecting."

"Thank you, friend Fool," said Leo.

I turned to congratulate Balthazar. I managed to keep my face expressionless as I did, but it was a near thing.

His wife was standing some feet away, talking to the Bishop. The henna designs had been washed off, and the sinuous figure was concealed under more modest garb, but I had no difficulty recognizing her as our missing dancer.

$\mathfrak{T}$EN

As for the infidels ... this city has become the nest of their treachery, the den of their ruses, the refuge of their exiles and their fugitives.

—EL-'IMAD

I did not speak with Balthazar's wife that day, but I trailed them after the celebration and marked where they resided. It was a small room in a building that belonged to Balian d'Ibelin in which laborers, soldiers, and transients were jammed together. It did not strike me as much of an improvement over the tents, but it had to recommend it those triple walls separating their new home from the hostile world.

The next morning, I watched the building from an alleyway. Balthazar and Leo emerged together in a crowd of laborers, but I did not follow them. Shortly thereafter, women began coming out, many with children clinging to their robes or shooting out in all directions as if launched by a wayward sling.

Balthazar's wife came out at the end of this group, looking around tentatively. She was alone. I hadn't spotted Leo's wife in the group. I had noticed her the day before, a skinny woman with a constant cough that she muffled with her cloak.

Balthazar's wife walked past my alleyway, glancing quickly inside as she did. I was deep in the shadows with my cloak around my motley and remained unobserved. When she continued on, I slipped out and followed her.

She proved to be wholly uninteresting in her wanderings, going through the stalls at the markets, looking longingly at some of the more expensive items, particularly the beaded necklaces that glinted in the sunlight. She purchased bread, dates, and a small skin of wine, then started back toward home.

I turned a corner and bumped into her. She frowned a bit.

"My apologies, milady," I said, then I pretended to recognize her. "I know you, don't I?"

"I don't think so," she said.

"No, no, I'm sure of it," I said, then I snapped my fingers. "Of course! I saw you dance one night out in the tents. I was sitting in with some musicians I had met."

"Oh, that's possible," she said. "I don't remember seeing you there."

"I am not surprised," I said. "You seemed very caught up in the dancing."

"It can be . . . rapturous," she said, smiling a bit shyly. "But I don't do that anymore."

"Really?" I said. "A pity. You were quite marvelous."

"Thank you," she said. "I enjoy it. But now that we live here, there's no more need for it."

"Ah, you've come up in the world," I said. "Congratulations."

"My husband gained a generous benefactor," she said. "We were very fortunate to leave the tents."

"No doubt," I said. "Such a dangerous place at night. Why, I heard a woman got her throat cut there only last week. Can you believe that?"

She turned pale suddenly and faltered in her step. I took her arm and steadied her.

"My apologies, lady," I said solicitously. "I did not mean to upset you so. Curse me for the fool that I am for speaking of such an indelicate topic to such a delicate woman. Did you know the unfortunate creature?"

"No, no," she said, recovering a bit. "It's just that it was upsetting to hear."

"Well, of course," I said. "I've seen so much death and destruction since coming to this world that I suppose I've become inured to it. But I shouldn't assume everyone is like that. Let me escort you home, lady."

"Thank you," she said.

"Which way?"

She indicated the route, and I took her arm again and guided her back. She thanked me again.

"I hope you change your mind about the dancing," I said in parting. "Entertainers can do quite well in Tyre. I'm sure that I could find you some work."

"Thank you, but no," she said. She took her leave and went inside.

I watched for a while to see if she would come out again and look for someone, but she remained there the rest of the day. When the men came home, I gave up and left.

Something there, I thought. A pity I couldn't bring any of the tent children into Tyre. I could have used some help watching her.

When I saw Isabelle on the following day, she was at her usual place by the window, staring out moodily. There was no sign of Ralph Falconberg this time, and the Queen was back to her royal paleness. I announced my presence with a soft chord on my lute, and she waved me languidly to a chair opposite hers.

"I enjoyed the show the other day, milady," I said.

"Are you referring to the ritual of baptism?" she said frostily.

"There was a ritual aspect to the performance, I agree," I replied. "Public roles are still roles, after all. I thought you played yours rather well."

"Not well enough, I see," she said. "If I had played it properly, you would not have known that I was playing."

"I think that your heart may not have been in it, milady."

"True enough," she sighed. "But one must put the welfare of one's kingdom over personal happiness."

"Nobly spoken," I said, applauding lightly. "And your husband? Was his heart in his performance?"

"His desire to retain his position was genuine," she said. "Strong enough to overcome his lack of integrity."

"You still believe him to be false," I said.

"I don't know anymore," she replied.

"Tell me something, milady."

"What, Fool?" she asked wearily.

"Did you believe him when you married him?"

"It didn't matter what I believed," she said bitterly. "I had no choice in the matter."

"But did you believe him?" I persisted.

"Of course," she said. "He was the savior of Tyre. Who could believe anything else? The mere suggestion otherwise would have been monstrous."

"Did you look at his face when he took his vows?"

"You are impertinent, Fool."

"I know, milady."

I waited.

"Yes," she said finally. "I looked at his face."

"How did he appear at the moment he pledged his soul to yours?"

"Happy," she said. "At that moment he was happy. But of what value was this soul? A worthless pledge, Fool, and his was the happiness of the successful swindler."

"Why do you believe this Greek sailor over your husband?" I asked.

"A woman knows when she is loved," she said. "And when she's being used. He's never loved me, Fool."

She stood and went inside to lie upon her divan.

"What of your investigation, Monsieur Droignon?" she asked.

"I have made some progress, milady."

"Tell me," she commanded.

"The dead woman had a sister who still lives. I have learned her identity, or think that I have. Her name is Mary. She is the wife of Balthazar, the man your husband sponsored at the baptism."

"I remember her," she said. "My husband has taken on Balthazar as a messenger. He's proving quite useful."

"I am happy to hear it," I said.

"Have you spoken to the lady?"

"I spoke to her," I said. "But she would not tell me much. I think that she may know something more."

She thought for a moment, then sat up.

"I need a new servant," she said. "I will employ her. Perhaps I can learn what she is concealing."

"Milady, I would not have you risk anything," I said. "Especially on my account."

"There's no risk," she said. "It's settled. I shall do it. Will you send for my lady-in-waiting?"

"Yes, milady," I said.

I left, wondering if I had done the right thing in roping the Queen into my own little investigation. I also wondered how much she would hinder it in her well-meaning way.

I wish that I knew you had this bias against spoiled inquisitive noblewomen before I married you, teased Claudia.

You were different, Duchess, I replied. *I've never met anyone like you, noble or otherwise.*

Isabelle made good on her intentions, and Mary was soon added to her personal retinue. We arranged for the dancer to be on errands outside the castellum at the hour of my daily visit, not wanting to spook the woman any more than I already had.

But the Queen made little progress. Mary was not used to service, and the more time she spent in the castellum, the more she seemed to shrink within herself. Balthazar escorted her inside every morning before leaving for Conrad's orders. When he left, she would stand stock still, watching him until the doors closed behind him, then she would take a deep breath and force herself up the stairs. It became harder and harder to see the ebullient dancer of my memory disappear into this frightened mouse of a woman. For all her talk of desiring the safety of the walls, she seemed trapped in Tyre.

A pigeon arrived a week later, heralding the departure of Scarlet from Saladin's camp. I announced the news to the novitiates, who cheered happily, then laughed as I feigned hurt over being so disfavored.

"But enough about him," I said. "Today, children, I will teach you about one of life's great passions. More importantly, I will teach you how you can make some money from it."

"Gossip again?" said one of the boys.

"No, my friend. I speak of nothing less than love."

The younger children made faces while the adolescents snickered.

"But isn't making money from love called prostitution?" asked Sara.

"Don't confuse mere acts with the ideal," I said. "Love is the foundation of chivalry. In the pursuit of it, any man of armor and ardor will need the services of poetry and music. That's where you come in. Let me demonstrate. Magdalena, I need you to play the object of desire."

"It's not playing, it's who I am," she said, batting her eyes at the boys.

"Perfect," I said. "Now, this normally would take place on a balcony.

Since we have none, I want you to climb that tree and sit on that first limb."

She looked at the tree, then took a running start and jumped. She planted her right foot on a bole and drove herself upward. She caught the limb with both hands and used her momentum to swing herself up into a handstand, then settled down on top of the limb. She smiled down at us.

"A unique method of climbing," I said, applauding. "One not generally favored by the nobility. All right, so you are a lady being sought by a knight. The knight, having attained his position by accident of birth, is a coarse and clumsy fellow."

"Then why should I want him?" asked Magdalena.

"You don't," I said. "But you soon will, because he has brought you the very sounds of love. A serenade if you will, Ibrahim."

Ibrahim picked up his guitar, stood before the tree, and began to sing to Magdalena. It was a song that I had taught him privately, one that had been composed by the troubadour Cercamon several decades before. I have sung it to many a lady on behalf of one swain or another, and I knew the power in it.

And now, that power belonged to Ibrahim. As with all who wield power effectively, he held back, letting his voice caress softly where his hands could not. I had never heard it sung with guitar before, and I must say that the instrument lent itself nicely to the occasion, entwining Magdalena in its chords until she seemed ready to swoon.

Ibrahim finished, and as the last chord seeped into the woods, the clearing was still. Even the birds seemed to have stopped their chirping to listen. And the girl in the tree was his.

Ibrahim laid down his guitar, stepped up to the tree, and held out his arms. Magdalena swung down from the limb straight into his embrace.

"And that, children, is how you conduct a serenade," I said, finally breaking the spell.

The novitiates looked at the young couple in awe, then started cheering. Ibrahim and Magdalena separated reluctantly, still holding hands.

The opposite of a serenade is an aubade, sung to alert illicit lovers of the coming of dawn and discovery. Such a song awakened me a few days later, the soft plunking of the guitar insinuating itself into my dreams. Funny, I thought. I never taught Ibrahim that one. And what is he doing in Tyre?

Then logic returned to me. I stepped outside the rooftop cottage to see Scarlet singing to his pigeons who regarded him with sleepy affection. The first glimmerings of the sun were appearing beyond the plains. I pulled out my flute and joined in, and we greeted the dawn together.

"Do the neighbors ever complain?" I asked when we finished.

"Only when I play badly," he replied. "And I never do."

I clasped his hand.

"Good to see you alive and unperforated," I said.

"Good to be that way," he replied. "It was an interesting journey. We were in Lydda, which is to the east of Jaffa. There were two Saracen camps, one with Saladin, one with Al-Adil, his brother. His brother is the negotiator, quite the shrewd diplomat. It turns out that they had separated into two camps so each could play to one of us. We were dealing with Saladin while Al-Adil was having Richard to dinner and continuing with his envoy. Guess who that was, by the way?"

"Humphrey of Toron again?"

"You've hit the mark in one. Isabelle's ex, making eyes at the serving boys while bringing Richard's proposals, the most interesting of which involved his sister."

"Whose sister?"

"Richard's sister Joanna. He brought her to the Holy Land as barter material. He's offering her in marriage to Al-Adil in exchange for good terms on the truce. They were talking about it in Saladin's camp. In fact, they were quite amused at the prospect, wondering what she looked like. I think they were worried that she might resemble brother Richard, which would be unduly formidable in a woman."

"Has anyone bothered to ask Joanna what she thinks about the idea?"

"Vehemently opposed, from what I heard, and ready to send for the Pope if the discussions persist. Richard has a niece in reserve just in case, but I don't think the Saracens will sell their souls for a little French flesh."

"What about your negotiations?"

"Conrad neglected to bring along a supply of female relations for trade bait. Quite careless of him. He is also not quite the influential figure that Richard is. But Saladin respects him more. Richard is the fierce warrior, running around and lopping off Arab heads like he was a deranged cabbage farmer, but everyone knows that he won't be staying here forever. Conrad is in it for the long haul, and determined to keep what he regards as his. But Saladin wants him to turn against Richard, and he won't do that."

"Is he that loyal to the Lionhearted?"

"No. He just realizes that Saladin is trying to play him off against Richard. So, we wait. If Conrad is recognized as the king, then Saladin will know where he has to go if he wants to end the war."

He stretched and looked out to the east, where the sunrise was obscured by a thick bank of clouds.

"Meanwhile, the rains are coming," he said. "The Fools' Guild cannot stop the Crusaders. Maybe the mud will."

"I have always suspected that we were lower than mud," I said.

"Tell me what's been happening here," he said.

"I've been looking into that woman's death," I said.

"Why?" he asked in surprise. "I told you that it was none of our business."

"None of your business, perhaps, but since I have a meddlesome nature and too much free time, I thought I would poke around a bit."

I told him what I had learned, and of Isabelle's involvement.

"Let me get this straight," said Scarlet in mounting fury. "There is a woman we know nothing about, who might be a thief, a spy, or possibly involved in the brutal murder of her own sister, and you have gotten her placed inside the castellum next to the Queen?"

"Well, when you put it that way, it sounds like a bad idea," I said.

"Unbelievable," he said, fuming. "I leave you alone for less than a month, and this happens. Thank Christ you didn't get the novitiates involved."

"Actually, they were a tremendous help," I said, and Scarlet howled into the morning air, sending the pigeons into a frantic flurry of beating wings. I heard dogs respond from around the city.

"I think the neighbors might complain now," I said.

He sighed.

"All right, what's done is done," he said. "I want to check this woman out thoroughly. Not because of anything you suspect, mind you. I just want to make sure the Queen is safe."

Scarlet reported the results of his journey to Conrad later that morning.

"Richard was in Lydda?" Montferrat asked. "But that's inland, isn't it?"

"Yes, milord."

"Could he be trying for Jerusalem before the spring?" wondered Conrad. "That would be the height of vainglory."

"I don't know," said Scarlet. "They say he's worried about the King of France being home while he's here and unable to defend his own kingdom. He may want to try and wrap things up quickly so that he may go back."

"He couldn't go home without resolving the question of who is king around here," said Conrad. "How do we stand with the Crusaders now?"

"The French favor you," said Scarlet. "Richard still wants Guy de Lusignan. The French are getting restless and homesick."

"Maybe Richard will concede the crown to me to appease the French," said Conrad. "Well, let's wait and see."

When we were admitted to the Queen's chambers afterward, we found her in conference with the Bishop of Beauvais. She smiled at Scarlet and waved us to our usual seats. The Bishop scowled in our direction, then turned back to Isabelle.

"Will you not try, Your Highness?" he pleaded with her.

"I will try, Your Holiness," she replied. "But you know that he rarely listens to me. You would have more success approaching him directly."

"My Queen, he cares for you more than you think," said the Bishop, patting her on the hand. "You must go to him. If he delivers the funds that we need, you will find me to be a most valuable ally."

"One would hope that you were an ally to all good Christians," smiled the Queen.

"Some good Christians are better than others," replied the Bishop, rising from his seat. "I take my leave of you, Your Highness."

He bowed and swept out.

"Scarlet," she said, holding out her arms. He stepped into her embrace, and she kissed him fondly on the top of his head.

"It is good to see you, Isabelle," he said. "I hope that Monsieur Droignon entertained you sufficiently in my absence."

"He did his best, but he's no Scarlet," she said. "An unfair comparison, I know."

"I hear he's brought you a new maid," said Scarlet.

"One with a mystery," she whispered. "A dead sister."

"Yet she does not mourn and she does not talk," said Scarlet. "Don't you think that odd?"

"But she does mourn," said Isabelle. "Twice I have come upon her when she thought she was alone and unobserved, and I discovered her weeping uncontrollably. I have sought to sound her out, to offer her sisterly comfort, but she just wipes her face and goes back to work. I think that she fears someone."

"That's interesting," I said. "Maybe her sister knew something and had to be silenced. Maybe Mary knows it as well. Or maybe her sister was killed as a warning to Mary."

"Maybe, maybe, maybe," sighed Scarlet. "Well, I want to know more about her before I feel comfortable about having her inside the palace. Their sponsor was Balian?"

"At first," I said. "But Conrad stood up for Balthazar."

"Probably just to make a point," muttered Scarlet. "What about before? Any connection between her and Balian?"

"Not that I can tell," said Isabelle. "She was from near Tortosa, which is north, while Ibelin is below Jaffa."

"There's always the tents," I said. "Everyone comes together at the tents. We have some good gossips in training out there. Shall we put them on the scent?"

"You've gone this far, you might as well follow it further," grumbled Scarlet. "All right. Isabelle, I want you to be careful around her."

"You're being silly," said Isabelle. "I have nothing to fear from her."

"Fear her anyway," commanded the dwarf. "To please me, if nothing else."

"You're the only person who can bully me like this," she teased him.

"Don't forget your mother," he said.

"I am trying my best," she said, sighing a bit.

The children took their next gossiping assignment with alacrity, but turned up no word of contact between Balian and Mary, Balthazar, or Leo prior to the night we saw them speaking together.

"Not that they couldn't have done it unobserved," I said to Scarlet as we supervised tumbling exercises.

"Well, I really don't suspect Balian of being anything other than what he is," said Scarlet. "Probably he just responded to their appeal out of the goodness of his heart. That's the problem with these good-hearted people."

December brought the rains, the cold, and the news that Richard had brought the Crusaders to Ramleh, even further inland. Conrad just shook his head at the news and went on with the business of managing Tyre. But even that was to take an eventful turn.

One afternoon, the alarum was raised from the watchtowers at the harbor. A small group of ships, several of them of Arab design, had appeared on the horizon. They were bearing straight for Tyre.

Conrad was out in minutes, ordering the raising of the chains barricading the harbor. His ships were manned and in position to take the battle to the opposing fleet, and Conrad himself took the command of the leader.

Those in the city not directly involved in its defense fled to the safety of their homes and barred the doors. Scarlet and I walked through the deserted streets to the seawalls and mounted them for a better look.

The ships drew near. Suddenly, an ensign was raised on the lead ship, followed by another. The first was the colors of Montferrat, the second of Tyre. A huge, red-faced man stood at the prow and waved his sword.

"Hallo, Conrad!" he bellowed. "I've brought you a present!"

"Oh, no," muttered Scarlet. "It's Bernard du Temple. What mischief has he brought?"

Cheers erupted from the walls and the ships in the harbor, and the chain was lowered. We went down to watch. The mystery flotilla came in peacefully and anchored, and Bernard jumped on the wharf to be met by Conrad in a bear hug.

"You bastard," roared Conrad. "What do you mean by scaring us like that?"

"Your pardon, milord," said Bernard, kneeling in mock humility. "Look in the holds. Enough provisions to keep you going for months, and goods and spices to trade for more! Five ships have I captured on your behalf."

"What about the crews?" asked Conrad.

"Alas, they could not swim this far," said Bernard.

Conrad looked at him.

"How many?" he asked quietly.

"Altogether?" laughed Bernard. "Maybe two hundred. I'd say God have mercy upon their souls, but they were infidels, weren't they?"

"Then God have mercy upon yours," said Conrad. "Well, what's done is done. We'll sort things out and give you your share. Come, Bernard."

They left, and Conrad's men began unloading the ships.

"Makes our little act of larceny petty in comparison," I said as we walked up to examine the ships.

"We didn't kill anyone," said Scarlet somberly. He looked at the prow of the first boat and read the Arabic lettering. "Damn, damn, and damn."

"What is it?" I asked.

He looked at me bleakly.

"He could have unloaded the ships and sunk them quietly in the middle of the night. But no, he had to come parading them in where everyone could see what they had done."

"What are you talking about?"

"These aren't just any Saracen ships," he said. "These belonged to Sinan."

"Who is he?"

"The Old Man of the Mountain," he replied. "The chief of the Cult of the Assassins. That's one person you don't want to be stealing from."

ELEVEN

And I John saw the holy city, new Jerusalem, coming down from God out of heaven, prepared as a bride adorned for her husband.

—REVELATIONS 21:2

They never made it to Jerusalem. They sat at Ramleh for six weeks while the weather grew ever worse. Saladin's raiders harassed the perimeter and carried off the herds of cattle that had been driven along with the army. Soon, the winter became so miserable that Saladin withdrew his raiders and sent half his army home, choosing to let the sleet and hail accomplish his work instead.

With the Crusaders growing more miserable and restless day by day, Richard finally made the decision to forge ahead to the Holy City. They slogged through the miles of mud and winds so fierce that all of the soldiers' energy was funneled into the normally simple act of setting up tent poles every night. They came within twelve miles of Jerusalem to learn that an Egyptian army had arrived before them to reinforce Saladin. The Templars and the Hospitalers scouted the muddy plains and informed Richard that if he attempted the city walls, his men would be caught with no footing between two armies, and even if they were fortunate enough to prove victorious, they could not hold the city against further attack, isolated as it was.

They sat for five days as the wet got into the provisions and destroyed them and the fever and chills made martyrs out of men and horses, then they gave up and returned to Ramleh.

I have often thought that if they had waited for spring, for good weather and good footing, and seen the Holy City illuminated by the unclouded sun, then things would have been different. But patience and religious fervor rarely go together.

"Richard will have to make peace with Saladin now," said Scarlet when we heard the news. "His men will be deserting by the day."

"He really did pick the worst possible time to go inland," I said. "I wonder if Blondel and Ambroise helped that decision along."

"They'll take credit for it even if they didn't," said Scarlet. "But this will be the most dangerous time for both sides, what with a frustrated army and no truce yet."

Tyre, being on the coast, did not suffer as much from the weather. The city and the tents made it through the Christmas holidays with a semblance of good cheer, especially when Scarlet and I led the novitiates through their first ever Feast of Fools. Peter, the boy who boasted of his sneakery, was selected as the Bishop of Fools, and rode an ass through the tents as we danced and tumbled about, with every musician we could find recruited to provide the appropriate raucous ruckus.

The one sour note was sounded by Sinan, to the surprise of no one once the provenance of the pirated vessels became generally known. One morning in December, the sun rose to reveal a grand pavilion erected in the middle of the tent city, its gay colors making the weatherworn tents surrounding it even more drab in comparison. No one had seen it set up. No one had even seen it brought in, yet there it stood, proudly flying the colors of the Assassins.

"Wonderful. Just wonderful," sighed Scarlet when we saw it from his rooftop. "Let's go watch the fun."

We assembled in the great hall to await the envoys. Conrad was deep in consultation with Balian, the Falconberg brothers were practically wrestling each other for seats close to the Marquis, and assorted nobles, servants, and soldiers muddled about, trying to look useful. I spotted Balthazar with some of the other messengers, watching the whole thing with awe. At the last second, the Bishop of Beauvais dashed in, blessing the assemblage as he darted by to take his seat at Conrad's left.

Scarlet and I set up in our usual corner and began playing softly. Conrad and Balian glanced briefly in our direction, then went back to their discussion.

"I wonder what he'll do," I whispered.

"What can he do?" replied Scarlet. "The deed has been done by one loyal to him, and he will suffer the consequences whether or not it was done at his behest."

A captain appeared at the entrance to the hall. Conrad waved him forward impatiently.

"They are at the gate, milord," said the captain. "What is your desire?"

"Bring them in with full honors," commanded Conrad.

"Yes, milord," said the captain. "Shall we search them for weapons?"

Conrad stepped down from his seat and shoved the captain so hard that he lost his balance and hit the ground.

"How dare you?" thundered the Marquis. "Do you think that I fear these men?"

"No, milord," protested the captain. "I just thought that for your safety..."

"They will be treated with all courtesy, do you understand?" said Conrad. "Not a hint of distrust, even if you have to throttle yourself to keep from speaking. Bring them here directly."

"Yes, milord," said the captain, scrambling to his feet and racing out of the room.

Conrad turned to face the rest of the room.

"The first man to show any sign of fear will be stripped of his arms and turned out into the tents," he said. "That applies to me as well. These people can smell weakness all the way from the top of their accursed mountain. Make them know that we are their match."

He scanned the faces of his men, then nodded, satisfied. He took his seat and waited.

The envoys were admitted. There were three of them, each somewhere in his thirties, boasting neatly trimmed beards and well-muscled forearms poking through their sleeves. In a display of bravado equal to that of the Marquis, they were unarmed, at least to the naked eye. Who knew what weapons were concealed beneath their flowing robes? Or if they needed weapons at all?

The leader stepped forward and nodded briefly, causing a brief murmur of anger from the knights in the room which was quelled by a sharp glance from Balian.

"Conrad of Montferrat, I bring you greetings from our lord Rashid ad-Din Sinan," said the envoy in fluent langue d'oc. "Peace be unto you from him, and from us."

"Peace be unto him, and to you," replied Conrad.

"Praised be Our Lord, Jesus Christ," added the Bishop, making the Sign of the Cross.

"How does your noble master?" asked Conrad.

"He grieves," said the envoy. "He sits in our castle at al-Kahf and mourns the loss of so many brave men who now lie unavenged on the sea's floor."

"Doesn't beat around the bush much, does he?" I whispered to Scarlet.

"Wonder what Conrad will say," said Scarlet.

But Conrad said nothing. He merely leaned back in his chair and waited, his hands folded on his stomach.

The envoys stood in silence as well, watching his face.

"Well?" said the leader after several minutes.

"Well what?" asked Conrad. "I am sorry that he mourns. Is there anything else?"

The envoys looked at him, puzzled.

"Are you not going to offer reparations?" asked the leader.

"No," said Conrad. "Why should I?"

"There has been peace between our two peoples," said the envoy. "Lord Sinan wishes it to continue, but he cannot let this go by."

"I know very well that he is too great a man to let a simple payment of gold appease his honor," said Conrad. "I will not insult him in that fashion. If he insists upon war to avenge the loss of his ships and men, then we are prepared. He knows where Tyre is. Let him come to us if that is his desire."

The envoys conferred briefly, then turned back.

"If that is your answer, so be it," said the leader. "Peace be unto you from him, and from us."

"Our blessing and thanks for your pains," said Conrad. "May you have a safe journey home."

They nodded and left.

Conrad signaled to Balthazar, who stepped forward and knelt before him.

"You know the territory near al-Kahf," said Conrad.

"Aye, milord," said Balthazar.

"Good. Follow them," commanded Conrad. "See who they speak with so that we may know who they are sending to Tyre. William?"

"Yes, Conrad," replied William Falconberg.

"Go with him. Anyone who speaks to them and heads in our direction, you are to waylay and kill."

"With pleasure, Conrad," said William, grinning wolfishly, and he and Balthazar left.

*　　　*　　　*

"Something bothers me about this," I said to Scarlet as we walked to the clearing later.

"What is it?" inquired Scarlet.

"Al-Kahf is maybe a week's ride from here. Those envoys got here too quickly if the news traveled just as normal gossip. They must have spies already in Tyre or the tents."

"Very likely," said Scarlet.

"And I was thinking about that dead woman," I continued.

"Her again?"

"The way her throat was slit—that deadly efficiency could have been the work of an Assassin."

"But why her?"

"Maybe because she recognized him for what he was."

We reached the clearing while he thought. The novitiates were running through several different foolish arts simultaneously, somehow managing not to collide with each other or bonk their colleagues on the heads with juggling clubs. Sara was up on the tree limb, begging one of the boys to serenade her. He ignored her.

Scarlet clapped his hands, and they quickly assembled, looking eager and ready to do anything. He looked at me, then turned back to them.

"We may have an Assassin somewhere in the tents," he said. "Maybe more than one. These are people of the Isma'ilite sect of the Saracen religion. They are fiercely loyal to their lord and quite happy to become martyrs for their faith. They are based in the Nosairi mountains, so if there is one here, he is likely to be in the guise of a Syrian Christian or a Frank from north of here."

"Will it definitely be a man?" asked Peter.

"The Guild has no record of any woman ever fulfilling a mission for the Assassins," said Scarlet. "That doesn't mean it's impossible, but I think it unlikely."

"What about a man disguised as a woman?" asked Ibrahim.

"I am not sure what the point would be, but that's possible," said Scarlet. "I understand friend Droignon has preached the values of gossip. Go ahead, but be circumspect. If there is an Assassin here, he will not hesitate to kill any one of you, even the children, and none of you is ready to take on one of them yet. You come straight to Droignon or me. We'll be checking for the signal several times each day."

We sat and watched while they did their stretches and tumbles, occasionally calling out a suggestion.

"What did you think of Conrad's strategy today?" I asked.

"He put up a strong front," said Scarlet. "I might have counseled some reparations, but he also has to keep the respect of the men here. The fault was in making Tyre a place that his thieving friends could think a haven."

"You mean thieves like us?"

"Well, I did that more to hamstring Richard than to help Tyre," said Scarlet. "I didn't think that I was setting an example for anyone. Conrad had those companions long before he came here. They all think he's stealing a kingdom now, and they are just along for the pickings. If Bernard du Temple had merely taken the crews as hostages, things probably could have been worked out peaceably. If, if, if. It was a done deed when he sailed into the harbor. We will just have to wait this one out."

"Would it help if we sought out the Assassins ourselves?"

He shuddered.

"The Guild has tried to place someone there a couple of times," he said. "They never came back."

"Maybe William and Balthazar will have some luck," I said. "Why do you suppose he chose William for this assignment?"

"I should think it would be obvious," said Scarlet. "First, because William excels at the sneaky and underhanded, which makes him just the person to intercept an Assassin."

"And second?"

"So that Balthazar won't have to worry about William going after his wife while he's away."

The novitiates turned up several potential candidates in the tents. Scarlet and I spent several days investigating them, but ended up ruling each one out for one reason or another.

One morning, while we were visiting Isabelle, she beckoned us to her window and leaned forward to whisper.

"I was talking to Mary yesterday about the rumors going around about the Assassins," she said. "I said that they would probably be living in the tents if they were here at all. She laughed and said, 'There's no one in the tents who could harm us. Not anymore.' Then she shut up and would not speak further on it. What do you think about that?"

"I think that you should drop her from your service at once," said Scarlet. "I have a feeling she's dangerous."

"Nonsense," scoffed Isabelle. "She's frightened of mice. How could she be dangerous?"

"Please, Isabelle," said Scarlet.

"And if I get rid of her, then I'll never find out what her story is," continued the Queen, ignoring him. "Frankly, I want to satisfy my curiosity more than anything else. It's not as if I have anything else to do besides get huger by the month."

"You're not even showing yet," scoffed Scarlet. "All that's happened is that you've become even more beautiful."

"That's excessively flattering even for you," said Isabelle, smiling nonetheless.

"She has finally caught on to you," I said. "Look, why don't I shadow Mary while Balthazar is away? Maybe she'll take advantage of his absence to follow her own pursuits. I can start when she leaves the Queen this afternoon."

"All right," said Scarlet.

Mary led me nowhere but to market and back, to market and back. She ate with Leo and his family at night and took no lovers while her husband was away. At least, outside the castellum.

Inside the castellum one day, however, she turned left in a hallway instead of her normal right. I hung back long enough to give her some breathing space, then poked my head around the corner just in time to see her vanish into a room and the door close behind her. I crept up to listen, but it was a thick oaken door that fitted too snugly to allow any distinct noise through. All I knew was that it was a man and woman conversing.

When she emerged, I was at the other end of the hall, watching. Her garments appeared unmussed, her hair still in place, and no clue from her skin as to what had transpired inside.

Then Ralph Falconberg stepped into the hallway and watched her depart. It was his room that she had visited.

Was it a liaison? A little fund-raising on the side?

Or was she acting as a go-between for the Queen?

"It could have been something completely innocent," said Scarlet when I told him about it.

"What connection could Mary have to Ralph Falconberg?" I asked. "He could be using her to communicate with the Queen, or to spy on her. He wants Isabelle, I'm certain of it. And she's in a vulnerable state right now between the pregnancy and the uncertainty over Conrad."

"Isabelle would not succumb to any man," said Scarlet. "Especially a man like Ralph. He's wasting his time if that's what he's doing."

"But what if it's something else?"

He shrugged. "Impossible to know what it is at the moment. In the meantime, I'll be spending more time with the Queen. That should give her some protection."

An unbidden thought crept into my brain. Who then will protect people from the Queen?

In the middle of Christmas dinner a week later, the doors opened and William strode in, followed by Balthazar, who was carrying a bulging burlap sack.

"The prodigal returns," observed Conrad, Isabelle sitting at his side. "What did you bring me for Christmas, my friend?"

"Show him," ordered William.

Balthazar walked up and upended the bag over Conrad's table. A pair of bloodied heads rolled out and tumbled across it like misshapen dice, sending a silver goblet spinning.

"There're your Assassins," said William. "Merry Christmas, Conrad."

Isabelle put both hands to her mouth and fled, retching. Conrad looked after her and sighed.

"There may have been a better time and place for this, don't you think, William?" he said.

William shrugged.

"I think thinking was a thing he didn't think about," chirped Scarlet.

"It never was my little brother's strong point," agreed Hugh Falconberg.

"Well, William, tell us who they are," commanded Conrad. "Or were."

"We followed the envoys north," said William. "They kept to the main road past Sidon, but turned inland just before reaching Beirut. We saw them meet with two men. The men went into their tent and came out a little while later dressed as Franks. We figured they were disguised Assassins, so we followed your orders. After the envoys continued north, we waited for the two men to come by. I am sorry to say that they did not live up to their reputation, milord. It was an easy pair of kills."

"Well done, William," applauded Conrad. "One who may become king thanks you."

"May I also say that Balthazar performed superbly in your service," said William. "He is an expert tracker and knew the terrain well. He kept us from capture by Saracen patrols on at least three occasions."

"My act of Christian charity in sponsoring you has been amply repaid," said Conrad, smiling at Balthazar.

Balthazar bowed, looking a little sick. It's one thing to track human prey, but quite another to carry the trophies back with you. I had the feeling that he did not enjoy the experience. Which was to his credit.

"What did you do with the bodies?" asked Conrad.

"We buried them where no one would notice," said William. "Shall I mount the heads at the main gate?"

"No," said Conrad. "It isn't a good idea to flaunt this. Let the Assassins wonder for a while. If they know for sure, they'll just keep sending more, and the next ones won't be so easy to spot. Bury these."

He grabbed the heads by their hair and tossed them to Balthazar, who caught them with distaste and put them back in the sack.

We all relaxed about the Assassins after that.

We shouldn't have.

Scarlet and I were entertaining the Queen a few days later when Balthazar appeared at her door, accompanied by his wife.

"Milady, I beg a moment of your time," he said, coming to kneel before her.

I was surprised and sensed the same of Scarlet, but the Queen nodded as if she had been expecting this and motioned him to stand.

"Please, speak freely," she said.

"I have come to apologize for my wretched conduct in your presence," he said, almost in tears. "It was not my wish to upset you so, especially in your present condition. I was merely obeying William Falconberg."

"As you were commanded to do," said the Queen sympathetically. "I assure you, Balthazar, that I hold you blameless for that incident. The Falconbergs vie with each other for the conduct that demonstrates the most bravado. It is not the first time that we have seen this competition degenerate into this kind of crude behavior."

"I thank you for these kind words, milady," said Balthazar, kneeling again. "Bless you for them."

"Good Fools, would you excuse us?" asked Isabelle. "I would speak with this gentleman alone."

"Certainly, milady," said Scarlet, concealing his surprise for the second time in minutes.

"Mary, be so good as to show them out," commanded the Queen, and before we knew it, we were on the streets of Tyre.

"What is she up to?" sputtered Scarlet. "What would she with that ambitious refugee?"

"Maybe she thought she could get information out of him that she couldn't get out of Mary," I speculated. "She does have this ability to bewitch lesser men, which is to say, all of us."

"Without me there?" he protested.

"Especially without you there."

"What if he's dangerous?"

"She seems not to fear him," I observed. "If anything, he seems afraid of her. Why else would he come to apologize?"

"Good manners? No, not from someone like him. Maybe Mary made him do it."

"Maybe," I said. "Or maybe the Queen suggested it to Mary so that she could get Balthazar alone for questioning."

"You like it when I am discomfited, don't you?" he said accusingly.

"Yes, I do," I said.

"I tell you, Scarlet, pregnancy has sapped me of my beauty," wailed Isabelle the next day. "Normally, I would have a man like that twisted around my little finger. But yesterday, I couldn't get anywhere with him."

"His wife was nearby," said Scarlet.

"That would discourage any man from reacting to you," I agreed.

She looked at us, tapping her foot expectantly.

"And you're still beautiful," we both added hastily.

"It took you long enough," she said. "The odd thing was when I offered my condolences over the death of his wife's sister. He replied that he didn't even know that she had a sister, but he thanked me for the information."

"Now, that's interesting," said Scarlet. "When a wife fails to mention a family member to her husband, then that's suspicious."

"As suspicious as a husband failing to mention a prior living wife to his current one?" asked Isabelle.

"Are you still convinced of that?" asked Scarlet. She nodded. "Well, Isabelle, I am going to have to add that to my list of things to change in the world. I swear that I will make you see some sense before this is over."

One morning in late January, we rose to hear cries from the southern watchtowers. We looked in that direction to see a small cloud of dust heading up the road toward us. It soon cleared enough to reveal a dozen mounted knights, one of them carrying the colors of Champagne.

Young Henry had changed since I had last seen him at the Lion-hearted's revels in Acre. Not physically so much—he still possessed the pale, almost unearthly beauty that had been the only benefit of his long illness. What was different was his mien. He walked with the swagger of the soldier who had bloodied his lance many times, and he looked with the eyes of a man far past him in years, one who had seen death coming from every angle already and no longer feared its approach. He led his men on foot through the streets of Tyre, and all who beheld him felt as if an archangel had come among them.

Mind you, not everyone was happy to see an archangel in town. It all depends on your perspective, I suppose.

Conrad had ample warning of Henry's arrival and was fully arrayed when the youth was admitted to his presence.

"Well, well, it's the nephew of many uncles," he said, rising to meet him. "You are welcome in Tyre, my friend."

"You are most gracious," replied Henry. "The King sends his regards."

"Where is he now?" asked Conrad. "We last heard at Ramleh, having, Moses-like, glimpsed his objective from afar without attaining it."

Henry smiled icily. "Having fought so far like a true Christian, he found his faith strong but his arm weary," he said. "He has returned to Ascalon to finish rebuilding the walls so that he has a strong base from which to set forth again. For which final task, he demands that you join him."

"Let him demand," said Conrad. "Let him cajole, plead, beg, threaten, bribe, or seduce. The answer will be the same. I will not jeopardize what has already been retaken at so much cost. With Ascalon, we now control a hundred miles of coastline with barely enough men to protect it. If we risk all on one more throw of the dice, then we can lose everything."

"Is that your final response?" asked Henry.

"It is," replied Conrad. "But I have a request of you, my friend. You must share with us as lavish a dinner as is at our disposal ere you depart."

Henry hesitated slightly. I expect that the moral struggle was between eating with a man he regarded as the Devil versus having a genuine feast for the first time in months. In the end, his stomach won the argument.

"It would be an honor," he said, bowing slightly.

"Good," said Conrad. "Someone show him to his rooms."

"I will," said William Falconberg, stepping forward and saluting. "I am William Falconberg, milord. I am your servant." He beckoned to Henry, who followed him out of the room.

"What do you think?" asked Conrad of Balian. "Does Richard truly mean to take on Jerusalem again?"

"I doubt it," said Balian. "We have already had French deserters showing up at the tents, looking for ships home. He is running out of funds to keep them in provisions. He will lose all the French soon."

"Then he must finally sue for peace," said Conrad.

"Yes," said Balian. "We should contact Saladin again as well. I suggest that you send your best man."

"And who do you think that is?" asked Conrad, smiling.

"Myself," said Balian modestly.

At the dinner, Conrad personally escorted Henry to the table, to the cheers of all in the room. As he introduced him to Isabelle, Henry knelt before her and kissed her ring.

As he looked up at her, we noticed a familiar expression cross his face, one common to many who were meeting the Queen for the first time.

"Look," I whispered to Scarlet as we played on in our corner. "Jerusalem has conquered Champagne. God's own warrior has been smitten."

But Scarlet did not reply. He was staring at Isabelle in shock. For the Queen was looking at Henry in the same way.

TWELVE

Then Dagonet made haste and sought and found
The Queen, and shaking gleefully his bells
Broke into sudden laughter. Then the Queen,
'Why laugh you now, Sir Fool?'
And quickly came
The answer back, 'I laugh, good mistress fool,
To think a queen should be a woman, too.'
—OSCAR FAY ADAMS, "THE PLEADING OF
DAGONET"

A m I to be king?" demanded Conrad the following morning.
Henry looked at him, stone-faced.

We were back in the great hall of the castellum. To Scarlet's con-
sternation, Isabelle had a newfound interest in the affairs of state and
was sitting contentedly at her husband's side, watching the two powers
battle.

"Well? Am I?" Conrad asked again.

"The King has other concerns at the moment," Henry replied, the
slightest trace of a sneer in his voice, if not his face.

"Yes, and he expects me to drop everything and join him, doesn't
he?" said Conrad. "As if I haven't already done enough since I've come
here."

"No one can say that they have done enough while Jerusalem remains in the hands of the infidel," Henry said.

"Jerusalem!" Conrad said scornfully. "You just don't get it, do you?
You are not going to take Jerusalem, with my help or without. It's over.
Saladin has it, and he's going to keep it, because he has several times

more men than we do. And do you know why that is, my young friend?"

"Why, old man?" smirked Henry.

Conrad leaned forward into the lad's face and shouted, "Because they already live here!"

Henry reeled back under the verbal assault. Isabelle turned toward Conrad.

"Husband, please," she said, placing her hand gently on his arm. "Henry is our guest."

Conrad shook her off impatiently.

"A guest," he said bitterly. "We are all 'guests' here, didn't you know? Our protectors have to be shipped in, our money has to be shipped in, sometimes even our food. All so that we can cling to this strip of land by the sea and moan about Jerusalem. Hear me out, boy. You want Jerusalem, then you make the deal with Saladin. Truce, and free access to the holy sites, and we'll split the profits from the pilgrims' progress right down the middle. We'll hit them at the coast, he'll finish them at the Stations of the Cross, the Church can collect the donations for the indulgences, and we'll all rest easy."

"This is sacrilege!" shouted Henry. "We are on a holy mission—"

"Then why did you retreat?" asked Conrad. "Why didn't you die hacking at the gates of the Holy City? The Gates of Heaven were waiting if you had, weren't they? Wasn't that the promise? Why didn't you all die there?"

"I wish that we had," Henry said softly.

"There're plenty of opportunities left to you," said Conrad. "We'll pray for you when you go. Won't we, Beauvais?"

"Milord, perhaps—" said the Bishop.

"Oh, no perhaps about it," said Conrad. "No, we shall pray for Richard, and for you, young Henry. A special Mass in your honor. That much we are willing to do. But no more."

"The King—" began Henry.

"You know, if I was a king, things might be different," mused Conrad, stroking his chin. "Might help Richard as one king to another. Noblesse oblige, or professional courtesy, or whatever royal whim I have. But not the way things are now."

"King Guy de Lusignan fights bravely by Richard's side," said Henry.

"He's no king," retorted Conrad. "And Richard is giving him Cyprus, everyone knows that. That should be more than enough for him. But his claim to this kingdom died with his wife. The claim lies with the man who is married to the Queen of Jerusalem. It used to be through his wife. Now, it's through mine. I am married to the Queen, so by all rights, the crown is mine. Don't you agree?"

Henry looked at her, his face carefully expressionless today.

"Yes," he said. "The man who is married to her would be a king indeed."

She beamed at him adoringly.

"Maybe he'll want us for a serenade," I muttered.

"Oh, please don't even think of such things," groaned Scarlet.

"We wish you a safe journey," said Conrad.

Henry stepped back and bowed. But he bowed to the Queen, not to her husband. Then he turned and left.

"Do me a favor and follow him," urged Scarlet. "See who he talks to before he goes."

"Right," I said, and I made my farewells quickly.

Henry's quarters were a suite of rooms on a lower level facing the curtain walls. The placement was deliberate—all he had to do was look out his window to see the inner wall blocking the view, a reminder of how secure the city and its putative king were.

I camped out on a windowsill at the end of the corridor leading to his rooms, idly playing my lute. No one took notice of me for more than a second. Henry emerged after an hour with his men, his gear collected. No one had visited during that interval, and no one local came out with him.

They passed by me and descended the stairs to the main entrance to the castellum. As I followed and observed, a figure detached himself from a doorway and intercepted Henry. It was the Bishop of Beauvais.

I crept down the steps, trying to hear what passed between them, but they spoke in tones too low to be heard. The Bishop nodded at something Henry said, held up his hands in blessing over the group, then turned and went back inside.

The Frenchmen retrieved their horses from the stables, mounted, and left without further contact. I followed them out the gates and watched until they vanished down the road to Acre.

The great hall was empty when I returned. I went to the Queen's chambers and found Scarlet there.

"Anyone?" he asked when he saw me.

"The Bishop," I said. "He blessed their departure."

"He's a choosy one for blessings," said the dwarf. "Probably trying to wangle some money from Richard for that cathedral. Maybe he'll send some of his men down to help in Ascalon. I'm not really concerned about Beauvais."

"Who are you concerned about?"

He indicated the window, at which Isabelle sat, looking moodily out at the city.

"How fare you, milady?" I called.

"The city looks so gloomy today," she said.

"The city looks fine," said Scarlet. "The sun is shining, the birds are singing, the laborers are laboring and the courtiers are doing whatever it is that they do."

"Does the sun truly shine?" she asked. "I had thought that it set in the south this morning."

"For heaven's sake, Isabelle," snapped Scarlet. "He's only a boy. You're married to a man."

"Such a beautiful, noble boy," sighed the Queen. "And truly, he is about my age, is he not? I thought that there was something almost tragic about him."

"If by almost tragic you mean immature, then I would agree with you," said Scarlet. "Now, stop being ridiculous."

"Yes, that's our job," I said.

"Oh, Scarlet," she said. "May I just have this little fantasy to amuse me? I felt as if I were Queen in the Courts of Love, and he was going to the Crusade because his love for me could never be requited."

"Very pretty," I said. "I've had some fantasies of my own. Would you like to hear one of them?"

"Shut up, Droignon, this is not the time," said Scarlet. "Now, Isabelle, I want you to remember who you are. The Courts of Love are a fancy notion that someone came up with to please Eleanor of Aquitaine. If they existed, you would be my first choice for queen, no question. But in the real world, you are the Queen of Jerusalem, and you can't be mooning over the nearest pretty boy like some romance-engorged maid. Half the court saw the expression you had on your face, and the other half will be saying they did inside a day. The only one who didn't see it was your husband. Remember him? The one you married? Whose child you carry?"

"I remember, Scarlet," she said. "I remember all the time. I remember every time I feel this new life move inside me. All I have to do is stand on my land and breed successfully, is that it? What good is being queen if I can't have my way once in a while?"

"If your way takes you through Champagne, then there will be consequences," warned Scarlet.

"I've had a noble beauty without manliness, and manliness without beauty," she said. "Yon Henry possesses them both."

"Yon Henry is a puppy," said Scarlet.

She looked at him, realization dawning in her face.

"You're jealous," she accused.

"Jealous?" exclaimed Scarlet, turning crimson. "Who am I to be jealous? I am your dwarf, your plaything, your slave. And your friend and confidant. If you want to fall for this green youth in the middle of your pregnancy and embarrass yourself and scandalize the city in the process, don't let me stop you."

He stormed out of the room.

"I'll go calm him down, milady," I said, bowing.

It didn't take me long to catch up with him, an advantage of longer legs. I grabbed his shoulder, then let go before he had a chance to throw me anywhere.

"Go away," he said.

"I was going away," I replied. "It just happened to be in the same direction you were going away, my jealous master."

"I am not jealous!" he shouted.

"Then stop acting as if you were," I said. "So she's gotten besotted. So what? Half the women who saw Henry acted the same way. People go through these little spates of madness every now and then. In Isabelle's case, it's probably just the pregnancy talking. It makes women strange."

Hey! said my wife. You did not think that about me, I trust.

Of course not, Duchess. I thought that you were strange even before you became pregnant.

Oh.

"It's not about Henry," Scarlet insisted. "It's the crown that I am worried about. We need Isabelle and Conrad to present a unified front if they are going to lead this small slice of Christendom successfully. If he cannot even hold the loyalty of his wife, he'll never get it from the people. He'll be a coronated cuckold."

"Look, Henry's gone back to Richard, so it will be months before he shows up around here again. Out of sight, eventually out of mind, say I."

"I hope so," Scarlet sighed. "We are so close to seeing the end of this Crusading debacle. I would hate to see something as petty as love get in the way of peace."

"She doesn't love him," I reassured him. "He's just a fantasy. Try having one of your own sometime. You'll be better for it."

"I have one," he said, but he spoke no further on the topic.

The French started showing up a few weeks later. First just a couple, skulking about the tents, nervously looking around to see if anyone would challenge their desertion of their oaths and fellows. More trickled in, then the trickle became a veritable torrent of overdressed soldiers waving their falchions in one hand and their goblets in the other.

There was no room for them in Tyre, of course. Most of them came with whatever supplies they could lift from their adventures, but they didn't bring much in the way of food.

Conrad welcomed them as a sign that the army was falling apart. He fed them as well as he could, all the while making certain that they knew where it was coming from. While the troops resisted his attempts to recruit them into his service, they felt enough goodwill in their full stomachs to start cheering him as King Conrad whenever he rode into their camp, spreading cheer and wine.

The novitiates latched onto them as a prime opportunity to practice their language and jesting skills. Little impromptu performances popped up all over the tent city. Peter, in particular, became a favorite of the new arrivals, a ready accomplice in the frequent practical jokes they would play upon each other.

It was Peter who brought us a morsel of information that kept us on edge for a few weeks.

"I've found two spies," he announced with the supreme confidence of a ten year old.

We sat him down in the middle of the clearing and gathered around him.

"They say they are deserters," he said. "But they don't get drunk and chase women like the others do. They've been watching, and sitting with other people and asking lots of questions."

"What kinds of questions?" asked Scarlet.

"About supplies," said Peter. "Mostly, where does the food come from, how often do the fishing boats come in, that sort of thing."

"Doesn't sound like Assassins," I said. "They already knew about the pirated ships."

"No," said Scarlet. "I have a feeling it was our little exploit with the supply ship. I was wondering when that particular chicken would come to roost. You've all kept quiet about it, of course."

They all nodded furiously.

"What are their names?" asked Scarlet.

"Pierre and Phillippe," said Peter. "Pierre is my name in langue d'oc, isn't it?"

"Yes, it is," said Scarlet. "Let me think. They suspected Conrad's dwarf, so I probably shouldn't be getting too close to them. But they don't know Droignon was involved."

"Then I should check on them," I said. "Peter, lead the way."

He stood, puffed his chest out, and beckoned to me imperiously as the other children giggled. He took me through the confusion of tents with the ease of a Roman guide in the catacombs until we came upon one that had been pitched with military rigor.

I did not recognize the two men sitting in front of it, which was a relief. I was thinking about how to approach them when Peter marched up and said, "Messieurs, I found a man who knows your language and can sing your songs."

Perfect, my lad, I thought as I walked up and bowed.

"What is this creature?" said one of them, a stout soldier who looked uncomfortable sitting on the ground instead of on a horse.

"I am Droignon, the jongleur," I said. "I have come to entertain you."

"For a fee, I suppose," he said.

"Some men will work for a song," I said. "But what is the song worth?"

"The worth of the song depends on the worth of the singer," he said.

"A worthy reply," I said. "Let me sing you a short one, and if you like it enough, then you shall hear more. Tell me where you are from, and I will sing the life of that place."

"We are from Toulouse," said the stout man.

"I know it well," I said, tuning my lute.

"Well, not from the city itself," he amended hastily. "From St. Sulpice, north of there."

"I believe I passed through there once or twice," I said. "Does it have a small wooden church with a flat roof on a hill and a tavern called the Blue Dog?"

"That's the one," he replied.

"Then let me sing you a song the farmers sing at their revels," I said, and I launched into something appropriate. Peter grabbed a tambourine from my bag and accompanied me vigorously. At the end, they clapped and the stout man gave us each a penny. Peter's eyes grew wide and he thanked them profusely, drawing their attention away from me.

Afterward, as the two of us walked away, I handed him the second penny.

"What's that for?" he said.

"Your finder's fee," I said. "You did splendidly back there."

"I was amazed that you know that little village so well," he said.

[161]

"I don't," I said. "Neither do they. I made up the church and the tavern. And their accents weren't quite right. They sounded more like Normans to me."

"So they are spies," he said excitedly.

"Poor ones," I commented. "I have seen a much better spy today."

"Where?" he asked, trying to look around without appearing he was doing so.

"Right here," I said, patting his shoulder.

He grinned all the way back to the clearing.

Scarlet decided to take this information directly to Conrad. We were admitted to his private chambers. He nodded when we told him, unsurprised.

"Outside the walls, they don't present much of a problem," he said. "There're a few more in the city that I have my men keep under surveillance. I think that these two are just trying to find out the extent of the French desertions, but I'll notify the watch at the city gates to refuse them entry. I thank you for the information, and more for your loyalty."

We bowed. He picked up a scroll from his desk.

"Another summons," he said.

"From Richard?" asked Scarlet.

"From Hugh, Duke of Burgundy," he said. "He's abandoned Richard and taken the bulk of the French troops with him."

Scarlet gave a low whistle. "Where is he now?"

"Outside Acre. And therein lies the problem. The Pisans and the Genoese are at each other's throats there. The Pisans are trying to seize the city for Guy de Lusignan, and they won't admit the French." He stood and stretched, then removed his cloak to reveal that he was in armor. "Burgundy seeks my aid. And we cannot let Acre fall into the wrong hands, can we?"

"You mean the infidels?" I asked.

"I mean Lusignan," he said, picking up his sword. "After all, it belongs to my Queen. I will see you when it's over. It shouldn't take too long."

We followed him down to the harbor, where several dozen troops were pouring onto galleys in a grim, orderly manner. They cheered when they saw Conrad. He drew his sword and held it aloft so that it caught the sun, and they cheered some more.

"I almost feel inspired," I said. "When he does go to battle, he appears quite competent."

"He is," said Scarlet. "And he knows when to go. I feel sorry for the Pisans, except for the fact that it's their own damn fault."

Isabelle had not come to see her husband off. There was some comment about that around the city, but most ascribed it to her condition and forgave her readily.

Still, with the castellum virtually emptied by the expedition, she needed entertaining more than usual. Ralph Falconberg tried to pay her a few visits in her husband's absence but was rebuffed. He had stayed behind with his brother Hugh to assist Balian d'Ibelin in running the city while Conrad was away.

I saw Mary approach him in a hall one afternoon. Once again, I was too far away to hear the brief conversation, but she left in tears while he stood there, smirking. I wondered if I had read her wrong. Perhaps she was not a go-between but another discarded conquest. But none of our attempts to elicit conversation from her had any success.

Conrad and his ships returned from Acre a week or so later, laden with booty and prisoners. There were cheers from around the harbor as he waved the Pisan standard from the forecastle.

The Queen awaited him in the great hall, along with the assembled nobles. The trumpets sounded, the drums beat out a triumphant clatter, and he led his men through the doors and knelt before the Queen.

"Acre is yours again, my love," he said, offering her the standard.

"We are glad to see you safely returned," she said, taking it and handing it to Mary. "All is well here."

"Is it truly?" he said quietly.

She gave an almost imperceptible shrug.

"Come," she said. "Sit in your accustomed place by my side."

As he did, a soldier came running in a panic.

"Sir, we have report of a great army approaching from the south," he cried.

There were gasps in the room, but Conrad merely smiled.

"I have been expecting them," he said. "My Queen, the Duke of Burgundy will be joining us for dinner."

"Will you look at that?" exclaimed Scarlet. "He's done it! He's turned the French."

"I suspect Richard had as much to do with that as Conrad," I said. "Armies need to be paid, no matter how holy their mission."

The Duke came in a little later and was escorted to the place of honor at Conrad's right hand as Balian graciously ceded the place. Conrad himself served the Duke, selecting the choicest morsels for his plate.

"You are most kind, my friend," said Burgundy. "I have something for you as well that may be of interest."

He handed Conrad a scroll. The Marquis glanced at the seal and slit it open.

"From Richard," he said. "He wishes to meet with me again. At Casal Imbert."

"But that's just a day's journey south," said Hugh Falconberg. "I thought he was in Ascalon."

"He came up to Acre to try and help settle everything," said Burgundy.

"What do you think?" Conrad asked Balian.

"For him to come this far just to meet with you is a compromise on his part," said Balian.

"And for Richard, compromise might as well be capitulation," crowed Conrad. "Well, I am willing to meet him less than halfway. I'll be off in the morning. Balian, time for you to go to Saladin and discuss terms again." He lifted his goblet to the Duke of Burgundy. "My friend, to peace. You are most welcome in Tyre."

The tent city doubled in size overnight with the arrival of the French army. The celebrating began immediately as they had shed their armor and only awaited the ships that would bring them home again. Every kind of drink that could be found within twenty miles was carted in and sold at a huge profit, while the prostitutes were so in demand that they began talking about forming a guild of their own, just so they could have regular breaks from their practice.

A week after the arrival of the French, I saw the emergency signal from the novitiates. I found Scarlet at the castellum, and we ran to the tent city. Sara was by the signal pole, tears streaking her grimed face.

"Hurry, please," she said. "It's Ibrahim."

She led us to a tent where some of the older boys were apparently loitering, but we could see that they were on guard. Inside, Ibrahim lay on a blanket, his face bruised and bloodied. I lifted his tunic to see that his body was much the same.

"What happened?" asked Scarlet.

"It was the soldiers," said Peter. "Ibrahim and Magdalena were performing for them. The soldiers wanted Magdalena to go with them. She refused, and they grabbed her. Ibrahim tried to help. He fought well, but there were too many of them. They did this to him."

Scarlet sat by Ibrahim, feeling his pulse.

"Get a stretcher from somewhere," he said, and two of the older boys ran off. "I know a surgeon in the city. We'll try and save him. Where did they take Magdalena?"

"To a tent in the middle of their camp," said Sara. "We heard her screaming. But she came out later and ran off."

Scarlet looked at me. "I suppose you're thinking that if I taught them to fight your way, this could have been avoided," he said heavily.

"No," I said. "If Ibrahim had killed one of them, they would have hunted him down and hung him. You take care of him. I'll look for Magdalena. Did you see where she ran?"

"No," said Sara.

"Be careful," warned Scarlet.

I left without replying.

I wasn't about to go into the French camp. I wouldn't find out anything, and she had to be long gone from there. I went over everything I remembered about the girl, then started toward the clearing.

The sun was setting when I got there, and it was dark under the cover of the trees. I looked around and saw the one that she had climbed when we had her serenaded by Ibrahim. There was a dark form crouching on one of the upper limbs.

"Magdalena," I called softly.

There was a slight rustle from above.

"Magdalena, it's me, Droignon," I said. "Ibrahim is still alive. Scarlet's taking him to Tyre for help. Come with us. He needs you."

A sobbing drifted down.

"He'll never want me now," came her voice. "No one will. Who would want me when I have been so shamed?"

"A young fool," I said. "One who loves you unconditionally. What happened to you was not your doing, and he knows that. I suspect that he feels shame for not saving you."

"He tried," she said. "He was so brave. How can I face him?"

"Because you are also brave," I said. "There are no cowards in the

Fools' Guild. Scarlet picked you because he knew your worth. Come down, Magdalena. I'll take you to Ibrahim."

She came down, almost falling. I caught her and brought her out of the clearing. In the waning light, I saw what they had done to her. I took my cloak and wrapped it around her, then put my arm around her shoulders and helped her walk.

As we walked through the tents, a loose escort of novitiates formed around us who kept the curious and the louts from coming too close. I talked the guards at the gates into letting her into the city. As we walked through, I looked back and saw over my shoulder the phalanx of children who we had brought into this strange profession standing and watching us, the younger ones huddling together for comfort. Then the gates closed.

THIRTEEN

[A] companion of fools shall be destroyed.
—PROVERBS 12:20

I t's my fault," said Scarlet as we sat outside the surgeon's door.
"How?" I asked.

"I gave them too much responsibility," he said. "Too much confidence in their abilities."

"Bad things happen to even the best of fools," I said. "Ours is a dangerous profession."

"But the novitiates are supposed to be protected until they are ready," he said. "That's the point of the Guildhall. That's where they should be, not with me."

"They look up to you," I said. "You gave them responsibility and confidence, but you also gave them hope in a world where there's little to be had. Look at all that they had been through before they came to you. They know the world can be a miserable place, and they know that it's nearly impossible to change it. But thanks to you, they know that it's worth the effort."

He gave me a wan smile.

"Where's Magdalena now?" he asked.

"At the castellum," I said. "I had carried her to your room. When I came down, Mary was waiting for me. I told her to go to the Queen and tell her that there was a girl who needed help. Isabelle insisted on caring for her herself."

"That's my Isabelle," said Scarlet. "Why was Mary waiting for you?"

"I didn't ask," I said. "I was concerned with helping Magdalena at the moment."

"Well," began Scarlet, then the surgeon opened the door and beckoned to us.

"He'll live," he said briefly. "His right arm is broken. I put it in a splint. If he's lucky and God provides, it will heal straight. If not, he'll have a bent arm. His nose was broken, but that's never serious, and he lost some teeth. He won't be as handsome as before, but that's the price of brawling. If he wants to fight, tell him to join the Crusade, not take it on single-handedly."

Scarlet gave him a coin, and we looked in on Ibrahim. He was stretched out on a table, unconscious.

"I gave him something to make him sleep," added the surgeon. "Best thing for him. Feed him hot broths, and check the arm twice a day. If the skin begins darkening, bring him here straightaway and I'll have it off in a trice."

We had brought the stretcher with us, and we managed to get him to Scarlet's building. Then I slung him over my shoulder and carried him up to the roof. He groaned with pain at every step. By the time I had dumped him on the pallet, I was spent.

"I am carrying no more bodies today," I informed Scarlet. "You attend your Queen, and I'll take care of him. And buy a chicken for broth on the way back, would you?"

"Right," he said, and left.

I sat with Ibrahim through the day, mopping his brow with a wet cloth. In the afternoon, he sat up suddenly, calling out, "Magdalena!"

"She is safe," I said. "She is with the Queen."

"Did they . . ." he began, then he hesitated.

"Yes, they did," I said.

He tried to stand, and I placed my hands on his chest and pushed him down.

"I have to find them," he said weakly. "I have to kill them."

"Then you'll die," I said. "You'll do her much more good by living."

"But she will be unavenged," he protested.

"Yes," I said. "Vengeance is not a useful thing, in my opinion. I come from a land where Christianity is a relatively recent phenomenon, and one of the old ways that the nobles refused to give up was the blood feud. As a result, we have a dwindling aristocracy, which is not necessarily a bad thing. My point is, once you set vengeance on its course, it never ends, and it will come back to hurt others that you care about."

"What will happen to the soldiers?"

"I don't know. The Fools' Guild is not here to punish. It's here to save."

"I don't want them to be saved," he said.

"Neither do I," I replied. "But that's the way it is sometimes."

He was quiet for a while, and I thought he had drifted off again. But then he looked at me with old eyes.

"Being a fool is more difficult than any of us knew," he said.

"If Father Gerald heard you say that, he would give you the rank of Jester on the spot," I said.

There was a noise outside. I glanced out, my hand on my knife, then stood back. Magdalena came through the doorway, Scarlet behind her. She looked at Ibrahim with trepidation. Then he held out his hand, and she flung herself onto him, sobbing as he embraced her awkwardly. Scarlet pulled me outside.

"We have to arrange two things," he said. "First, let's get them married. If she is pregnant as a result of this violation, it will legitimize the baby. Second, we have to get them out of Tyre."

"Good idea," I said. "Where shall we send them?"

"To the Guildhall," he said. "I've been saving up to send two novitiates there. I was going to send two of the younger ones who could benefit more from the training, but things just changed."

I dug into my pouch and pulled out some gold. "Here's my contribution," I said, handing it to him. "That's what is left of the money I conned out of Conrad, plus what I've made since."

"But how will you live?" he asked.

"I've lived on no money before," I said. "That should be enough for you to send two more children."

"Twenty Venetian ducats a head," he calculated. "Plus food for the voyage and travel from Venice to the Guildhall."

"As for that, they could probably earn their way by entertaining," I said.

"If Ibrahim's arm doesn't heal, he won't be able to juggle or play the guitar," said Conrad.

"I knew a one-armed juggler once. He did quite well. People were impressed that he even bothered."

"All right. We have enough for four. Of the younger children, who would you pick?"

"Peter and Sara," I said.

"My choices as well," he said.

The wedding was performed by a Syrian monk two days later in the clearing. All the novitiates were there, of course, along with Scarlet and me. When the ceremony was done, Scarlet announced his news.

There were cries of joy, and tears from all. We made a modest feast from what was available and finished with sweetcakes that we had smuggled out of the castellum kitchen. As it ended, Scarlet and I each presented the newlyweds with a bundle tied with string.

"What is it?" asked Magdalena.

"Open them," commanded Scarlet.

She undid both knots, Ibrahim still hampered by his splint, and pulled out two pairs of motley.

"Discarded scraps of cloth from all over, brought together in a unified whole," I said. "Much as the Fools' Guild has been assembled from the discards of the world."

"Wear them well, my children," said Scarlet. "You've earned them."

"What about us?" demanded Sara.

"You've earned a few years with Father Gerald," said Scarlet. "You may or may not thank me for it."

We lent the newlyweds Scarlet's room and sat in the courtyard below, playing our instruments through the night, Peter and Sara sleeping at our feet. The next morning, we took them to the harbor where Scarlet had arranged things with a sympathetic sailing master. At the wharf, the four shook my hand solemnly, then suddenly burst toward Scarlet and hugged him hard.

"Will we ever see you again?" wailed Sara.

"Of course," said Scarlet smiling cheerfully. "I'll pop up at the Guildhall sometime, and you can buy me a drink and tell me your adventures."

A drum sounded from within the boat, and the children hurried on board. The oarsmen took their stations; the anchors were pulled up, and the boat slowly pulled out of the harbor. We waved until it was a dot on the horizon.

"You know that it's unlikely we'll run into them again," I said.

"I know," said Scarlet. "But it's my job to keep them hoping, isn't it?"

"Come on," I said. "I'll buy you a drink. But you'll have to lend me some money first."

"So, that's how you do it," he said.

Conrad returned from his meeting with Richard in a state of rage.

"That obstinate buffoon!" he bellowed as he heaved his helmet in the general direction of his servants. "Richard the Lionhearted! Richard the Bullheaded, they should call him. Richard the Pig would do."

"What happened?" asked Isabelle as pieces of armor continued to fly about the hall.

"He threatened me," Conrad said in amazement. "Me! Said that if I did not send every able-bodied knight that I have down to Ascalon to help rebuild the walls, he would seize my lands as forfeit."

"Our lands, you mean?" she corrected him gently.

He stopped and looked at her as if he had suddenly realized to whom he spoke.

"Your lands, my Queen," he said quietly. "Of course, they are yours. Which is why it is nonsense for him to make these threats. Every bit of land that has been recaptured is yours, not Richard's, and not the Crusaders'. And everything that I do to preserve this land is done for you."

"How nice," said Isabelle.

"How were things left?" asked Hugh Falconberg.

"They were left the same," said Conrad. "He's there and I'm here. He's King of his country, and I am the Queen's husband. Has Balian returned from Saladin?"

"Not yet," said Hugh.

"Then I will speak with the Duke of Burgundy," said Conrad. "He understands the situation. Without a King of Jerusalem, no truce will last. It has to be done now."

The last piece of armor shed, he kicked off his boots, wrapped his cloak around him, and sat petulantly next to the Queen.

"Such a lot of noise from a husband," said Isabelle that afternoon. "I think it's helping me prepare to be a mother. He wants his own way, and he stamps his feet and throws tantrums until he gets it."

"He'll relax when he gets the nod," said Scarlet. "It's been a long time for something that's so obvious."

"Do you know, I never really wanted to be the queen of anything?" said Isabelle. "Everyone wants me for what I own, and yet I have no power to choose anything."

"You have power, Isabelle," said Scarlet. "You just haven't asserted it publicly."

"If I gave my husband a command, and he refused it, what could I do to force him?" she mused. She looked at Mary, who was bringing in a tray of food. "Mary, could you make your husband do something that he didn't want to do?"

The woman looked startled.

"How could I do that?" she replied.

"By a woman's wiles," I said.

"You call them wiles," Mary said. "Men go for women for all the wrong reasons, then say it was our wiles that snared them. If you want a man to do your bidding, then you have to marry that sort of man. Otherwise, there's no hope."

And what's the fun of that? said Claudia.

Am I your ideal husband, Duchess?

There is no such thing, Fool. No more than there is an ideal wife.

Spring sneaked up on us one morning. We woke to see the plains shimmering greenly and the scent of new things in the air. Everyone was waiting to see which way Richard would go, east or west. The Duke of Burgundy went south to attend a council of French nobles and to urge that the question of the kingship be settled.

[174]

Richard was still holding out for Guy de Lusignan, but he had also received word that he was desperately needed in England. With Easter approaching, Burgundy threatened to pull out the few remaining French troops. Richard gave up.

Around the third week of April, the cry went up along the watch-towers: "Champagne! Champagne!" The cheer was picked up in the French encampment and soon echoed by those in the tent city, many of whom cheered without knowing precisely who he was.

With a blare of trumpets, Henry of Champagne returned to Tyre, his troops in their finest regalia. Isabelle, given the advance notice, assembled herself into a proper regal beauty, bulging belly notwithstand-ing, while Conrad elected to have the meeting on the steps of the cathedral.

The semi-royal couple stood to meet Henry, with the Bishop of Beauvais on one side and Balian d'Ibelin on the other. All Conrad's men lined both sides of the steps, and as much of Tyre as could fit crammed into the piazza to see.

Henry ascended to the step just below Conrad and Isabelle and knelt before them. Isabelle, her face glowing, bade him rise. He did so and held out a hand. His sergeant slapped a sealed scroll into it, and Henry held it aloft for all to see.

There was a flourish of drums, then silence as he broke the seal.

"My gracious sovereign Isabelle, Queen of Jerusalem," he said. "What I have to read here concerns your happiness, and by extension that of your kingdom. I beg your permission to address your husband and consort."

"We grant it," she said.

Henry turned to address the crowd.

"By designation of the assembled lords and barons of the armies of the blessed Crusade, with the full accord of Richard, King of England, and Philip, King of France, by his representative Hugh, Duke of Burgundy, we name as King of Jerusalem and its environs Conrad, Marquis of Montferrat and husband to the Queen of Jerusalem."

Huzzahs greeted this proclamation. Henry turned back to face Conrad.

"Seigneur Marquis, the Christian host of Ascalon, Jaffa, Acre, and Tyre have elected you the King of Jerusalem. Will you accept this great honor and greater burden?"

Conrad stepped forward to take the proclamation from him. Then he knelt before the Bishop for a quick blessing, kissed his wife's ring, and turned to face the crowd. He looked toward Heaven and held his arms to the skies in supplication.

"Gracious God," he cried, "who made me, and placed my soul within my body: You are the true and just King of Jerusalem and of all Creation. As you know me to be the worthy governor of Your kingdom here, see fit to have me crowned here in Your Church two weeks hence. If You do not know me as such, never consent to it. I pledge my life to You, to my Queen, and to my subjects, whose servant and guardian I will be until life itself has left my body and my soul has rejoined You in Heaven."

At this, the crowd cheered so that the echoes seemed to shake the very buildings, and flocks of pigeons and gulls shot into the air, bewildered by the onslaught. The drums boomed, the trumpets blared, and the taverns opened.

I mention this last because it was where Scarlet and I immediately repaired to for our own celebrations.

"Did he have that crowd eating out of his hand?" crowed Scarlet. "What a performance! He's done it. He's won the crown."

"Yes," I said. "It would be nice if the Queen looked happier about the whole thing. She had eyes only for Champagne."

"Yes, well, she'll be in the public eye from now on as never before," said Scarlet. "She'll keep up proper appearances. Now, we'll be needed throughout the festivities. Could you put together a group show with the novitiates?"

"Certainly," I said. "Too bad we have four fewer to work with."

"Yes," said Scarlet. "And it's too bad that we couldn't send all of them to the Guildhall."

"Maybe the Queen could help with that."

"I could never ask her for money," he said, looking into his cup.

That afternoon, as I was returning from working with the novitiates, I was hailed from the French encampment. I looked over to see a familiar pavilion set up. King Denis, my patron, stood in front of it, waving to me.

I dashed up and knelt before him.

"My liege, I am happy to see you alive and well," I said.

He motioned me to my feet.

"It gladdens my heart to see you, Droignon," he said. "You were right about my not needing any distractions. My life nearly ended on so many different occasions that I have been jumpy ever since. Since my arrival, I've killed three mice in my tent for the petty crime of startling me."

"I promise never to approach you from any direction but the front, sire," I said. "What brings you to Tyre?"

"The Duke of Burgundy has summoned the remaining French here for the coronation," he said. "I thought that I would stay for that, then we could go home."

"A good plan," I said, then I hesitated. "We?"

"Of course, Droignon," he said. "I would like to have stayed and seen Jerusalem, but by the time Richard settles everything with Saladin, we will have missed the next sailing season. There's not even enough time to make a proper pilgrimage. Pity. I dearly would have liked to behold the Holy City. However, as this may be the only real travel I ever do in my life, I thought we should visit Constantinople on the way home. They say it's one of the marvels of the Christian world."

"Very good, milord," I said. "Now, with your permission, I have duties to perform for the coronation myself. I am to be part of the entertainment. If you will grant me my time until the King is crowned, then I will be your fool again afterward."

"By all means, Droignon," he said.

I walked back to the gates, my heart sinking within me. I had not realized how fond I had become of living in Tyre and working with Scarlet. I had been postponing in my mind the question of what I would do when Denis returned. Foolish of me, considering that I had never settled anywhere for long in my career once I had finished my training. I had been Across-the-Sea since we came with King Philip to the siege of Acre, and if the king who was my assignment was going to leave, then that was it for me.

Well, at least the kingship was settled satisfactorily, and the truce seemed finally at hand. I would never find out what had happened to that poor woman killed in the tent city, but that was not part of my mission. I could leave without too much impeding my conscience.

I walked through the inner gate in a foul mood, realizing that I was going to have to break this news to Scarlet. A pair of faces passing in the crowd drew my notice momentarily, then disappeared. It was about a block later that the jolt restored my memory. I went dashing back to see where they went, but they had vanished.

I ran up the steps to Scarlet's rooftop. He was watching the sunset, gently petting one of his pigeons.

"They're inside the city," I said, panting.

"Who?" he asked.

"Those spies of Richard's," I said. "Pierre and Phillippe. I saw them walking in a crowd, but I lost them."

"I don't think Conrad countermanded the order to keep them out," said Scarlet, getting to his feet. "I don't like this. We had better go tell him."

The king-to-be was in his chambers, standing on a footstool and being measured by a brace of tailors.

"Greetings, my friends," he said. "How do I look?"

He held his arms out, and purple silk swirled about him.

"Very much a king," said Scarlet.

"Practically an emperor," I added.

"You think so?" he said, pleased. "It's modeled on something I saw in Constantinople. I think it looks rather grand."

"Milord, Droignon saw those two spies inside the city walls," said Scarlet.

Conrad stepped down from the stool, trailing silk and tailors behind him.

"I gave no order permitting them in," he said.

"Then someone erred, or was bribed," I said. "Either way, they are here."

"And that concerns us," said Scarlet.

"It is good of you to think of our safety," said Conrad.

"You're not royal yet," said Scarlet. "We want to see you sitting on that throne almost as much as you do."

"But do you have any reason to believe these men threaten us?" asked Conrad.

"We suspect them because they behave suspiciously," I said. "No reason not to be careful."

"Then I will be careful," said Conrad. "I will keep guards about me. Maybe one of the Falconberg brothers could join me as well. If they see these two fellows come near, they'll have free rein to cut them in half."

"Good enough," said Scarlet.

[179]

We went to entertain the Queen after that, only to find her entertaining Henry. He was seated next to her, nibbling on a cookie from a tray before them.

"Scarlet, Droignon, how wonderful!" exclaimed Isabelle. "I need your music to accompany the Count's tales of his adventures."

"The Count recounts," I said.

"No accounting for taste," muttered Scarlet, but he dutifully tuned his guitar and began to play.

"So, as I surmounted the hill overlooking the Holy City," Henry continued.

"A surmounting count!" interrupted Scarlet. "Mounted on a mountain."

"Hush, Scarlet," scolded the Queen. "Pray, continue."

"I looked across at Jerusalem," he said, gazing into her eyes. "Never have I seen a sight more beautiful, more sacred. It seemed to be lit from within by some celestial fire, and I thought that I beheld the Kingdom of Heaven lying before me."

"I thought that you had stopped miles from the city," chirped Scarlet. "And that it was all rainclouds and mud. Did you have your own personal weather, Count?"

"Really, milady, this fool should know his place better," said Henry, exasperated.

"As should you," muttered Scarlet.

"What was that?" thundered Henry, getting to his feet, his hand at his sword's hilt.

"Achoo. Forgive me, I sneezed," said Scarlet. "Pray, continue. You were at the part about beholding the Holy City lying before you like a strumpet waiting to be taken."

The Count was livid.

"My Queen," he said. "I beg that you have this impudent scoundrel flogged until he knows proper behavior in your presence."

[180]

"Please, good Henry, abate your anger," she begged him, suppressing a smile. "In our court, Scarlet has a license to say whatever he pleases, and it generally pleases me to hear him say it."

"Very well, milady," he said, bowing stiffly. "But in your radiance, alas, I have lost track of the sun. I am wanted by the Duke of Burgundy for counsel. I must take my leave of you."

He kissed her ring, turned without glancing at Scarlet, and left.

"Now, Scarlet," said Isabelle, frowning. "Why are you being so cruel to this upstanding young man?"

"I don't like him," said Scarlet.

"And your reason?" demanded the Queen.

"Something somewhere about coveting another man's wife," said Scarlet. "Seems to be wrong, somehow. Especially when her true husband is worthy of her trust."

"We've discussed that overmuch," sighed the Queen.

"Don't talk, Isabelle," said Scarlet, producing a letter from his pouch. "Read."

She took it from him uncertainly, then unfolded it and read it quickly, her eyes widening. Then she read it again, more slowly.

"Who wrote this?" she asked.

"I'm sorry it took so long to get the information," said Scarlet. "It was a while before I could find a sympathetic courier to Constantinople. But my correspondent is the Emperor's Fool there, a fellow called Chalivoures. He's a supreme gossip, knows everything that there is to know about everyone worth knowing. He confirmed that your husband left that city a widower, Isabelle. Conrad has been telling the truth."

She crumpled the letter and let it fall.

"It's too late for the truth," she said.

FOURTEEN

That did not go as well as I had hoped," said Scarlet as we left her chambers.

"Give her some time," I urged him. "Remember, she's been living with that false information for months. She can't just switch moods in an instant, no matter how good your source is."

"I just want her to be happy," said Scarlet. "I thought this might help."

"It will," I said. "Now, while we're on the subject of news, I have some for you. King Denis has arrived to reclaim me."

Scarlet stopped and looked at me in dismay.

"You're not going home, are you?" he asked.

"Not immediately," I said. "But soon after the coronation. I was hoping to be around for the truce, but looks like I'll miss out."

"By David's lyre, I shall miss you," he said. "I haven't even taught you how to play the guitar decently yet."

"Well, don't say good-bye," I said. "Plenty of fooling to do before I go."

We passed the Duke of Burgundy, who was heading toward the great hall, and Henry of Champagne, who was talking to William Falconberg.

"All these soldiers with no battles to fight," observed Scarlet. "I hope they can handle peacetime."

The next morning, after leading the novitiates through exercises and rehearsal, I paid a visit to King Denis. To my surprise, Henry of Champagne was sharing a morning meal with him. I bowed to them both.

"Good morning, Droignon," called my king.

"Good morning, sire and milord," I said. "Some music to ease the digestion?"

"This was one of the fools who caused me indigestion yesterday," said Henry.

"Actually, sir, that was my brother fool who did all the talking," I said. "I apologize if you think that I shared his sentiments. All I did was play my lute."

"That was well said, Droignon," said Denis. "Will you forgive him for me, Henry?"

"For you, cousin Denis," said Henry. "And you are right, Fool. It was that barnacle who clings to the Queen who aroused my ire."

"He does that to everyone," I said. "Even to me. But his heart is good underneath it all, and he is devoted to his lady."

"I have yet to see this Queen," said Denis. "They say she is a rare beauty."

"She is, my liege," I said. "With child, now, which adds to her charms, in my opinion. So, Count Henry, I hope that you have earned the right to indulge at last. When we spoke in Acre last summer, you felt that you did not deserve to partake of the splendors of this world."

"I spoke as a child would," said Henry. "One who was feeling sorry for himself because he lay abed while the others were playing in the sun. Now that I have tasted battle and survived, I truly appreciate what life has in store for those who would partake of it."

"A good lesson to take home with you," I said. "Will you be departing with the French after the coronation?"

"Actually, I must return to Richard today," he said. "My path is with him until the truce is signed. Cousin Denis, I thank you for your hospitality. I hope that we will meet again this side of Heaven."

"My hope as well," said Denis fervently as he clasped Henry's hand. "But if not, we have the assurance of Heaven awaiting us, and shall certainly meet there."

Henry's men were waiting nearby. He mounted his horse, and they rode south.

"Where is Richard these days?" I asked.

"Still in Ascalon, I think," said Denis. "He didn't want to come to the coronation after backing Guy de Lusignan all this time. I think he was angered by the council's selection. I'm not surprised that Henry isn't staying. I hear Conrad treated him pretty roughly when he was here."

"If the boy can face battle, he should be able to take a few angry words well enough," I said.

"Sometimes those can be worse," said Denis.

In the afternoon two days later, Scarlet and I were in our usual corner of the great hall. I was playing my flute just for the change of pace when I noticed that Scarlet had stopped playing. I looked up to see Isabelle standing in the entryway, watching her husband with an expression of . . . well, I'm not sure what it was. My thought was regret or sorrow, but I could not see below the surface.

Conrad saw her about the same time and stopped speaking to Balian d'Ibelin, who had returned from his latest diplomatic mission. The Marquis stepped down from the throne and stood in the center of the room. She came to a decision and walked slowly to him. Then she put her arms around him and kissed him long and hard as the men in the room applauded and cheered.

He wept, to my astonishment. This aging warrior wept before all, and held onto her for dear life.

"Careful, milord," called Hugh Falconberg. "Don't crowd the heir."

"Forgive me," said Isabelle.

"There is nothing to forgive," replied Conrad. "My dear, I am so happy to see you this way. Please, come with me to dinner tonight. I have been invited to the Bishop's table."

"Yes, do join us," called Beauvais. "You would grace our simple repast beyond measure."

"I must ask your indulgence and refuse," said Isabelle. "With all of this excitement, I must save my strength so that I will be a fitting queen at your coronation. I am going to bathe tonight in preparation."

"So be it, my love," said Conrad. "I will look in on you upon my return."

She kissed him again, gently this time, and left.

"You were right," said Scarlet. "Time healed the marriage."

"It does look that way," I said. Yet there was something staged about the whole scene, I felt, much as it had appeared at Balthazar's christening.

The Bishop of Beauvais stood and stretched, then adjusted his miter.

"Milord, I will go on ahead and prepare the table," he said. "I will see you at sunset."

"With all my heart," said Conrad. "Since you are providing the meal, I shall provide the music. Scarlet, though you are my wife's fool, will you do me the courtesy?"

"Milord, this is the first time that you've ever bothered to ask," said Scarlet. "Don't lose your command just when you have gained the throne."

"Quite right," said Conrad. "Scarlet, you and Droignon come to the Bishop's with me for dinner. I command it."

"And we obey," said Scarlet, smiling.

The Marquis of Montferrat rode a magnificent white stallion captured from the Saracens, while his escort, including Hugh Falconberg, rode lesser beasts. We walked ahead of them, playing and singing all the way from the castellum to the Bishop's house near the cathedral.

The Bishop himself opened the doors.

"Welcome," he cried. "Our humble house is honored beyond all worth by your presence. Come join us for dinner."

The humble house was nearly the size of the cathedral, and the simple repast was a seven-course feast, of which the poor working jesters could only sample three.

"Is the ceremony prepared for the coronation?" asked Conrad as they brought in the pastries for dessert.

"It is, milord," replied the Bishop. "I have drawn upon a number of different ceremonies, including those used for David and Solomon. I thought it fit for the King of Jerusalem."

"Not in Hebrew, I hope," said Conrad.

"Oh, no, milord," said the Bishop. "Done in the appropriate Latin, certainly. The Church requires no less."

"Good," said Conrad.

"Speaking of the Church," began the Bishop.

"Are you asking more money of me again?" interrupted Conrad.

"After all I have done to bring you to this point, I don't think it unreasonable," said the Bishop.

"If you had done as much as you had promised, I would have been king months ago," said Conrad. "It was Burgundy who clinched it for me. My first duty is to him. We'll get to the Church when the money starts coming in from the pilgrims."

The Bishop looked as if he had swallowed something that didn't agree with him.

"Very well," he said curtly. "Just remember that charity is good for the soul."

"My soul is fine, thank you," said Conrad. "And my belly is full, which is even better. Don't worry, my friend. You will get yours."

The meal ended on this unpleasant note. The horses were brought around, and Conrad mounted with Hugh on his right.

"Can you believe that bastard?" exclaimed Conrad as soon as we were out of earshot of the Bishop.

"Humor him, Conrad," said Hugh. "He's still . . . who's that?"

Two men were walking out of the shadows. Hugh clapped a hand to his sword, and Scarlet and I tensed. We had been seeing Pierre and Phillippe in every doorway both coming and going.

"It's all right," said Conrad. "It's Balthazar and Leo."

And so it was. We relaxed as the two came up on either side of Conrad, Balthazar with a scroll in his hand.

"Milord, we apologize for disturbing you," he said. "But it's a message from Balian. He said it was urgent."

"Not at all," said Conrad. "Give it over."

He reached down toward Balthazar, who was on his left, and in that moment a poignard appeared in Leo's hand and then buried itself in Conrad's side.

Conrad bellowed in pain, straightening on his horse, and Balthazar stabbed him from the other side.

"Conrad!" cried Scarlet, racing toward the Marquis as he fell from his horse.

"Traitor!" screamed Hugh Falconberg, and he drew his sword and charged at Leo. Balthazar looked on in shock as his companion was cut down before him. Then he took to his heels.

"Get him!" cried Hugh to his men.

"Wait!" shouted Scarlet. "Conrad still lives."

Hugh hesitated, unsure as to how he should divide his men. But I wasn't one of his men. I took off after Balthazar, knife in hand.

He cut down an alleyway that would have proved too narrow for pursuit on horseback. I proceeded cautiously, not knowing the terrain and not wanting to be the second man to be on the receiving end of that poignard. There was no moon, and the little starlight that was available was obscured by the buildings around me. I heard footsteps a distance ahead of me, and I followed as silently as I could. Behind me, the alarum was being sounded.

Then I heard a door open and shut ahead to my right. I edged up to it and eased it open, knife at the ready.

It was a side door to the cathedral. The central apse was the only part lit, a pair of torches burning. I feared a cat-and-mouse game among the pillars and pews, but my prey was unconcealed and most conspicuous.

He was kneeling before the cross, hands folded, praying for all he was worth, which was not much in my consideration. The poignard, still stained with blood that was two days short of being royal, lay by his side.

I stepped into the center aisle directly behind him.

"If you think that this place is a sanctuary, then you are wrong," I said.

He neither turned nor reached for his weapon. He simply maintained his supplicant posture.

"They would have no compunction about staining the altar with your blood," I said. "Neither, for that matter, would I."

"I know that," he said softly. "I am a dead man. Let me finish my prayers."

"Who do you work for?" I shouted.

"I don't know," he whispered.

[188]

"They'll tear it out of you," I said. "It will be a slow death."

"You have to save her," he said, turning to face me for the first time.

"Who? The Queen? Is she in danger?"

He shook his head. "My wife. You have to get her out of Tyre."

"Why the hell should I?"

He smiled sadly. "As an act of Christian charity."

"I should let her be torn to pieces by the mob," I said. "Tell me what you know. It may be your last chance."

"I can't tell you anything," he said. "My only salvation is in silence now. Please, I beg you. Save her."

The doors burst open behind me, and Ralph Falconberg strode into the cathedral, sword drawn, ten soldiers fanning out behind him.

"Balthazar!" he shouted.

Balthazar stood, his knife still on the ground.

"I arrest you in the name of . . ." barked Ralph, then he hesitated. "In the name of the Queen."

Balthazar looked at me, his face drawn, then held his hands out, crossed at the wrists, and walked past me to the waiting soldiers. Ralph suddenly lashed out, and Balthazar fell to the floor moaning, blood gushing from his forehead.

"Bind him," commanded Ralph. "Take him to the castellum."

Balthazar was trussed up and carried away. Ralph noticed me standing there, my knife still in my hand.

"Well done, Fool," he said, then he turned on his heel and walked away.

I walked over to the cross and retrieved the bloody poignard from where Balthazar had let it fall, then I ran back to where the Marquis had fallen.

They were no longer there. I heard shouts and cries coming from every direction. I didn't know if it was still the search party, or if this assassination was the prelude to some armed insurrection within the city. I decided to take my chances at the castellum. It seemed the mostly likely destination for the Marquis.

The normal pair of guards at the entrance had been reinforced by an entire squadron, many sleepy and some still wrestling on their armor.

I was admitted and ran up the steps to the great hall. More guards were posted outside this doorway, and I was barred from entry. Scarlet came out while I was arguing with them.

"Come on," he said to me.

"Conrad?" I asked.

"Dead," he said tersely. "The Bishop was rushed over to give extreme unction, and Isabelle was told to come down and see him before he died, but it was too late. Hugh Falconberg told her that Conrad's last words were to her."

"Were they?"

"I couldn't tell," said Scarlet. "It was a kindness of Hugh to say so. I must go up to be with her now."

"I'll go with you," I said.

"What can you do?" he asked.

"I don't know," I said.

The Queen sat by her favorite window, a single candle on the table beside her. She was so still that she might have been a statue carved from pure alabaster. Her hands rested on her swollen belly.

"He's gone," she said without turning toward us. "He's gone, and I remain, with his child nearly ready to be born. That's all I have from him—his child. What else do I have?"

"The Kingdom of Jerusalem, for a start," I said.

"And us, Isabelle," added Scarlet. "I told you before that you had power. It's time for you to assert it."

She turned and looked at him for a long time, then nodded slowly.

"Mary!" she called. "Mary . . . no, she's gone. Cynthia!"

[190]

A maid ran in.

"Tell the Falconbergs and the rest of Conrad's men that I will speak with them here."

The maid flew out of the room, and Isabelle turned back to us.

"How do I rule?" she asked bitterly. "I've been Queen for two years and haven't had to do that yet."

"Treat the men as you just treated Cynthia," said Scarlet. "They'll jump just as quickly."

"What happened to Mary?" I asked.

"I have no idea," she said. "She never came back from some errand she had to run."

Scarlet shot me a glance, and I slipped out of the room.

There were doubled patrols throughout the city, and torches at every window as people woke to find out what was going on. Rumors were shouted across from building to building, transforming with each gust of wind into something more frightening or outlandish.

Knife drawn, fearing the worst, I burst into the room that Mary had shared with Balthazar. What I found was emptiness—all their possessions gone, a single kerchief left on the floor apparently in hasty flight. I checked the apartment next door, where Leo's wife and daughter should have been, but they had vanished as well.

I ran to the city gate but was stopped by the guards.

"No one's going in or out," said a captain.

"Earlier, did you see any women leave? One of them was Mary, one of the Queen's servants."

One of the guards nodded. "Around sunset, I think. They were taking some food out to friends in the tent city, they said."

"Have they returned?"

"No, and they'll be stuck there tonight until the all clear's been given."

[191]

I had a feeling that they were nowhere near the tent city by now. They probably had a six-hour head start, and who knows in what direction?

I trudged back to the castellum and whispered my news to Scarlet. The Duke of Burgundy, the brothers Falconberg, Balian d'Ibelin, and others of Conrad's disreputable crew were filing in somberly to kneel before the Queen.

"Please, stand," she commanded them. "Tell me what is happening outside."

Hugh Falconberg stepped forward and cleared his throat.

"The city gates have been barred as a precaution," he said. "We have doubled patrols and have the towers and ramparts at full alert until daybreak. The garrison protecting the tent city is out in force, and the French have been notified."

"The French also stand ready to defend Your Highness," added Burgundy.

"As soon as they sober up," muttered Scarlet.

"And the captured murderer?" said Isabelle, almost choking on the word. "What information did he give?"

Ralph Falconberg stood beside his brother.

"I was the captor of the Assassin," he said, puffing up his chest. "I took charge of the interrogation personally, milady. He finally confessed, before he died, to being of the Cult of the Assassins, he and his confederate. They acted upon orders of Sinan to take revenge upon your husband for the taking of his ships and the slaughter of their crews, all of which were righteous trophies of war. I assure you that this traitor's corpse will be dragged through the streets for all to see what happens to our enemies."

"Which will do nothing to bring my husband back," said Isabelle, deflating Ralph a bit.

"I just thought ..." he stammered.

"No, go ahead, drag the corpse around Tyre," she said. "It's what the people want to see. We shall give it to them."

There was a shocked murmur among the men.

"Well?" she said, looking around the room. "Did you expect me to behave any differently? You feel no shame at boasting before me of torturing a man to death and desecrating his corpse. If I am to lead you, then I must do what a ruler is expected to do. Balian, what of Saladin?"

"He will see this as an opportunity," said Balian. "We must keep the armies on constant vigil."

"And Richard?"

"He will also see this as an opportunity," said Balian. "With all due respect, my Queen, you are too young and ... and ..."

"Too female," finished the Queen drily. "I am aware of my apparent shortcomings, to which you might also add too grief-stricken, too weary, and too pregnant. Nevertheless, I am still the Queen, and I carry the heir to the throne within me. I demand your respect and your obedience. My Lord Duke of Burgundy, I ask you, as a friend, to order your armies on alert and to share command with Hugh Falconberg."

"I will, milady," answered Burgundy.

"Let the castellum be barred to all but ourselves," she said. "Give out the news of the Assassins, and let all others know that the Queen of Jerusalem still lives and will turn the keys of the kingdom over to nobody but the true representatives of the Kings of France and England. That should buy us some time."

"Very good, milady," said Balian, and they all bowed and left.

When the doors closed, Isabelle collapsed onto her seat, sobbing hysterically. We rushed over to comfort her.

"You were magnificent, Isabelle," said Scarlet.

"How can I do this?" she cried. "They're already scheming. I could see it on their faces. That pig Ralph won't even wait until my husband is buried to press his suit, I can tell."

"You are twenty-one and the Queen, Isabelle," said Scarlet. "You don't have to do what you're told anymore."

"No, I suppose I don't," she said, blowing her nose. "But it's so hard, and I am so tired."

"You should sleep," I said, pulling Scarlet away from her. "There is nothing more that you can do tonight. We shall guard your door ourselves."

"Thank you, Monsieur Droignon," she said. "Thank you, my sweet Scarlet."

We closed the door behind us and sat against it.

"So, the official story is that Balthazar and Leo are of the Cult of the Assassins," I said.

"A plausible story," said Scarlet. "The Cult trains its members to insinuate themselves into a community and wait until they are ordered to strike. They can live for months or years before they take action. The only problem is, I don't believe it."

"Neither do I," I said. "Why don't you?"

"Before they took Conrad away, I took a quick look at Leo's corpse," said Scarlet. "I sniffed around his mouth and nose for a moment."

"Ugh," I said. "What on earth for?"

"In the Cult of the Assassins, the warriors and killers use a substance called hashish before they act. It is a potent drug with a distinct sickly sweet scent. I could not detect it on Leo. I doubt that we would find it on Balthazar, either. And the two of them were in the city long before Bernard du Temple captured Sinan's ships. Sinan has never bothered with petty spying. He only sends his men in when he wants someone killed. How about your reasons?"

"When he fled, Balthazar went to the cathedral," I said. "I found

[194]

him kneeling before the Cross, praying with all his heart. He was a murderer, no question. But no Isma'ilite would have done that in his final moments."

"True," he sighed. "I guess the conversion took, didn't it? Maybe Leo was of the Cult, and he had some hold over Balthazar to force him to join the plot. Too bad we can't ask the Assassins about them."

I took a deep breath. "I could go, if you want," I said.

There was a long pause. "I have no problem with sending a man to his death," he said. "But there has to be some point to it. All we could get is information, and I don't know how much good it would do us now."

"You know my Arabic's good," I said. "I can pass for Egyptian or Syrian. I can get away with this."

"No," he said. "Thanks for offering, but no. I don't want your blood on my hands. I feel bad enough thinking we could have stopped this somehow."

"If not Sinan, then who?" I asked. "Saladin? He could have paid Sinan to do it."

"Not his style," he said. "He prefers killing people in battle. This is too sneaky and underhanded for him. And why Conrad? If anything, Saladin respects him more than Richard."

"Maybe that's his reason for killing him," I said. "Too strong a king to remain here."

"Maybe," he said. "But I doubt it. There is one person we haven't mentioned, speaking of sneaky and underhanded."

I looked at him. "You mean Richard," I said.

"I do. After all the trouble Conrad has caused him, to see him become king of everything Richard recaptured would be the ultimate slap in the face. I wouldn't put it past him to get in his parting shot before he goes back to England."

"Neither would I," I said. "But unless we turn his operatives, we'll have no way of proving it."

"And maybe we shouldn't try," said Scarlet. "It won't bring back Conrad, and it will just fragment the Christians here. If those remaining aren't united, and if they don't receive support from home, then they'll be ripe for the plucking. What's done is done."

"Then Richard has won," I said. "Conrad goes unavenged. But that's not our problem. Is it?"

"No," he sighed. "More's the pity. We were so damn close. Now, it's back to uncertainty."

He picked up his guitar and began playing softly, disconsolately. I didn't join him in the music. I had thought of one more person who may have wanted to see Conrad dead and who had ample access to at least one of the murderers. She had begged off accompanying her husband to dinner, choosing to stay home and bathe instead while he was cut down by the husband of her maid. But to bring the Queen up as a suspect to Scarlet while he mourned the death of his master and the hopes that hung upon him would have been cruelty indeed.

Scarlet plinked on into the night. Below us, a man who wasn't king was being prepared for a burial that would not be royal. Behind us, in a room I once thought was Paradise, the Queen of Jerusalem cried herself to sleep.

$\int$IFTEEN

The glory of young men is their strength; and the beauty of old men is the grey head.

—PROVERBS 20:29

We took turns sleeping outside Isabelle's door. When the first rays of the sun came through the window at the end of the hallway, I got up stiffly and began my stretches. Get limber in the morning, Theo.

Scarlet woke when Cynthia arrived with two trays of food. Wordlessly, she handed one to us and went inside with the other.

"Thoughtful girl," said Scarlet as we dug in. "Times like these, you forget to eat."

There was a sudden tumult from without. We went to the window and saw a crowd gathering, calling for the heads of Balthazar and Leo. Then there was a clatter of hooves, and a pair of horses came out, dragging the brutalized corpses behind them.

The crowd erupted, pelting the bodies with stones and screaming, "Assassins!" The riders pulled their grotesque cargo away from the castellum, and the mob followed them.

"They seem satisfied that it was the Cult of the Assassins behind this," I said.

"Why shouldn't they be?" said Scarlet.

"What about Ralph Falconberg?" I asked.

"What about him?"

"I've been thinking while you were asleep. You snore, by the way."

"I do?"

"Yes. Do you really think that Balthazar admitted being an Assassin during Ralph's tender ministrations?"

"He might have, just to get him to put an end to it," said Scarlet. "Men being tortured can confess to anything."

"Let's say that Balthazar was not an Assassin. Let's say that he would not have confessed to anything like that because above all else, he was trying to protect his wife from further persecution. Do you think that Ralph would have given out that story to cover up the truth?"

Scarlet thought for a moment.

"Ralph might also have done it just to cover the fact that he managed to kill the only person who had any information without finding out what it was," he said.

"There's that," I said. "I also wonder how Ralph knew to look in the cathedral for Balthazar. And I am remembering how Mary met with Ralph. I had thought she was being a go-between for Isabelle, but maybe it had something to do with her husband."

"Maybe," said Scarlet. "But she's gone, her husband is dead, and we have no way of leaning on Ralph. He's too powerful. And what would be his incentive?" He stopped abruptly and pounded his fist on the windowsill. "Isabelle," he growled. "Could he murder his lord just to get at the wife?"

"Not just a wife," I said. "The Queen of Jerusalem."

"Well, he won't have her," he said. "Not if I can prevent it."

Conrad was laid out in the apse of the cathedral with his head toward Jerusalem as if he was a Church dignitary. The Bishop presided over the funeral mass with as much grandiosity as he could muster, all of the subsidiary holy men flanking him in a show of ecclesiastic force. I was back with the servants, as usual, but Isabelle took Scarlet with her to the front row, clutching his tiny hand while weeping under her veil. An assortment of local nobility sat behind her. I noticed that the Duke of Burgundy was not present. I supposed that he was persuading his troops that they were still an army under his command.

When all was said and done, they took the Marquis of Montferrat to the vaults below. I don't know which noble Tyrean family had been evicted from their eternal rest to make room for Conrad. Maybe there was an extra vault available. The city hadn't been in Christian hands that long.

My mind wandered idly during the mass. I wondered about Isabelle. Every public occasion was a stage for her, it seemed to me. Now, she played the grieving widow for all to observe and sympathize. If she had shown this much feeling for her husband while he was alive, maybe . . .

Maybe he would still be alive.

Did you really suspect her so much?

I did, Duchess. Especially with what was to follow.

As we emerged from the cathedral, those who could not squeeze inside started cheering, "The Queen! All hail Queen Isabelle!" Women wept upon seeing the brave expectant widow face her public. Ralph Falconberg gallantly stepped forward to take her arm as she approached the front steps, but she froze him with a glare and signaled Balian d'Ibelin to help her.

Then a different roar reached us from outside the city walls. Soon the cry was picked up from the soldiers on the ramparts and towers: "Champagne! Henry of Champagne approaches!"

We hurried to the castellum. The Queen took the throne, Scarlet sitting at her feet, d'Ibelin standing at her side. A herald came into the great hall.

"Henry, Count of Champagne, has arrived and seeks an audience with Your Majesty," he said.

"I will only speak with the representatives of the Kings of England and France," she informed him.

"And I am both," proclaimed Henry as he strode into the hall without permission.

"How do you claim both?" demanded d'Ibelin.

"I am by the designation of my uncle, Richard of England, his representative to Jerusalem," said Henry.

"And France?"

"Through me," said the Duke of Burgundy, who had come up behind Henry. "Although I am sure his other uncle would do the same. And I am certain that both uncles would happily assent to what I am about to propose."

"Propose, my lord Duke?" responded Balian. "This is hardly the time for proposals."

"But that is the very thing that I am proposing," said Burgundy. "And as for the time—there is little to waste."

"I am tired, my lord Burgundy," said Isabelle. "I buried my husband just now while you were somewhere else concocting schemes, and I lack the patience for riddles. Speak plainly."

"Very well," said Burgundy. "Your kingdom needs a king. Any delay in finding one will lead Saladin to attack. We all know that. The ten thousand Frenchmen under my command are here because they are tired of fighting and want to go home. Without them, you will be under siege within a fortnight. But they will stay if there is a king to whom they would show loyalty without hesitation."

"Does such a paragon exist?" asked the Queen.

"He stands before you," replied Burgundy.

She looked at him quizzically. "But are you not married, milord?"

Henry stepped forward.

"He means me, my Queen," he said, and he knelt before her. "I have been asked to be your husband by the men who have fought in

God's name and for yours, and I ask on behalf of the ones who have died doing so."

"But what of your own desires, good Count?" she asked softly.

He took her hand and kissed it. "I could think of no better fate than to be your husband," he said. "It is impossible for me not to love a creature as fair and gentle as you. And I swear that I will be as loving a father to your unborn babe as if it had been my own."

She looked at him, then around the room. Many of the men were nodding and smiling to each other. She looked at Balian, who was expressionless in the face of this performance, then back at Henry.

"Give me leave to think about your kind offer," she said. "I will pray to God tonight for guidance, and give you my answer on the morrow."

"We need—" started Burgundy, but Henry cut him off with a wave of his hand.

"I would expect no less, my Queen," he said, rising and bowing. "I place my fate and happiness in your hands. Until tomorrow, then."

He left with the Duke of Burgundy.

Isabelle followed them with her eyes, lingering a bit too long for decorum, then turned back to the room.

"I pray that you leave us to our thoughts," she said. "Good Balian, tarry with me. There is no better mind in Tyre than yours."

"I will, my Queen," he replied.

The other men in the room filed out. Scarlet stayed by her feet but nodded at me to play quietly where I was. Soon, the hall was empty but for the four of us, and the servants closed the doors.

"Balian, speak openly," she commanded him.

"It's a smart move by Burgundy," he said. "Henry on the throne will keep the army complacent for a while. They've been running wild since they came here. We'll have a whole generation of bastards with French features within a year. More importantly, it guarantees support from both kings, even after they leave. Frankly, I could not think of a better choice politically."

"Scarlet?" she said, holding her hand down. He took it, and she pulled him up to a seat beside her.

"I agree with Balian," he said.

She looked at him in surprise.

"I thought that you disapproved of Henry," she said.

"I don't like how he romanced you under the nose of your husband," said Scarlet. "But that situation, sad to say, is over. Burgundy's right about the need to act quickly. If there's a king on the throne, Saladin will stay on course for peace. And you could do a lot worse than Henry."

"Meaning Ralph," she said.

"I meant in general, Isabelle," said Scarlet.

"Monsieur Droignon?" she said, looking over at me.

"It is not my place to say, milady," I said, strumming away.

"I command you to answer," she said.

"Put aside the questions of truces and armies," I said. "As a woman to a man, how do you feel about him?"

"I feel that I could love him," she said simply. "I was too young for my first husband. My second was too old for me, which is something altogether different. Here is a man not much older than myself who swore his love to me before any of this happened. I have never had a marriage where love came before politics."

"Don't be fooled, Isabelle," said Scarlet. "This is nothing but politics."

"But love may come," she said. "And that was never a possibility before."

"Conrad loved you," said Balian.

"Conrad loved this," she said, slapping her hand on the throne.

She stood, and we rose around her.

"I wish to be alone in my chambers tonight," she said, and we bowed.

"I was surprised that you went along with the choice of Henry so easily," I said to Scarlet as we walked back to his place.

"I thought that the Guild would prefer it," he replied.

"Lie to yourself, my friend, but never to me," I said. "You just didn't want Ralph to be the one married to her. You struck while the iron was hot, just like everybody else. She hasn't even had a chance to mourn decently."

"Henry is the lesser of two evils," he said.

"But still evil?" I asked. "Or was that just jealousy speaking?"

"I am not jealous," he protested, but his heart wasn't in it.

As I settled in for the night, I heard his guitar. I don't think he stopped playing until the sun rose.

We hurried to take our places in the great hall. Those who had followed Conrad assembled quickly, exchanging knowing looks as Henry entered with the Duke of Burgundy.

The heralds announced the Queen, and all knelt as she walked into the room, Balian at her side. She settled herself onto the throne as comfortably as her pregnancy would allow and motioned the room to relax.

"Is the Bishop of Beauvais present?" she asked.

"I am here, my Queen," he said, stepping forward.

"What is the policy of the Church toward remarriage after the death of one's husband?" she asked.

"Normally, to wait one year before remarrying," he said. "But that is more advisory than compulsory in nature and may be waived during extenuating circumstances."

"Such as?"

"Such as war or pregnancy, milady."

"But the war will be ending soon," she protested mildly.

"In God's name, I hope so," he said, pressing his hands together fervently. "Yet until the truce is signed, we are in a state of war."

"And we are certainly in a state of pregnancy," she said. "Well, that settles one question. Good Count Henry, I have thought and prayed about your gallant proposal. I ask that you accept certain conditions before I give my answer."

"Name them, milady," he said.

"First, that I designate my unborn child as the heir to the throne of Jerusalem," she said. "No matter how many children follow of my new husband's getting, the first shall be first."

"I accept," he said. "The child of Montferrat will be the next king of Jerusalem at such time it pleases God."

"And that goes for the rest of you," she said, looking about the room. She stood and walked about the room, holding her swollen stomach with both hands. "Do you swear to this unborn child that you will be his loyal subjects?"

"We swear," chorused the room, many placing their hands on her belly as they did.

"Good," she said. "Second: That Balian d'Ibelin will be the regent if I should die before the child is of age."

"There is no better man for the job," said Henry. "I accept."

"Third," she said. "That Scarlet remains with the household staff for as long as either I or the baby shall live."

"The dwarf?" exclaimed Henry.

"The same," she said.

"But . . ." he began, then he thought better of it. "Very well. I accept."

She stepped down and faced him, holding out both hands. He took them in his.

"I accept as well," she said. "I will marry you and make you the King of Jerusalem."

He kissed her, holding her gently so as not to bump up against her belly, and the room burst into cheers.

Excepting Ralph Falconberg, who looked furious. And myself.

"Did you ask her to do that for you?" I asked Scarlet afterward.

"No," he said, looking pleased. "She thought of it on her own. Between Balian and myself, she should have plenty of good advice."

"Yes," I said. "Nothing like good advice when your husband is the one running the kingdom. I hope she enjoyed her little taste of power. She's going right back where she was."

The wedding and coronation were held a week later. Two lines formed outside the cathedral, one of men and one of women. The trumpets blared, and the happy couple emerged and posed for the people.

The banquet was held outside at a square from which the normal market stalls had been removed. All of the preparations for Conrad's coronation were still in place, so the festivities proceeded as originally scheduled, with just the occasional name change inserted into the script.

The novitiates, many of whom were seeing the interior of Tyre for the first time after so long a sojourn in the tents, performed splendidly, finishing with a pair of six-man pyramids juggling clubs across to each other. Scarlet beamed at them proudly from his place by Isabelle's side, and Henry solemnly presented each of them with a silver bezant.

Scarlet sang an encomium composed for the occasion; Balian and Burgundy gave long-winded speeches, and everyone got drunk, with the exception of Isabelle. And Henry, I noticed. Amidst the celebrating in his honor, he smiled politely and kept a cold, sober eye on everyone. Not the worst quality in a young king, I suppose, but I thought he could have been happier. At the end of Scarlet's performance, he joined in the general applause hesitantly and stopped before the rest.

Given the recent history, the normal wedding jibes were abandoned. The usual folk customs for the wedding chamber were dropped as well, due to the bride's advanced stage of pregnancy. I hoped Henry was a patient man. Indeed, that seemed to be the theme of many of the speeches made. Everything good comes to those who wait, slow and steady wins the race, and so on. In other words, give her a chance to produce the heir before you go heaving your crusading loins at her, young Henry.

My own king, Denis, partook in the revels heartily. The next day, he decided to tour the city with me as his guide. I made a point of showing him the ruins under the waves of Old Tyre as Scarlet had once shown them to me, and Denis was duly impressed.

"Comes to us all, jesters and kings, doesn't it?" he mused.

"Aye, milord," I said. "Should the jester go first like a good servant and prepare the way?"

"No rush, no rush, my friend," he said. "Let us live as long and as well as we possibly can. The world does not need our lives so badly."

One of his men came running up.

"Sire, I have found a boat to Constantinople," he said. "It leaves in two days."

"Excellent," said Denis. "Book passage for all of us." He turned to me. "Should be quite a trip. I've never been there."

"Nor I," I said. "May I take my leave of you now, sire? There are some friends to whom I wish to bid farewell."

"By all means, Droignon," he said. "Meet us at the harbor two days hence."

In the morning, I went to the clearing for one last session with the novitiates. They were still buzzing with the success of their performance and were already taking requests to repeat it for various companies of soldiers. I gave them some more material to work with, then gathered them around me.

"My children, my students, my friends, my colleagues," I said. "It has come time for me to leave you."

There were cries of dismay, which secretly pleased me, I must say.

Egotist!

What?

Well, if you insist that I play Echo to your Narcissus, I'll say it again. Egotist!

My dear wife, all performers are egotists, and all teachers as well. What should a teacher of performers be?

Smug, apparently.

Perhaps. But remember, these children were orphans and refugees. If Scarlet had become their father, I had become something to them as well.

A mother?

More of an uncle. Let me continue. This story is still my performance.

Egotist.

"Now that you have had a taste of performing before royalty and crowds, you may be spoiled for what I have to share with you," I continued.

"Nonsense!"

"Tell us!"

"Please, Monsieur Droignon?"

"Then sit," I said. They did, quickly and quietly. "The Guild will always tell you not to let your love of performing interfere with your mission. Fair enough. But what I want to tell you is this: do not let your mission interfere with your love of performing. It's why you want to become fools. It is a way of life, not just a way of carrying out the obscure and frustrating tasks that the Guild will send you. We entertain, whether it's before a hundred thousand at the Hippodrome or one lowly shepherd in exchange for a night's shelter. To bring laughter to the world is as sacred a mission as to bring peace. We may bump into each other again someday, in which case I expect each of you to buy me a drink."

They cheered at that. I held up my hand.

"But in the event that we do not, remember me, and I will remember you. And now, I want to see if it's possible to embrace all of you at once."

It wasn't, as it turned out, but we certainly tried.

I came back to Scarlet's cottage. He wasn't there, so I fed the pigeons and gathered my belongings. When I was done, I went to the castellum. To my surprise, I was stopped at the entrance.

"Is there anything wrong?" I asked the guard at the gate.

He looked around to make sure no one was watching, then leaned forward to whisper to me.

"Sorry, Droignon, but there's orders from the King. No jesters in the castellum anymore."

"What? But the Queen—"

"Orders from the King," he said. "That's what I said."

"What about Scarlet?"

"He's inside with the Queen," he said.

"So, there is a jester in the castellum," I said.

"No, there isn't," he said.

"But you said—"

"I know what I said, Fool," he barked. "Now, go away!"

I saw one of Henry's captains standing at the entryway, the source of the guard's increased hostility.

I went back to Scarlet's place, hurt and puzzled. After all this time, I wanted to pay my respects to Isabelle. I also wanted to see how she appeared in private. At the wedding, she seemed happy, but I had my suspicions of her public performances.

At sunset, I heard Scarlet climbing the ladder to the roof. I came out of his cottage to see him standing at the edge of the roof, looking out to sea.

"Scarlet?" I said. He turned, and I winced.

He was no longer clad in his scarlet motley, cap and bells. He was wearing the dingy garb of an ordinary palace servant.

"He promised that I would remain with the household staff," he said quietly. "But he never promised that I would remain a jester. I am to be his lackey. Scarlet the Varlet."

"Bastard!" I shouted.

He shook his head.

"As long as I am with Isabelle, it doesn't really matter," he said. "And I will still have time to teach the novitiates once a week. If they can support themselves. With peace at hand, everyone in the tent city will be leaving Tyre. We may not be able to keep the children together. We'll have to find places for them to do their fooling, but I have a feeling that it won't be easy with this young king."

He noticed my packed gear for the first time.

"Well," he sighed. "Looks like you're leaving."

"I could stay," I said. "You're the Chief Fool. If you tell me to stay here, the Guild can't second-guess you."

He shook his head.

"What I would like personally is not what I think should be," he said. "When do you leave?"

"In the morning," I said.

"Then tonight, we will get roaring drunk, and I won't give you a head start this time."

We walked to the wharf, and I stowed my gear aboard the ship.

"I solved one of our minor mysteries," Scarlet said as we walked to the nearest tavern.

"What's that?"

"When I was in the great hall, fetching wine for my new master, who should walk in but Pierre and Philippe."

"Really?" I exclaimed. "So they were working for Henry?"

"No," said Scarlet. "Your guess was right. They were spies for Richard. But they were spying on the Duke of Burgundy. After the French abandoned the Crusade, Richard wanted to make sure that they wouldn't try to seize any territory on their own."

"And they had nothing to do with Balthazar and Leo?"

"Apparently not."

I hesitated, took a deep breath, then plunged.

"Scarlet, what about Isabelle?" I asked. "What if she was behind Conrad's murder?"

He darkened.

"Don't ever mention that again," he said. "I know that she had nothing to do with it."

"But—"

"I trust her as I trust myself," he said. "If you value our friendship, then drop this now and forever."

"All right," I said reluctantly. "But I haven't any other ideas on the subject."

"Even if we found out who was behind it, we couldn't do anything to bring Conrad back," said Scarlet. "The wheel has turned once again. Alexander the Great's Tyre lies under the sea, Conrad lies under the cathedral. In the morning, you sail away. I'll get some wine."

The first words he ever said to me, I thought.

It didn't take him long to get drunk, and the pressure of going through the day without jesting caused him to burst into a constant riot of song and storytelling. Soon, everyone in the tavern was crowded around the dwarf who sat on a high stool in the middle, his eyes flashing like twin suns. Only the daylight streaming into the tavern broke his chain of foolery.

"Well, looks like we all forgot to sleep," he said merrily. "Gentlemen, good day. I must escort my brother to his place of departure."

We all staggered out, looking like wrecks and smelling like men who had spent the night carousing. I espied Denis and his retinue moving their supplies and horses onto the ship.

"I guess this is it," I said.

"Seems like it," he said.

I knelt down to embrace him.

"Come back to the Guildhall someday," I said. "If I hear that you're there, I'll drop whatever it is I am doing and come see you."

"Maybe," he replied. "But there's Isabelle. And the baby. Someone has to watch out for them."

"She's safe," I said. "Good-bye, Scarlet. I owe you a few drinks."

"It all works out in the end," he replied. "It has been a pleasure. *Stultorum numerus . . .*"

"*Infinitus est,*" I said, and boarded the ship.

I stayed on the deck as the oarsmen pulled us slowly out of the enclosed harbor, watching Scarlet shrink into an even tinier version of himself, one hand raised.

Peace is at hand, I thought. Not as much bloodshed as there might have been. One king home already, one king to return soon, I hope. Maybe the alliance here would carry over to France and England, but somehow I doubted that. More work for the Guild.

Yet there was a murdered marquis, and a poor woman no one remembered who had her throat slit. Not our problem, said Scarlet, and he was right. Still, I was not satisfied with how things were left in Tyre. But that would be the last time that I would set foot in that city.

$\mathscr{S}$IXTEEN

Excellent. Why, this is the best fooling, when all is done. Now a song!
—WILLIAM SHAKESPEARE, *TWELFTH NIGHT,* II.iii

A nd that was it?" exclaimed Claudia, startling Portia into crying. We stopped and dismounted so that she could soothe and nurse the baby.

We had left the Adige river behind at Bozen and were now following the path of the Isarco, hoping to reach the hospice at Brixen by sunset. It was the same route that the Romans had once used to go from Verona to Innsbruck, the old *per vallem Tridentinum*. It was the easiest of the passes through the Alps, which was a good thing for us, lacking the elephants Hannibal used for the western passage.

It had been perhaps ten days since we left Niccolò. The rivers were getting some snow melt even now, but the road wasn't too muddy and the horses got through without much complaint. We had switched our guises back to those of returning pilgrims, realizing that merchants without goods would arouse undue suspicion from the toll-collectors. It also gave us access to the hospices, which saved us some money. The inns were dear, especially with the increased flow of traffic in the spring.

The inns, however, were a useful source of information. The Guild kept a few jesters posted along the road, and they often worked the inns, entertaining travelers and picking up all kinds of gossip. At Bozen, we learned from a colleague that the traveling Guild was just five days ahead of us, having tarried to repair the wagons. We also learned that the wine at Bozen was outstanding.

When Portia was asleep, I took the sling from Claudia and climbed back on Zeus. He seemed to know that the baby was in his charge now, for he didn't raise his usual nasty antics. Claudia mounted Hera and looped the mule's reins around hers, and we rode on.

"No, that was not it," I resumed.

"But you said that was the last time you set foot in Tyre," she objected.

"And so it was. The story would continue elsewhere some years later."

"Oh. I still can't believe that you, of all people, would leave so many loose ends like that."

"I wasn't quite the avenging busybody that I have become of late," I said. "Nor was I my own master. I had specific directives from the Guild and from Scarlet. What other choice did I have?"

"I suppose," she said.

"What would you have done?" I asked.

"Well, since at least two people were lying, I would have gone after them somehow," she replied. "Probably starting with the lesser."

I shook my head in admiration. "I wish that you had been with us then," I said. "Where were you when we needed you?"

"At home, raising a child while waiting for my first husband to come back from the Crusade," she said. "All while running his city and his estates. Anyhow, it's easy enough for me to pick up on the lies from the story. I'm sure it was much more difficult when you were living through the experience."

"It was, unfortunately. Had we understood more as the events actually happened, we might have averted some of what was to come. But I'm getting ahead of myself."

✲   ✲   ✲

Denis and I ended up spending a lengthy period of time in Constantinople, thanks to a romantic entanglement.

Is Thalia part of this story? Because if she's not, I'd rather not hear about her.

She was not part of this story. We stayed more on account of Denis's lover than anyone I was involved with. But I'll move on.

After we left, we traveled overland to Durazzo, sailed to Apulia, and continued west to Pisa. From there, it was a short journey to Denis's kingdom. I was hoping to guide him into a suitable marriage once we came home, but he was in no hurry to settle down with anyone. About two years after that, having survived the armies of Saladin and the fleshpots of Constantinople, he fell from his horse while hunting and died of his injuries a week later.

A young death, a sad death, but not a mysterious one. Since he died without issue, the throne passed to his father's younger brother, a hale former soldier with three daughters, two of whom were married with children of their own. I stayed on for a while to help ease the transition, but the kingdom was in stable hands, so I requested permission to return to the Guildhall.

It was actually my third visit there since returning from Tyre, Denis having been most generous with my requests for the occasional journey. I came sometime in early July of 1197.

Having arrived unexpectedly, I was hoping that my surprise appearance would be good for a few rounds of drinks from my brethren. To my disappointment, however, the Guildhall was relatively devoid of visiting fools. The hall held mostly faculty and novitiates, and they were too busy to give the prodigal his just deserts.

But my coming did not go entirely unnoticed. As I was unpacking my gear, a novitiate knocked respectfully at my door.

"Father Gerald wants to see you," he said. "Right away."

I tossed my weapons under the bed and followed him through the old tunnel that cut through the mountain from the Guildhall to the monastery on the opposite slope. The boy vanished behind me, and I tapped on Father Gerald's door.

"Come in, Theophilos," he called, and I stepped inside. He was an ancient man, knife-thin and more weathered than an Alp. There was constant speculation at the tavern as to his age, but none had the courage to ask him about it. He could still see back then, and his glare hit me like a shovel before I could adjust to the dim light of the room.

"So," he said. "Thought you would pay us a little social call, did you?"

"Nice to see you, Father," I said. "You're looking . . . well, rather old."

He smiled, stepped from behind his desk, and embraced me. I returned it carefully.

"It turns out that your appearance is most opportune," he said, sitting down again. "Are you up for a little more travel?"

"Wouldn't mind it at all," I said. "Things are rather dull where I am, which is a good thing. Where are you sending me?"

"Acre," he said.

I felt a thrill of both joy and anxiety shoot through me.

"Did something happen to Scarlet?" I asked.

"No, no, nothing disastrous," he said. "But I need someone to take some information to him and to get a fresh sense of what's going on there. By the time we hear anything about the area, the news is three months gone. Given your familiarity with the territory, you're the ideal fool."

"I would be delighted," I said. "I enjoyed my time with the little fellow immensely. What's the information?"

"Pisa," he said. "They're sending a fleet to Acre, and that's always trouble. They have intrigued in that area before, and Henry bears them no love. I don't want Scarlet to find this out by seeing them sail into the harbor. With some warning, he may be able to work on Henry to reconcile with them."

"Fine," I said. "How much of a lead do I have?"

"They leave in a week, according to Fazio. You know Fazio, don't you?"

"Met him in Pisa a couple of times," I said. "One of the best. All right. How do you think I should go?"

"I'd say from Brindisi," he said. "There's regular pilgrim traffic going from there, and you'd be more likely to find passage than in Venice. You may want to consider stopping in Cyprus on the way. The fool with Lusignan is named Lepos."

"In Nicosia or Famegusta?"

"Lusignan is in Nicosia. And one more thing, Theo. You'll be taking another fool with you."

"I will? Why?"

"He's going to be assigned to Acre. Scarlet could use another pair of eyes and legs in the area."

"Fine," I said. "Who is he?"

"See for yourself," said Father Gerald. "He's standing right behind you."

I whirled to see a tall young man grinning at me from two feet away. He was in full motley, yet had crept up behind me without making a sound. Not easy when you're wearing a cap and bells.

"Well done," I said. "I never heard you coming. Not many can catch me unawares when I'm sober."

"I was always good at sneaking," he replied. "But you knew that."

I stared at him for a moment in shock.

"Peter?" I exclaimed. "Is that you?"

"*Stultorum numerus*, Monsieur Droignon," he said, and he grabbed me in an immense hug.

[216]

I pried myself away, stepped back, and looked him up and down. He was maybe fifteen or sixteen by this point, with the build of an acrobat and a devilish glint in his eyes.

"And he's graduated," I said to Father Gerald. "Did he do well for you?"

"Took to it like a duck to water," said Father Gerald proudly. "He already spoke Syrian and Arabic, so he seemed the right man for this job. He's done some apprenticing, including four months with Fazio. I expect that you could add a little more to his education on the trip."

"It shall make the journey a pleasant one," I said. "Very well, youngster. Pack your gear. We leave at dawn. What is your name now, by the way?"

"Perrio," he said. "Something close to my own."

"Ibrahim and Magdalena are in Thessaly," Perrio informed me the next morning as we left the Guildhall. "They have two children, and from all reports are quite happy. Sara is breaking hearts in Brittany. And the others . . ."

"What do you mean, 'the others?'" I asked. "I thought only four of you came to the Guild."

"You didn't hear?" he exclaimed. "Scarlet managed to send every single one of the novitiates to the Guildhall. We don't know how he did it, but somehow he got the funds together."

"Remarkable," I said, shaking my head in wonder.

"Some of them are still in training," he continued. "But the older ones are all out and fooling. If Scarlet ever decided to come back to Europe, he could go from country to country and never have to pay for a drink."

"What of Scarlet himself?" I asked.

He looked gloomy for a moment.

"They say that Henry treats him most cruelly," he said. "The King of Jerusalem never misses an opportunity to insult or abuse him. Yet Scarlet merely smiles and continues serving him. He has never once considered leaving or given Henry the opportunity of getting rid of him."

"And Henry considers himself honor bound by the promise he made the Queen," I said. "Poor Scarlet. To go so long without launching even one retort or insult. That must be hell for a fool as talented as he is."

We found a merchantman shipping out of Brindisi to Cyprus and paid for enough space to rig two hammocks, one over the other. The trip took about three weeks, and we were heartily glad to put our feet back onto solid ground when it was over. We docked at Kyrenia—not the most convenient port on the island, but the most fortified. This close to the eastern end of the Mediterranean, piracy was a real threat. In particular, the emir of Beirut, Usamah, was raiding Christian shipping so prolifically that the odds of completing a pilgrimage to the Holy Land without being killed or enslaved were about one out of two.

From Kyrenia, it was a day's journey south to Nicosia, the capital of the conquered kingdom. I say kingdom, but there wasn't actually a king at this point. Guy de Lusignan had died in 1194, alone and disgruntled, and the mantle had fallen to his brother Amaury. It took some time and political maneuvering to get recognition for Cyprus as a new kingdom, but it finally had been done and Amaury was set to be crowned in September.

The years of Crusader rule had not made much of a change. The island was still very much a Greek place. The people spoke Greek, the churches practiced the Greek rite, and the food was Greek, which was fine with me. The mountains of the interior made for good vineyards, as we discovered. Perrio had not yet learned to drink properly, so I took it upon myself to further his education, as per my mandate from Father Gerald.

Nicosia was a central market for the island and could have passed for any reasonably bustling Greek town, except that the men were clean-shaven, a concession to their to their Frankish masters. Still, everyone looked prosperous and contented, which shows how little the loss of a beard compares to five years of peace and stability.

In the center of the city was a keep, dating back to Byzantine rule, and still being repaired and built up. The Templars had used it when the island had been given to them by Richard, and they had barely held out against the subsequent revolt of a populace not in tune with the Templars' tender methods. The city was not walled, although a number of defensive towers were under construction around it.

A man in motley appeared in front of us as we crossed the market.

"Do I even have to bother with the password?" he said merrily. "My brothers, welcome to Nicosia. I am Lepos. Come, come, my room is yours."

"*Infinitus est* anyway," I said, shaking his hand. "The name is Droignon, and the recent newcomer to manhood is Perrio. I'm supposed to watch him until he starts shaving."

"Hm, looks like you'll be a while," said Lepos, examining the boy critically. "Well, I suppose you're just passing through."

"Not just," I said. "Father Gerald told us to check in with you. It is a welcome diversion after the sea voyage. How are things here?"

"Rather good," he said, taking me by the arm and guiding us to the keep. He had a small room in the cellar next to the stables. Not much in the way of sight or smell, but he had it to himself, which meant there was enough room for the three of us to cram in. He lit a small lamp and pulled out a wineskin and three cups.

"I've been saving this for a special occasion," he said, pouring the wine and handing the cups around. "To the Guild."

"To the Guild," we echoed, and drank.

"It's difficult being on an island and keeping contact," he said. "Especially being inland. There was another fellow stationed down in Limassol for a while, but he died two years ago. Now, I have to depend on the sporadic visit."

"Ever hear from Scarlet over in Acre?" I asked.

"Scarlet came over in '94 when King Henry dropped by," he said. "Quite the coup for us. We finally got Henry and Amaury reconciled. There had been a lot of bad blood between them."

"Why?"

"Henry kicked the Pisans out of Acre in '93. Amaury went over to try and patch things up, and Henry threw him into a dungeon. It took the Masters of both the Templars and the Hospitalers to get him released. Scarlet worked on Henry for months and finally got him to see that Cyprus was a useful ally and trading partner, especially after Guy died and Amaury took over."

"So they've settled?"

"Let me put it this way," he said. "Amaury's three sons are now betrothed to Isabelle's three daughters. We won't be celebrating the weddings just yet, as none of them is more than ten, but it shows the good feelings."

"Three daughters," I said. "I didn't know about them. So the first was Conrad's?"

"Marie of Montferrat," he said. "And two more with Henry, Alice and Philippa of Champagne. That's why Isabelle stayed at Acre. She had to take care of the children. And she probably needed a break from the amorous attentions of her king. So, what brings you through here?"

"More Pisans," I said. "They're sending a fleet to Acre."

"Oh, dear, that does sound like trouble," he said. "Well, if they come looking to Amaury for support, they'll find he's allied with Henry now. Maybe that will discourage them."

"Maybe Amaury could persuade them to ally with Henry as well," I said. "Now that we're all one big happy family."

"Sounds good," he said. "I say, why don't you come to dinner to-night? We can do some three-man work. Amaury's boys will love it. They are always after me to give them juggling lessons. I'm trying to keep them away from the sharp objects."

"But those are the most fun," said Perrio.

"I want them to live until their weddings," said Lepos. "And get married in full possession of all of their fingers."

"All right," I said. "Let's see what the graduate can do."

We planned out the evening's entertainment and walked upstairs.

"One thing you should know," said Lepos. "Amaury's wife died a few months ago, so stay away from marriage and such topics."

"We will," I said.

Lepos entered the great hall first.

"Sire, or sire to be," he announced grandly. "I bring you a company of fools—well, anyway, three!"

I launched myself into the room, performing a series of handsprings that ended with me in kneeling position before Amaury. Perrio burst in with a double somersault in midair that carried him a good twelve feet before he hit the ground. Lepos caught my eye and nodded approvingly.

Amaury was a stout fellow in his late forties with a face that looked accustomed to cheerfulness in better circumstances. He brightened when he saw us, and he beckoned to his three boys, who clambered up onto his lap and the arms of his chair and remained there for the performance.

We pulled out a number of chestnuts, most of them new to the room. Always a boon to a resident fool when colleagues come to visit— it gives him a chance to do the routines he cannot do by himself. Perrio turned out to be spectacularly good with the tumbling and more

[221]

than capable with the music. When we shifted to the comic sketches, he went from the wide-eyed rustic to the befuddled virgin with ease, and we had the room roaring for over an hour.

We finished by each hauling one of the sons up onto our shoulders and dashing about the room while they squealed in terrified delight. Then we linked arms and did a silly song-and-dance bit, the boys bouncing gleefully along. Amaury stood and led the applause when we were done.

"Wonderful, Lepos," he said. "Where did you find these fine fellows?"

"They found me, milord," he said. "The older one is Droignon, a colleague from long ago. The newer one is Perrio. They were passing through, looked me up, and kindly consented to join me in performance."

"Just passing through, eh?" said Amaury. "Our good fortune, then. Where are you off to, gentlemen?"

"To the Holy Land, milord," I said. "A fools' pilgrimage. We are trading entertainment for lodging along the way."

"Well, here's your passage east," said Amaury, tossing us some silver. We bowed. He motioned us close and pointed to the boys, who were running around, imitating our antics. "That's the happiest I've seen them in months," he said softly. "For that alone, you should be blessed."

"I understand, milord," I said. "If it be not too forward for a fool to offer condolences to a lord, let me express my sympathies."

"If it not be too forward for a lord to accept them from a fool, let me thank you," he said, holding out his hand. We each clasped it in turn.

"Will you be sailing from Limassol or Famegusta?" he asked.

"I thought we would go from Famegusta to Acre," I said.

"Acre, eh?" he said. "I would ask you to give my regards to the King and Queen, but I don't think Henry likes fools much."

"So I hear," I said. "Maybe we could improve his disposition. You could make our performance a gift to your future daughters-in-law. He could hardly refuse that."

"Capital idea," he said. "I wouldn't mind seeing him lighten up a bit, and surely the Queen would enjoy it. I wish her well. Not merely a beauty, but a woman of quiet strength and virtue."

"Her worth is great in your eyes, then," I said.

"I was married to a woman of higher worth than I deserved," he said. "I did not treat her well when we were young, for I was headstrong and foolish. But as I grew older, I came to know the value of a good and loving wife. I tried to be a husband equal to such a wife."

"You succeeded, milord," said Lepos. "All know that."

"It is kind of you to say so," said Amaury. "Would that she had lived long enough for me to fully make amends. All I can do now is raise my boys to be the kind of men I should have been from the start."

"The best possible tribute to her," I said.

He called for his secretary and instructed him to prepare our introduction to the court at Acre. The three of us ate quietly in a corner of the hall.

"Not bad, youngster," said Lepos affably. "Let me suggest one thing."

"Certainly," replied Perrio.

"The double midair somersault is a wonderful trick," said Lepos. "But too much to open with, unless you have something even better reserved for the finale."

"I do," said Perrio. "We just didn't get to it. But I take your point, Master Lepos."

"What a polite fool," Lepos said to me. "Does he know how to be rude and insulting as well?"

"We spent two entire months on retorts," said Perrio. "Brother Francis taught us."

"Does he still live?" laughed Lepos. "Nastiest fellow I've ever met. He's beaten vipers in contests of venom. Good, youngster. You'll do fine."

Amaury's secretary came over with the sealed scroll. We rose and bowed, and he waved to us.

"Safe journey, my foolish friends," he said. "Come see us on your return. You are welcome in Cyprus any time."

"We will, milord," I called, and we turned in for the night.

From Nicosia, it was two days' journey overland to the port of Famegusta on the eastern end of the island. This was a bustling trading town, with sizable Venetian and Genoese quarters, along with a smaller contingent from Pisa. The tiny Byzantine castle on the hill overlooking the city was abandoned, the guard garrisoned in a new, squarish tower of Frankish design. Other towers were going up around the city and the harbor.

We found a ship that was leaving for Acre the next day. We stowed our gear aboard, then decided to wander the city. There were plenty of taverns catering to both the visiting ships and the inland farmers who came to sell their crops at the market. We checked out all of them, performing at some, drinking at others. As we came to one at the end of a particularly dingy street, I heard music coming from inside.

"I've heard that before," I said, reaching for my tambourine. "I never forget a tune once I've learned it."

"Sounds like it comes from Outremer," said Perrio.

"Let's go see if it's the same musicians I learned it from," I said.

We stepped through the doors. The musicians, mostly guitar players, were on a crude raised platform at one end of the tavern. The room was filled with men who were clapping along enthusiastically as a woman whirled and dipped gracefully among them, her face and arms decorated with henna designs.

I was right. It was the musicians I had played with in the tent city. And that was Mary dancing before us.

SEVENTEEN

Afar, a dwarf buffoon stood telling tales
To a sedate grey circle of old smokers,
Of secret treasures found in hidden vales,
Of wonderful replies from Arab jokers.
　　　　　　　　—BYRON, *DON JUAN*

Recognize her?" I muttered to Perrio.

"I do," he replied. "And I heard what happened in Tyre after I left. What would you like me to do?"

"Stay by the door," I said. "If she makes a break for it, grab her."

"What about you?"

"I'm going to sit in with the band."

I worked around the outside of the room, keeping the spectators between the dancer and myself. When I got to the platform, I tapped one of the guitarists lightly on the shoulder. When he turned, I held up my tabor in question. He nodded, smiling, and I sat on the bench next to him.

I still remembered the rhythms. In fact, I had used them a few times at Denis's court, trying to liven things up when we had dances, but it never really caught on. As I started playing, the other musicians glanced over for a moment to see the source of the percussion. Some of them recognized me, but they raised no warning.

Mary was whirling about at the other end of the tavern, bells at her ankles and a tiny pair of cymbals in one hand. As she danced back toward us, she glanced in my direction and nearly stumbled. She recovered and finished the dance as the drunken louts about us applauded and whistled. Then she walked quickly to a door at the rear of the tavern that I hadn't noticed before.

The tavern was back in full riot when the performance ended, and it took me a precious minute to push through to the rear exit. There was another room in back and an open door leading out into an alleyway. Cursing under my breath, I pulled my knife and ran out.

She was there, writhing in Perrio's grip. He had one hand clapped over her mouth and another around her waist, and he was bobbing and jerking his head back as she slashed at his eyes with her nails. Blood dripped from his chin.

"Enough," I said to her as I held up my knife. "I only want to talk. Make a noise and I'll see to it that the authorities will know everything."

She looked at the knife, then back at me, and she nodded.

"Let her go," I commanded Perrio.

He held onto her wrist and dabbed at the blood on his chin.

"Those cymbals are sharp," he muttered.

"Where can we go to talk quietly?" I asked her.

"I have a room nearby," she said. "You will pay me?"

"Depends on what I hear," I said. "I can also make sure that you never work on this island again, so you had better make this worth my while."

"And my chin," added Perrio.

"Poor little boy," she said teasingly, turning to stroke his face with her fingers. He slapped her hand away.

"You've drawn enough blood for one night," he said.

We walked quickly to a boarding house and slipped in without drawing much attention, though I had the feeling that the sight of two men going in with such a woman was not uncommon for the area.

The room itself was surprisingly clean, with a straw bed in one corner.

"Sit down, keep your hands in view," I said. "I'm interested in knowing more about your husband."

"He's dead," she said.

"I know that," I said. "The last thing Balthazar said to me before he was captured was to get you out of Tyre safely."

Her eyes welled up with tears.

"Of course, when I got to your room, you were already gone," I continued.

"You tried to help me?" she said in surprise.

"I did," I said as Perrio suppressed a smirk. "You left a handkerchief behind. I'm afraid that I do not have it anymore."

"But why were you trying to help me?" she asked.

"Because he asked me to," I replied. "And I thought that you were innocent of his crimes. If I thought otherwise, I would be handing you over to the guard right now."

"He was a good man," she said, lowering her eyes.

"He was a murderer and a traitor," I said, and her head snapped up as if I had struck her.

"He had no choice," she said. "He did it to save me. That's what he told me."

"Start from the beginning," I commanded her.

"We were burned out of our farm by Saladin's army in the winter of 1190," she said. "We had no money, just the clothes we fled in. We fell in with a group of traveling musicians. I knew how to dance; I knew I could make men look at me while I did it. So we joined them, and eventually ended up in the tents outside Tyre."

"Where did you meet Leo?"

"Leo was from our village," she said. "He and Balthazar were old friends. When I was out performing with the musicians at night, Leo would take my husband drinking. Balthazar told me that seeing men watch me like that made him depressed and angry, so he needed Leo to cheer him up."

"Did either of them ever have any dealings with the Assassins?"

"Balthazar, never," she said firmly. "Leo—I don't know. There was a time when he left and was gone for a few years, but he never said where."

"Tell us about your sister," I said. "Tell us about her death."

"She was a greedy, headstrong girl," said Mary. "She ran away when she was younger, thinking she would find a wealthy husband in Tiberias. She ended up selling herself to men. One day, she showed up at the tent city, penniless. We took her in, made her promise to behave, but she was soon back to her old ways. She would disappear for days at a time and come back with some trinket she would show off to the women. She usually ended up selling it later.

"One night, she came back and pulled me aside. 'I'm going to make some real money,' she said. 'I've found something valuable, and I'm going to sell it back to the owner.' 'Found what?' I asked her. She wouldn't tell me."

"Did she tell you who the owner was?"

"No," she said. "And I didn't want her to. Somehow, I knew she was heading to a bad end, but she never listened to any of us, no matter how we begged her to change her ways.

"She didn't come back that night, but that was nothing new. The next day, Leo came running in. He told us she was dead. We came out as the soldiers carried her body through. I wanted to go take care of her, but the men held me back. They were afraid that we would be thrown out of the camp if some connection was made to us.

"That night, Balthazar came back drunk, weeping. He kept muttering, 'That damned Falconberg.' He wouldn't tell me why."

"Did you ever find out?" I asked.

"No," she said. "He kept telling me never to mention it, that we were in danger."

"From who?"

"He wouldn't say. But he said that what happened to Rachel was a warning."

"What happened when you got inside the city?"

"William Falconberg was constantly after me," she said bitterly. "I tried to fend him off, but he persisted. My husband feared to confront him.

"When I became maid to the Queen, things became worse. Balthazar drank more than ever, and he would disappear with Leo late into the evening. He would come home some nights shaking with terror, but he would not speak to me.

"I was frightened, not knowing who had this hold on him, not knowing what lay in store for us. Finally, out of desperation, I approached Ralph Falconberg."

"Why Ralph?"

"First, to see if he could intervene with William. Of the Falconbergs, Ralph was the smartest. I thought he might have the most influence over his brother's behavior. He was quite courteous at first. He asked me a lot of questions about William and about my husband. I confided in him, thinking he was sympathetic."

She sighed. "Only it turned out that he was the worst of all of them. He wanted from me what William wanted, and he threatened to have all of us expelled as spies if I did not consent. I had no choice. I consented."

She started to cry.

"Balthazar came home one night. He looked even more terrified, but to my shock, was sober. 'I have something to tell you,' he said. 'What is it?' I asked him. 'I am being forced to commit a great crime,' he said.

'I am doing it only so that you and I will be safe. I have been assured that we will be protected.' 'What are you talking about?' I asked. He shook his head. 'Let's flee this place,' I said. 'Surely there is somewhere we could go that is better than here.' 'There is nowhere,' he said. 'Those who threaten us can find us anywhere on the coast, and the infidels control everything inland. This is the only way.'

"I was frantic. I didn't know where to turn. I thought of coming to you."

"I remember now. You were waiting when I brought Magdalena back from the tents."

"Yes," she said. "But you were concerned only for her. There was no chance for me to talk to you, and after that I lost my nerve."

"What about Ralph Falconberg? Did you tell him?"

She looked down, ashamed.

"Yes," she said. "I did. He said to find out everything I could and to bring the information to him."

"What about Leo's wife? Did she know anything?"

"I never trusted her," she said. "So I never talked to her about it."

"What about the night Conrad was killed? Did Balthazar tell you that it was going to happen?"

"He and Leo came to us in the afternoon. They told us to pack up everything and to wait for them in the tents. They would leave word with a friend about what we would do next. We did as they commanded. Then word reached us about what happened."

"What did you do?"

"We fled," she said simply. "We split up. I eventually met up with my musician friends again, and we've been traveling ever since then. And that is all that I know."

I reached into my pouch and tossed a coin onto the floor by her foot.

"For your time," I said. "I would say for your troubles, but no payment could compensate for that."

We left her there and walked back to our boat.

"How's the chin?" I said.

"Sore, but I'll live," replied Perrio. "Tell me more about what happened in Tyre."

I sketched in the parts of the story with which he was unfamiliar.

He yawned. It was well past midnight.

"Do you think she was telling us the truth?" he asked sleepily.

"Impossible to know," I said. "But if she was, then Leo may be the one who killed her sister."

"Really? What makes you say that?"

"When the soldiers came for her body, they covered it with a blanket before they carried it back to the tents. The only way Leo could have known that it was Rachel was if he knew she was dead in the first place."

"Which means he killed her, or saw it happen," said Perrio. "Too bad you can't ask him about it. Still, her story puts you on the trail to one of the Falconbergs."

"Yes," I said. "Ralph always seemed a good candidate to me. We'll bring this to Scarlet when we get to Acre."

We docked in Acre on the fifth day of September. The city, while physically much the same as I had remembered, was completely different. The markets were busy, the ships in the harbor were jostling each other for room, and there was continuous traffic of cargo and pilgrims both coming and going. The air was filled with a dozen languages, and the people who spoke them appeared contented and, more importantly, fed.

It took us some time to find a room at a reasonable rate. Most of them preferred charging by the day at premium prices to transient dwellers. Since the time I had last ridden from Acre, in borrowed armor, a small neighborhood had sprouted north of the city wall, absorbing some of the overflow of the population, and it was here that we found a boarding house run by an amiable widow. The city walls were in good repair, and the rebuilt towers had been joined by outlying ones to the east. I pointed out to Perrio where the catapults had once flung their stones, where King Richard had built a portable fort overnight, and where the slaughter of the Saracen civilians had taken place.

He looked at this last spot for a while.

"Did they bury them?" he asked quietly.

"Burned them, I think," I replied. "We were out of Acre by then."

"It's a wonder that anything grows there," he said, looking at the farmers going about their harvesting. "One would think that the very ground would be cursed."

"It may be," I said. "But so much evil has taken place in the Holy Land that there may be no stone that is untouched by it. Yet things still grow."

We sat down to a decent dinner for the first time since Nicosia, then slept in beds that did not sway for a change.

The next morning, we presented ourselves at the entrance to the castellum. I had told Perrio how Blondel, Scarlet, and I had borrowed King Richard's seal, and he glanced up at the central tower with a bemused smile as I handed the letter from Amaury to the captain at the gate. He had us wait while he went inside.

"Think this will get us in?" asked Perrio, idly juggling three balls with his left hand.

"I think so," I replied.

The captain came back a little while later.

"You are commanded to return on the morrow to entertain the princesses," he said.

We bowed and thanked him. He beckoned us forward.

"The King's varlet bids that you await him tonight in the usual tavern," he said, winking at us.

"Even more thanks for that message," I said. "If you care to join us, the first round's on me."

"Duty calls, alas," he said regretfully.

Perrio and I passed the time performing in the fish market. Acre apparently had not seen any fools in a while, for we soon drew a good crowd. I was happy to see children back in the city again. So many had left or died during the last Crusade, but here was a fresh crop, giggling and singing along.

Of more interest to us was a band of German soldiers. Their captain approached us during a break and engaged us to entertain them the following Friday, when it was their custom to feast.

"As happy as I am to get paying work, I am surprised to see the likes of them in Tyre," I remarked to Perrio as we packed up.

"Oh, I guess you hadn't heard," said Perrio. "A bunch of them were sent here by Barbarossa's son. He's never gotten over the poor showing the Germans made during the Crusade, so he's trying to stir things up again. Fortunately, Henry doesn't seem interested in renewing hostilities."

"Thank God for that," I said. "Let's sing them some peaceful German songs Friday."

"I didn't know there were any," said Perrio.

As the sun began to set, I guided my young charge to the tavern where I had first met Scarlet. The same barkeep was there, sporting the same beard, only longer and dirtier. I called for a pitcher and three cups, and we commandeered a table in the corner.

We were watching the door intently. When it opened to reveal a pair of eyes flickering about halfway up the door frame, Perrio whistled a quick tune between his teeth. Scarlet came over to us, blinking to adjust to the dim light. I leaned forward so that my face was illumined by the candle, and his face lit up.

"*Stultorum numerus,*" he said, holding out his hand.

"*Infinitus est,*" I returned, taking it, and he jumped into my arms.

"By the First Fool, Our Savior," he said, laughing. "I never thought that I would see you again. Welcome back, Theo. Or is it still Droignon?"

"In Outremer, it's Droignon," I said. "Good to see you, my friend. I owe you a drink. Have one."

He pulled up a stool and allowed me to fill his cup.

"To the Guild," he said.

"To the Guild," we choarused, and we drank.

"I'm Scarlet," he said to Perrio.

"I know that quite well," said Perrio, smiling at him.

Scarlet squinted at him, then his mouth fell open.

"Is that Peter?" he exclaimed. "Stand up and let me greet you properly, boy."

Perrio stood and embraced his teacher, then Scarlet stepped back and looked him up and down.

"You look like a fool," the dwarf said critically, and Perrio looked as if he would burst with pride.

"He's called Perrio now," I said. "He's a full-fledged jester, and Father Gerald has sent him to join you."

"This is an evening of wonders," said Scarlet, his eyes tearing. He pulled out a handkerchief and blew his nose loudly, laughing to cover his emotions. "Well, Perrio, tell me about all my children."

Perrio rattled on for an hour, with Scarlet interspersing questions, exclamations and occasional snorts of laughter. Then he turned to me.

"Will you be staying, or are you merely my new assistant's escort?" he asked.

"I am also bringing word from the Guild," I said. "There's a Pisan fleet on its way, maybe a few days behind us. We left before they did, but we came overland through Cyprus."

"Damn," he sighed. "Just when I thought we had reined in the Germans."

"What's been going on with them?"

"They went pounding off on their own without so much as a by-your-leave to Henry, then came scampering back when the Saracens retaliated. Now, Al-Adil's up in arms and on the march toward Jaffa."

"Will he negotiate?"

"Probably," said Scarlet. "Balian's counseling diplomacy, but the Falconbergs want battle. Fortunately, Henry tends to side with the smarter man whenever there's any disagreement, and that's always Balian."

"The Falconbergs are still around?"

"The same three. Otto's still up north, but the others are deeply involved with Henry."

"Interesting," I said.

"Why so?"

"We met up with an old friend on our way here."

I told him of our encounter with the dancer. By the time I was done, his merry demeanor had vanished.

"That makes sense, somehow," he said pensively. "Mary's sister went to Tiberias. That's where the Falconbergs came from. A pretty maid like that would not have escaped their notice, and who knows what secrets she could have heard coming out those drunken mouths?"

"Unless Leo was connected with the Cult of the Assassins," I said. "Conrad's death could still have had its roots with the Old Man of the Mountain."

"No," he said.

"How can you be so certain?"

"Because I've been there," he said.

We looked at him, dumbfounded, and he laughed.

[236]

"No, it was not nearly as daring as you think," he said. "We were invited."

"The Assassins must be getting lazy," I said. "Used to be, they would come looking for you. Now you have to go there to be killed?"

"New regime," he said. "Sinan died in '93. Since Conrad was already dead, there was no one who really wanted to continue the quarrel. The next spring, Henry was traveling north to settle the latest dispute between Antioch and Armenia. I was with him, of course."

"I have a feeling his intervention was your idea," I said.

He shrugged. "He generally pays no attention to me," he said. "He lets me blab away when I'm getting his wardrobe together in the morning. Maybe some of it sinks in, I don't know. Anyhow, he traveled north, along with his escort and retinue, including me with the servants. Just after we left Jabala, an embassy came down from the Nosairi mountains carrying the Assassins' colors. We were, to put it mildly, apprehensive, but they greeted us with all civility and decorum and invited us to dine."

"And Henry actually accepted?"

"He thought it was worth the risk to restore good relations with the Assassins. So we followed the embassy into the mountains to al-Kahf, and my God, what an amazing place! Someone must have said, 'What would be the most completely inaccessible place in the world?' and then found al-Kahf and stuck a castle on top of it. We thought Tyre was impregnable—you can't even get an army near al-Kahf. There's no place where they can set up for battle. We passed through a tunnel in the rock, approached the castle single file, and at the last second a drawbridge was lowered over a ravine. The master, Abu Mansur bin Muhammad, stood alone inside the entry, welcomed us, and personally escorted Henry to dinner."

"Did Henry have a food taster along with him?"

"That also was me," said Scarlet. "And this was one of the times that I truly appreciated the job. It was one of the most lavish feasts I have ever eaten, and all I did was taste each course as it was brought in. Dancing girls, music, knife-throwing, all manner of entertainment. But then came the grand finale. Abu Mansur pointed to one of his men, who stepped forward and knelt before him. The master then pointed to the window, and the fellow promptly goes up to it and jumps out."

"My goodness!" I exclaimed.

"Now, I mentioned the layout here. We dashed over and looked out the window, but all we saw was a ravine so deep that we couldn't even see the body.

"Henry sat down, looking quite pale. Then what do you think happens? The lord points to another man, and out the window he goes!"

"What?"

"Now, this is carrying the point too far. Henry begs that this portion of the entertainment cease. Abu Mansur says, 'A small demonstration of the devotion and obedience of my people. I offer this loyalty to you, my neighbor. As a token of my love, should you ever have need to end the life of one who troubles you, never fail to call upon us.' Henry thanked him, and dessert was passed around.

"When the dinner was over and everyone had repaired to their rooms, I went down to the kitchen, which was on a floor below the room in which we dined. I wanted to get what I needed to serve Henry breakfast before we left. There were several of the Cult there, indulging in a late meal after waiting upon the dinner guests, and they greeted me cordially, especially when they found that I spoke their language. I dropped a joke or two, and soon had them laughing. Well, it was a long time since I had an audience, so I indulged myself. Right in the middle of the story, I looked at one of them and stopped.

" 'You're the man who jumped out the window!' I said. He looked at me and shook his head. Then I spotted the second recent suicide

slinking to the rear of the group. I started laughing. 'That was marvelous,' I said. 'How on earth did you manage it?'

"They started laughing as well, and they showed me the setup. There
was a pair of poles that were shoved out of the window below the one
the men jumped through, and ropes tied between them. All they had
to do was catch on, then swing through the kitchen window and pull
the poles in before anyone looked."

"One hell of a trick," I said. "If they miss, it's a long way down."

"Absolutely," he agreed. "But they don't miss. It's something one of
us could do if we were stupid enough to try it. So, anyhow, they asked
me to keep it a secret from Henry, since we were all such good friends
now. I said, 'I will do this, if you will answer me one question.' 'What
is it?' said a large man who seemed to be in charge. 'What connection
did the Assassins have with Conrad's death?' I asked.

"Well, they weren't expecting anything like that. They looked at me
as if I was mad. The leader leaned forward and said, 'We could have
killed you for discovering the trick we played at dinner. For information
like this, a man would certainly have to die.'

" 'I am sure of it,' I replied. 'But as your guest, I would hope that
you would keep to your tradition of hospitality. In any case, this is for
my own personal curiosity, not for any other use. I have no influence
over matters concerning Henry.'

" 'If you were a man, I might challenge you for it,' said the leader.
'But since you are only a dwarf...'

" 'Only a dwarf?' I said. 'Well, this little man hereby challenges you
to a little wrestling match. If I win, you give me an answer. If you win,
you may name your price.'

" 'Ridiculous,' he scoffed. 'An Assassin wrestle with half a man?'

" 'If you are afraid of me, then withdraw,' I said.

"They all laughed. 'The imp has courage, if not wisdom,' my opponent said. 'Very well. Two falls out of three.' The other men cleared

a circle in the kitchen, and the two of us stepped into it and saluted each other. He stepped toward me, reaching for my head. I feinted to the left, ducked under his clutches, and swept his feet out from under him. He landed rump first on the stone floor as the other men laughed and jeered.

"He sat and laughed along with them. 'I have underestimated you, my little friend,' he said as he regained his feet. 'You have tricks of your own, and my balance was wrong. I see that fighting a small man requires a different approach.' He suddenly crouched and came swiftly at me. I tried to sidestep him but found myself flung hard to the stones. I rolled to ease the impact, then stood up.

" 'And now we are even,' I said, bowing to him. He bowed back. We commenced circling each other as the men in the room started cheering both of us. He feinted several times, but I refused to take the bait. Then he straightened and beckoned me to him.

" 'Come, if you are truly a man, and attack me,' he said. 'I weary of chasing you.'

" 'If you insist,' I said. I walked up to him, then suddenly accelerated, crashing into his legs. I didn't budge him an inch.

" 'A poor choice, my friend,' he said, reaching down to me. 'You lack the weight.'

" 'For what I am doing, little weight is needed,' I said, and then he became aware of the precariousness of his situation. I had wrapped my arms around his legs just below his knees when I hit him, locking my hands together in the tightest grip I could manage. I braced my feet and leaned into his body. His knees bent under the pressure, and he toppled backward, his arms flailing."

"I remember you teaching us that trick," said Perrio.

"The rest of the Assassins cheered and clapped. I was worried that I might have pushed his dignity too far, but he started roaring with laughter as he lay there, me still holding onto his legs. 'You're no ordinary dwarf,' he said, holding out his hand. I shook it, and helped him up. 'A wager is a wager,' he said. 'And you have risked much for nothing, my friend. The Assassins had nothing to do with Conrad's death. We were not unhappy to see it happen. We owed him a hundred deaths for the loss of our ships and men, but such are the vicissitudes of Fate. The two men we sent were intercepted by two of yours and cut down, curse them for their incompetence. We did mete out punishment to that wretched pirate who seized the ships, but Conrad's death, ordained though it may have been by Allah, was not of our doing. I swear this by all that is holy.' "

"And you accepted that?" I said.

"Oddly enough, yes," he replied. "You and I never thought it was really the Assassins behind it, and I sensed honor guiding my kitchen combatant. Call it mutual respect between warriors."

"Which brings us back to Leo, Balthazar, and the Falconbergs," I said.

"Yes," he agreed. "And that is disturbing, because that means the man behind the murder of the claimant to the throne of Jerusalem may still be within striking distance of the current occupant."

EIGHTEEN

. . . That was September,
the end of summer, my window was open, a dwarf
was singing in my bedroom.
—GERALD STERN, "MY DEATH FOR NOW"

I awoke to the soft strummings of a guitar, and there was Scarlet perched in the window. For a moment, I thought I was back in his rooftop cottage in Tyre, but then I saw the King's livery on his tiny body and Perrio stretching at the other side of the room.

"Good morning, Fool," said Scarlet. "I have been sent to fetch you for the noon entertainment. I told Isabelle of your arrival, and her daughters of your performance. All were delighted, although I'm not sure how much the baby understands."

"That's the official statement," I said. "What's the truth?"

"Henry was most displeased," he said. "But that letter from Amaury made it impolitic for him to refuse. He's putting the best face on it by inviting all the children of the court to the performance so that all may praise his generosity."

"My favorite audience," I said. "I don't suppose his largesse extended to the servants' children."

"His didn't, but Isabelle's did," he replied.

"Three cheers for the Queen," I said. "How does the lady?"

"She's had three children in five years," he said. "She's tired."

"But still beautiful, of course."

"Of course," he replied.

"And Henry—is he beautiful as well? Or tired?"

"Not tired enough," he said, scowling. "It's funny. Conrad, for all his faults, and I could list them until the sun went down, knew how to run a kingdom and keep his subjects happy. Henry, on the other hand, this paragon of Christian virtue, has become a petty tyrant. He spends half of his time banning one sinful activity after another, and the other half reminding people that he's in charge. When people criticize or disagree, he throws them into prison. He even did that to the local bishops when they elected a new patriarch without consulting him. He'll have a servant whipped at the drop of a goblet, and at the end of the day, he'll throw himself at the Queen as if he's never had a woman before and fears that he may never have one again."

"I take it you've dropped your share of goblets," I said gently.

"My sins have been more verbal in nature," he said. "But I've paid for them just the same. Well, not the right mood for a performance. Start smiling boys, we're off."

It was odd walking back into the castellum, remembering our burglary of years before. The building hadn't changed much, but it was no longer a wartime fortress. A set of marble steps had been added to the front of the building on which a number of petitioners sat, fanning themselves in the sun. Children scampered about until their mothers herded them into the great hall.

"By the way," muttered Scarlet as he left to announce our arrival. "I mentioned the Pisan fleet to Henry. He'll probably ask you a few questions about it."

"Fine," I said. He vanished through the entryway, and Perrio and I waited patiently until a servant stuck his head out and beckoned to us.

The hall had changed in appearance since I last played here. The gaudy silk hangings from the Crusaders' revels had been replaced by more austere but regal decorations—mounted shields, crossed spears, and religious icons wherever one looked. Where once I had seen Richard the Lionhearted dance a drunken warrior's caper, I now saw Henry seated, stone-faced, on an ornate throne, William Falconberg chatting quietly with him. Where a thousand soldiers had crammed in for a final debauch before marching to martyrdom, a few dozen children shouted gleefully when they saw us. We did a two-man version of the show we had done for Amaury's sons, throwing in some juggling with brightly colored silks for the princesses. Marie, the oldest, definitely had the stamp of Montferrat on her face, the same look of wolfish combativeness planted on a five-year-old girl. Alice, the middle child, sucked her thumb and watched with wide eyes, while Philippa, the toddler, clapped and squealed on her mother's lap.

Isabelle watched our antics with a wan smile. She had always looked pale to me, but there was something almost unhealthy about her aspect now. It was not merely that she was tired. She was weary, as if the attentions of her young, virile husband, so desired at first, had sapped her of her vitality.

From a distance, Henry watched us, barely registering any reaction even as William guffawed at his elbow. Nearby, I noticed Scarlet watching us, especially Perrio. My little friend's body, hands, and mouth twitched along with each routine and song, straining to join in. I wished we could have roped him into performing with us, but that would have left him in bad standing with the King.

We finished by plucking flowers out of the ears of the astonished little princesses and presenting one to each of them, the Queen accepting on behalf of the baby. The children clapped enthusiastically, but our most welcome approval was the surreptitiously raised thumb from Scarlet, who then casually left the room.

The Queen herself came up to us as we packed up. We dropped everything and bowed. She motioned us up immediately.

"It is good to see you again, Monsieur Droignon," she said.

"Your Ladyship is too kind," I said. "May I present my colleague, Perrio?"

"Milady," said Perrio, bowing again.

"Have you come to Acre to stay?" she asked. "Perhaps I could prevail upon my husband to have you here again."

"And perhaps you will not," said Henry coldly as he appeared by her side. "Please, my Queen. I would not have you consorting with common fools." She flinched, then regained her composure and walked out of the hall.

"But she has not, milord," I said. "For fools are not at all common around here."

"And even if they were, the two of us are most uncommon fools," added Perrio.

"Do you dare address the King of Jerusalem?" he asked, his face darkening.

"Let's see," I said. "I've addressed the Kings of France and England in my time. A pope or two, and a smattering of patriarchs. Oh, and at least one doge. How about you, Perrio?"

"Emperor Henry," Perrio said proudly. "Quite a nice fellow with a charming baby boy."

"You see, sire, we are fools," I explained. "We do not discriminate. We'll talk to anyone. It would be an offense if we didn't address you."

Henry looked more closely at me.

"We've met before, haven't we?" he asked.

"I am flattered that such a great one remembers," I said. "I was on the last Crusade. I was the fool of your cousin, the late King Denis."

"Yes, of course," he said. "I should have recognized you. You favor those green diamonds under your eyes."

"I do, sire."

"You sang to me in this very hall," he said, glancing around.

"I did, sire, and you thanked me."

"So many things have changed since then," he mused. "So many men have died. And many more will, I fear."

"How so, milord?"

"If what you say is true, we may be in for an attack," he said.

"What I say?" I exclaimed. "All I said in here was in jest."

"You were heard in a tavern last night mentioning a Pisan fleet coming our way," he said. "Your old friend Scarlet told me about it."

"I had no idea it was of any importance," I said. "I was merely telling him of my journey here."

"How came you by this knowledge?" he asked sharply.

"By my own eyes and ears," I said. "I left the kingdom of your late cousin to make a pilgrimage to Jerusalem in his honor. My path initially took me to Pisa, where I saw the fleet in preparation. I entertained some sailors at a wharfside tavern that night, and learned that they were coming to Acre."

"For what purpose?"

"Truly, milord, I do not know, for they were just simple seamen."

"How many ships?"

"I saw about twenty-five," I said. "But my purpose was not to count them, so I cannot vouch for that number."

"What could they want?" he asked William Falconberg, who was listening to our conversation.

"They've always wanted Acre," said William. "We'd better stand ready to fight."

"You're always ready to fight," said Henry. "Do you know Pisa well, Fool?"

"Well enough," I said. "We have both spent time there. In fact, I met my new partner in folly in Pisa."

"You, boy," he said to Perrio. "Do you believe they intend to attack us?"

"I think they want what they always want," said Perrio. "Money."

Henry looked at the lad, a thin smile forming on his lips.

"Out of the mouths of fools comes wisdom," he remarked to William. "We don't have to fight them. We could buy them off by giving them their quarter back for trade, and use them for something that would benefit us all."

"What's that?" asked William.

"With a fleet that size and our unwanted German army, we could take Beirut," said Henry. "Wipe out Usamah, split the take three ways, and make this sea safe for shipping again."

"Will the Pisans go along with that?" asked William.

"They could fight us here with the outcome uncertain, or they could get part of what they came for peacefully and regain the love of the King of Jerusalem," said Henry. "With some Beirut booty thrown into the bargain. We'll negotiate when they arrive. How far behind you were they, Fool?"

"Not long," I said. "We gained a few days traveling across Italy and shipping out from Brindisi. I would expect them soon. May a fool offer his help in this venture, milord?"

"Help, Fool?" he said. "What help could you possibly give us?"

"This, sire," I said, holding up my lute. "The two of us know the music of Pisa quite well. It would be a nice welcoming gesture to have us there when they arrive for negotiations."

"I suppose you expect to be paid for this help," said Henry.

"Milord, we have already made enough to provision the last leg of our pilgrimage," I said. "I offer music in the service of reconciliation. It would be churlish of me to request payment for that noble cause."

"It would be churlish of me not to pay you," replied Henry. "Very well, Fool. Come on the day of the fleet's arrival."

We bowed and exited the hall. Scarlet was waiting for us.

"Well?" he whispered eagerly.

"He wants to use the Pisan fleet to go after that pirate emir in Beirut," I said.

"Not a bad idea," said Scarlet. "He's a menace worth stopping. Who suggested it?"

"He came up with it himself," I said. "But your student here guided him neatly into the ways of greed as our salvation. Well done, boy."

"I was just following your lead," Perrio replied modestly.

"We will have to teach you about hogging credit," said Scarlet. "Good performance, both of you. Everyone enjoyed it."

"Everyone but Henry," I said. "It was strange seeing him on the throne talking with William. I kept thinking of when I first saw them together, virtually in the same spot. Who knew that they would end up being the King of Jerusalem and his right-hand man?"

"The wheel of Time keeps turning," said Scarlet. "In another five years, things could be completely different again. I must attend my King. Isabelle told me to tell you she'll work on him to have you back for the children. Marie was quite smitten with Perrio."

"She'll have to get over it," said Perrio. "She's already betrothed. Her love life is too complicated for a five year old."

"See you at the tavern later?" I asked.

"Maybe," said Scarlet. "I can't always get away." He thumbed his nose at us in salute. We returned the gesture, and left the castellum.

"What did you think of the Queen?" I asked Perrio.

"I kept thinking of how Scarlet would describe her to us when I was a boy," he replied. "In my mind, she had to be the most beautiful woman who ever lived. Meeting her in person was a little disappointing."

"No one can compare with the imaginings of a child," I said.

"It's not just that," he said. "She's so old. What is she, twenty-five?"

"Oh, dear," I said.

"I remember Magdalena saying that to see the Queen was to fall in love with her. I didn't believe it, but what did a ten-year-old boy know of love?"

"What does a sixteen year old know of it?" I teased him. "I espied no waving handkerchiefs when we left the Guildhall."

"They were all too exhausted to wave when I left them," he riposted.

Scarlet didn't show up at the tavern that night. A boy from the castellum sought us out and gave us the message that the King was keeping him occupied.

Having broken the ice by performing at the castellum, we found ourselves in great demand. Word spread that fools had returned to Tyre, and we ended up playing to so many dinners and parties that we didn't even bother hitting the markets. The German soldiers, in particular, were quite enthusiastic, demanding every song and heroic poem in our repertoire while the ale flowed freely.

On the ninth of September, a horn sounded from the top of the castellum's central tower, alerting Acre to the approach of the Pisan fleet. Having planned to come into the city by surprise, the Pisans were quite astonished to see their colors hoisted all over the harbor and banners in their dialect welcoming them. Henry himself in full royal regalia, accompanied by a regiment of bishops carrying reliquaries and icons, stood at the head of the wharf to greet them.

The Pisan leaders were understandably suspicious, but they accepted his invitation to parley and dine the following day. Fresh provisions were sent to each ship, and that evening, small boats carrying some eager young women went out to soften the resolve of the troops a little more. I doubted that this was at Henry's bidding; it smacked more of the style of the Falconbergs, but a good idea, nonetheless.

We still hadn't seen Scarlet since our performance at the castellum, but a hastily scribbled note from him carried by a messenger boy advised us to arrive early for the noon meal so that we could set up in advance of the Pisans' arrival. Perrio and I had been practicing every song we knew from that city of towers, and as the sun approached its peak, we walked up the marble steps and presented ourselves at the entry.

We were expected, and a guard escorted us to the King's chamber, a large room two floors above the great hall with a number of large windows running from the floor to the ceiling enclosed with iron bars.

The King stood by a washbasin, scrubbing his face vigorously, while Scarlet stood by him holding a towel. Balian d'Ibelin and all three of the Falconbergs were there, along with a number of other men I didn't recognize but who wore the colors of Champagne. Balian smiled when he saw us and came over to greet us.

"I remember you well, Monsieur Droignon," he said as he showed us to the corner from which we were to play. "Now, this is no occasion for jesting. Stick to music, and nothing that will stir up the blood."

"We will, milord," I said, bowing.

We began playing softly, and Henry turned and scowled at us, snatching the towel from Scarlet.

"About time the fools got here," he snapped. "I was wondering if they would ever arrive." He threw on a golden breastplate that caught the sun coming in through the windows, then added a crown and a purple cape.

"A moment, sire," said Scarlet, reaching to adjust the breastplate.

Henry slapped him.

"If I need you, I will tell you," he said. "How many times must I remind you of that?"

"Forgive me, sire," said Scarlet, kneeling.

I glanced over at Perrio. His jaw was clenched in anger, but he continued to play without interruption.

There was cheering from outside, and Scarlet scurried to a window and peered through the bars.

"They are here, sire!" he called. "What a glorious sight! Come and see your new army."

The King walked toward the window, craning his head to see as Scarlet came up to him to retrieve the towel. Then, and to this day I am not sure how it happened, Henry stumbled and pitched forward toward the window. He reached for the iron bars to steady himself.

And the iron bars gave way.

"My liege!" cried Scarlet as Henry fell through the window. The dwarf flung himself onto Henry, grabbing his legs and clinging with all his might. "Save the King, for God's sake!" he yelled. But the weight of the monarch was too much and, to our horror, he disappeared from view, dragging Scarlet with him.

There were shouts from the men in the room and screams from the people outside. We all dashed down to the front of the castellum and burst out to find a small crowd already surrounding the body of the monarch, blood gushing from his head to stain the white marble steps.

Scarlet lay on his back some feet away. No one paid any attention to him. I thought him dead as I knelt by his tiny body, but his eyes opened and flickered toward me.

"Theo," he whispered.

"Hush," I said. "We'll get you some help."

"No," he said. "No need. I can tell."

I started to weep, I couldn't help it.

"Don't," he said. "No point. I would like to have seen the Guildhall again. When you get back, make sure you buy everyone a drink, and tell them it came from me."

"You'll find a good tavern in Heaven," I said. "Someplace where they will let you be a jester again."

"Somehow, I don't think that's my destination," he said.

"Nonsense," I said. "You'll watch over all of us. Make sure the novitiates behave."

"It's good to have friends in high places, Theo," he whispered. "Look to Jerusalem. Remember that. Tell Isabelle . . ."

He stopped, looking at the entry to the castellum. I turned to see the Queen standing there, looking at the scene in horror. Then I turned back to Scarlet. He smiled. I still saw a flicker of light in his eyes. Then it faded.

"The King is dead!" someone shouted.

Isabelle shrieked with anguish and collapsed, sobbing. Balian and Ralph Falconberg immediately went to her and helped carry her inside. Several of Henry's men called for a stretcher, while a few servants came out with a blanket and started to gather up Scarlet's body.

I was going to help them. I wanted to prepare my friend's body for burial, but I was interrupted by Perrio pulling urgently at my sleeve.

"Come with me," he said. "We may not have another chance."

"What are you talking about?"

"Just come with me before they come to their senses and kick us out."

He ran quickly and silently up the steps into the castellum. I followed him, and he led me back into the King's chambers, now deserted. He went over to the window from which the pair had fallen and motioned to me to join him.

"Look," he said, pointing at the top of the frame.

Where the bars had been inserted, the frame had been gouged out so that just a sliver of wood held them in place. I knelt carefully to examine the base. The same thing had been done there.

"Someone tampered with the window," I said. "Someone wanted Henry dead."

"Who brought him to that window?" said Perrio softly. "Who came up to him just before he stumbled?"

I looked at the boy, not wanting to believe what had become all too evident.

"I think Scarlet did this," he said, fighting back his tears. "I think Scarlet killed the King."

NINETEEN

. . . this is my last jest.
—EDGAR ALLAN
POE, "HOP-FROG"

C ome on," I said. "Let's get out of here. We don't want to draw
any attention to this."

We ran back down as silently as we could. No one marked us. When
we reached the ground floor, I looked until I saw the steps leading
down to the cellars.

"This way," I said.

"Where are we going?" asked Perrio.

"I want to find Scarlet's belongings," I said. "Maybe there's some
clue there as to why this happened."

The castellum's stables were in the cellars along with the kitchens
and storerooms. We were directed to a corner at the end of the stalls
where the stench from the mucking out was strongest. There, we found
a tiny pallet. On top of it, Scarlet's motley was laid out, freshly laun-
dered and pressed.

"He knew he was going to die," said Perrio. "He has his burial
clothes ready."

"Why?" I muttered. "Why would he do this?"

"You saw how the King treated him," said Perrio, the tears streaking
his whiteface.

"But the King's been treating him like that for years," I said. "Why now?"

"Even the strongest men can snap after constant torture," said Perrio. "That's what it must have been like."

"Not Scarlet," I said. "He wouldn't kill a man for something like that. He wouldn't kill—" But I stopped there.

Something small and white caught my eye. It was a tiny piece of paper, shoved into a crack in the wall. I pulled it out and unrolled it.

"T," I read aloud. "I sent my instruments to Perrio. Look to Jerusalem."

I heard people approaching and quickly shoved the note into my pouch. Some of the castellum's servants came up.

"Oh, good, you got it out already," said one of them, gathering up the motley. "We thought he'd want to be buried in this. We'll take care of it."

"Thank you," I said. "The least I could do for a brother fool. Come, Perrio."

We went back up to the entryway.

"It must have been something recent that caused this," I said.

"Maybe something to do with the arrival of the fleet," guessed Perrio.

"Maybe," I said. "Or maybe it had something to do with the arrival of a pair of fools."

"Us?" exclaimed Perrio. "We caused this? How?"

"Something we said that meant something to Scarlet, if not to us," I said. "Somewhere in the information that Mary provided."

"I can't think of anything," he said.

"Go back to our room," I told him. "I want to check something out. If you hear that I'm in prison, try and get me out. If you can't, you've just become the Chief Fool of Jerusalem."

"But—"

"Just do it, boy," I snapped. He looked stricken, but he turned and left.

I had a hunch, based on Scarlet's last words and what I knew of him. I found the steps leading to the central tower and started climbing. I paused for a moment as I passed the room where Blondel and the Lionhearted had passed some tumultuous nights, but it was guards' quarters now. I kept climbing until I emerged into the bright afternoon sun.

The tower gave a bird's-eye view of Acre and its surroundings for several miles. I had never been up here before, and the scenery took my breath away for a moment.

"Takes everyone that way the first time," said a voice, and I turned to see a solitary guard sitting on a stool, munching on some bread. His skin had been burnished to a deep bronze tone, and his beard was grizzled. He had only one arm and a wicked scar running across his hairless scalp, yet he seemed amiable for all that. He waved me over to another stool, put the bread down, wiped his hand on his breeches and held it out to me.

"Name's Aldo," he said as I took it.

"Droignon," I replied. "I'm a fool."

"I can see that," he said. "Thought you might show up one of these days."

"Really?" I said. "How so?"

"Friend of mine," he said. "Scarlet, the King's lackey. Asked me to give you the tour if you had a mind to."

"You know what happened today?" I asked him. He nodded mournfully. "I'm sorry. He was a friend of mine as well. Was he up here much?"

"Whenever he had a free moment," he replied. "Said he spent too much of his life with his view of the world blocked out. I didn't mind it at all. He was good company."

"He was that," I agreed. "He told me that it's good to have friends in high places. I realized that he must have meant you. Are you the only watchman here?"

"From sunup to sundown," he said. "Only use they have for a one-armed soldier in peacetime. My job is to look at the world and make sure there's nothing ugly on the horizon."

"What if there is?"

"If I see a signal from the outlying guard towers, I ring this," he said, holding up a large cowbell. "If I see a large fleet approaching, I sound this horn."

"I heard it yesterday," I said. "You have a fine set of lungs."

He chuckled. "Scarlet used to say the very same thing," he said. "We used to watch the world together and chat. He knew a wondrous amount about it."

"Did he ever talk about the King?" I asked hopefully.

"No," he said. "He talked about birds, and music, and all the people he's met. He told me a little about you. He liked you, Droignon."

"Thanks for that," I said. I looked out to the east. "Is that the way to Jerusalem?"

"More to the southeast," he said, pointing.

I walked over to that corner and traced my fingers idly along the surface of the sandstone blocks. Sure enough, I came across a piece of thread, much the same color as the stone to which it was fastened. I pulled it carefully toward me, and a tiny, rolled up piece of paper rose into view. I slipped it into my pouch and gazed out over where the armies of the Third Crusade had once laid siege to this beautiful city.

"Have you been to Jerusalem?" I asked Aldo.

"No," he said. "Don't really see the point. It's just another place."

"I heard that you can see the Holy City from up here."

"Nonsense," he scoffed. "It's a week's journey from Acre. You can't even see Tyre from here, and that's only two days away. Now, there's an interesting city. You should go visit."

"I've seen it," I said. "It was interesting indeed. But thanks for the thought. Friend Aldo, it has been a pleasure meeting you. I hope to come up to visit again soon."

"The pleasure was mine," he said. "Maybe I will see you at Scarlet's funeral if they let me have the day off."

We shook hands, and I began the long descent to the ground.

When I passed the guards' room, I took the note out. It was too dark to read in the staircase, so I stepped inside the empty room and sat on the windowsill.

T, the note read. *You were right. Sometimes there is no other way. Henry was going to launch a new Crusade to retake Jerusalem using the Pisans and Germans. I overheard him planning it with the Falconbergs. Thousands would have perished. I could not live with that. Maybe the Assassins have the right approach—remove the head, and the body can no longer function. Forgive me. S.*

There it was. The explanation. Logical, sensible, even justifiable. After all, peace was the primary objective of our guild. Every word in the note rang completely true.

And I didn't believe it for a moment.

I cannot say why. Perhaps it was the timing. Henry hadn't even reconciled with the Pisans yet, though his desire to do so may very well have been motivated by his plan to retake Jerusalem.

But if Scarlet killed him for another reason, then where in Mary's story was that reason?

I stuck the note back in my pouch and ransacked my brain, trying to figure it out. The window overlooked the area north of the city wall, and I realized with a start that this was the very window from which Blondel lowered King Richard's locked box. I peered down, trying to remember where Scarlet had waited in the sapper's trench, but the ground had been filled in. I could see Perrio in the distance trudging disconsolately toward our boarding house. So strange to see a neighborhood growing where armies had once waged war. It seemed like another lifetime since I rode to Tyre in borrowed armor with a dwarf by my side and a stolen supply convoy driven by children.

Tyre.

It was two days' journey to Tyre.

I stood up with a jolt.

I paced the room, adding things up, testing the theory for flaws, but I kept coming back to the same conclusion.

The information that sent Scarlet and Henry out that window didn't come from Mary.

It came from me.

I rushed down the stairs, then found my way to the Queen's chambers. I knocked respectfully on the door. Her maid opened it, expecting somebody, but was surprised and distressed to see a fool standing before her.

"Go away," she whispered.

"I would like to pay my respects to the Queen," I said quickly.

"This is not the time," she snapped.

"Please," I said. "Tell her it's Droignon. Tell her I have a message for her from Scarlet."

She was puzzled, but she turned without telling me to go away. I waited, and a short time later, she opened the door and reluctantly bade me enter.

Isabelle lay upon her bed, sobbing. Only the one maid was attending her, and the children were nowhere in evidence.

"Monsieur Droignon is here, milady," whispered the maid.

I sat by her bed and took her hand in mine as the maid gasped in shock.

"Good lady, you weep," I said.

"Yes," she cried.

"Why do you mourn?" I asked.

Her maid looked at me in horror. The Queen sat up, clutching a silk handkerchief which she used ineffectually to dab at her tears.

"Fool, I mourn my husband's death," she said bitterly.

"I see you weep, and I believe that you mourn," I said. "But not, I think, for your husband."

Isabelle looked at me in shock.

"Milady, I apologize for this rude intrusion," said her maid, rising to her feet and heading for the door to summon a guard.

"*Stultorum numerus,*" I said quickly.

"What?" said Isabelle.

"You heard me," I said.

She looked at me, then nodded slowly.

"Bess, leave us," she called suddenly.

Well, of all the shocks this maid experienced during her short exposure to me, this was the greatest. She started to protest, then saw the steely look on her mistress's face. She curtsied quickly and backed out of the room, closing the door behind her. I turned back to the Queen, who had stopped crying.

"Well?" I said.

"*Infinitus est,*" she whispered.

"I thought that was the case," I said. "When did Scarlet recruit you?"

"When I was twelve," she said. "I was so lonely. He was my only real companion. I had learned enough to know that I was in a sham marriage put together for political reasons, and I thought I would be trapped in it forever. Nobody else understood my misery. I asked him to teach me things, and he did. Then, one day, I saw him talking to another jester, and I asked about it. He became secretive, which was not at all like him. I kept at him, and eventually, he told me about the

[259]

Guild. It sounded grand and noble and fun, and I wanted to be a part of it."

"Juggle," I commanded her, reaching into my bag for my clubs. Before I could hand them to her, she reached into a drawer in a table by her bed and took out three of her own. She sent them expertly into the air for a minute.

"Enough, milady," I said. "You pass."

"You mentioned a message from him," she said.

"His last words were of you," I said. " 'Tell Isabelle . . .' he began, but then he saw you. He died with a smile on his lips and your loveliness in his eyes. I think that he meant to say that he loved you."

"I know," she whispered, the tears rolling down her cheeks again. "And I loved him."

"Too bad about those rules forbidding marriage between the nobility and the serving class," I said, a bit harshly.

She looked up, stung.

"I had no choice!" she cried.

"Neither did he," I said. "Here. Read this."

I tossed her the note he had left on the tower. She read it, and I watched her face carefully. Her expression was an attempt to look shocked, but there was a palpable sense of relief underlying it.

"I don't know what to say," she said. "I cannot believe it."

"Neither can I, unfortunately," I said.

"But Henry was planning the Crusade," said Isabelle, looking at me. "He told me so himself."

"Oh, that may be true enough," I replied. "But it's not why Scarlet killed him."

"Why, then?" asked the Queen.

"He did it for you," I said.

"What?" she cried in outrage. "How dare you!"

"Please, hear me out, milady," I said, holding up my hand. "He may very well have had good reason to do this. I now believe that Henry was the man who instigated the murder of Conrad."

The outrage vanished. "Whence comes this belief?" she asked me carefully.

"From nothing that would hang a man in court," I said. "But from a small handful of circumstances that all point in that direction. Your husband, your previous husband, I should say, was killed by a pair of men named Leo and Balthazar. They were recruited, or perhaps threatened, into becoming the henchmen of one of the Falconberg brothers. We learned this from Balthazar's widow, Mary. Her sister, who was killed near the tent city outside Tyre, had lived in Tiberias. I suspect that she learned of Leo's connection to the brother, and possibly of the connection to Henry later on, but we'll never know for certain."

"Which of the brothers?" asked Isabelle.

"Which did Scarlet pick?" I responded. She refused to take the bait. "Very well, milady. I believe that it was William. When Henry arrived in Tyre to speak with your husband, William Falconberg made a public display of introducing himself to Henry and greeting him as if for the first time. But I had seen William speaking to Henry on quite familiar terms before that, right here in Acre. William is not a smart man. He felt it necessary to establish that he had no connection to Henry when in fact he did. And that is suspicious.

"I think that it was my casual mention of that to Scarlet last week that set him on his fatal path. It started him thinking about Henry and William just as I did today. And he remembered something that we all failed to notice at the time of Conrad's death, thanks to the general shock and confusion of the event."

"What was that, Fool?" she asked.

"That it takes two days to travel from Acre to Tyre," I said. "Even at the gallop with a change of horses. Henry left two days before Conrad's death, supposedly to rejoin Richard. *Yet he showed up in Tyre the morning after!* If he had received the news by messenger during the normal course of events, it would have been at least four days after Conrad's death before he would have shown up. Yet in he marched, all dressed up and with the support of the French army, ready for marriage to you with your husband's body still cooling in the vault. How could that have happened unless he knew in advance that Conrad was going to die? Henry made a show of departing, but didn't go anywhere. He hid out nearby and waited."

"How could he be sure that Leo and Balthazar wouldn't talk?" she asked.

"Because of the Falconbergs," I said. "William probably told Leo and Balthazar that the other brothers were in on it with him. And Ralph may have been, although I think that he merely figured out what his brother was doing and decided to let events play out. He's too smart to let anyone tie anything to him. But Hugh was never told, and that leads me to one other instance: When Leo and Balthazar killed Conrad, Hugh responded by cutting down Leo. And Balthazar was visibly shocked by that. He could only have been surprised by that if he had been expecting all the Falconbergs would protect them, and that Hugh's position as the King's escort was part of the plan. Perhaps he had been led to believe that the murder was part of a larger, general revolt against Conrad, and it was only when Leo was killed that he realized that he had been betrayed."

"But why didn't he confess?" asked Isabelle.

"You know the answer as well as I, milady. Because his captor was Ralph Falconberg, and that's when the false story about them being Assassins began. Whether Ralph was in on it from the start, or whether he did it to protect his brother, only he can say. But after that, Henry had the crown and you, and the Falconbergs all came along for the ride."

"If what you say is true," she said slowly, "then Henry deserved to die."

"Maybe," I said. "But Scarlet didn't."

"I didn't know that he would take his own life," she said, the tears flowing anew. "You're right. He did figure all of this out, and he came to me. I learned that the man I thought married me for love had only done so out of ambition, just as I had learned too late that the man who I thought married me out of ambition truly loved me."

"I am sorry for it, Isabelle," I said.

"I couldn't live with him after knowing this," she said. "Knowing that the man who came to my bed every night had killed my husband for that privilege. I would have gone mad."

"So Scarlet saved you," I said.

"He said he would take care of everything," she said. "I won't pretend that I didn't know what that meant. But I never knew that he would kill himself as well."

"How could he do anything but that?" I shouted, and she cowered against the headboard. "You knew him better than anyone. You knew how he abhorred killing. Do you think that he could have lived another moment with you, knowing that he had violated his most sacred precept and did it at the behest of the woman he loved above all else? Every intimacy, every memory of the two of you would forever have been tainted by this act. Every day in your presence would have eaten away at him. Believe me, lady, he had no other choice. Death was a mercy."

"What else could I have done?" she whispered.

"You could have killed the man yourself," I said. "Poisoned him, got him drunk and then shoved him out a window to look like an accident, done it a dozen different ways, and let Scarlet think no less of you for it. But you let him die for you, Isabelle."

"What will you do?" she asked fearfully. "Denounce me? Take vengeance upon me?"

I looked at her, clutching a cushion to her stomach and rocking like a little girl. I wondered if that's how she spent her first wedding night.

[263]

"No, lady," I said softly. "Scarlet taught the children not to kill. I taught them to shun vengeance. I know all too well where it can lead."

"Then what shall I do?" she said. "Call upon my oath to the Guild. Command me, Fool. Name what penance I must pay."

"Let me think," I said, and I sat with my legs crossed on the bed, leaning back for a minute. "Very well. You must rule as Queen of Jerusalem. That is your role and your punishment. Remove the Falconbergs from any position of influence. Scarlet trusted Balian. You do the same."

"Is that all?" she asked.

"It is a heavy burden as it is," I said. "But there's more. There will be pressure upon you to remarry." She turned pale and looked down. "Resist it. There is no urgency. Take the normal period of mourning this time. Reach out to Al-Adil and make peace, and give the Pisans their quarter in exchange for their loyalty. A grieving young widow should appeal even to their shriveled sense of chivalry.

"And, if I could put my two mites in, should you consider marrying again, there is a man I could suggest."

"Who, Fool?" she said in surprise.

"Amaury of Lusignan," I said. "His boys are already betrothed to your daughters, and he is to be a king in his own right, so he will stand before you as an equal. Cyprus would be a valuable ally as well, being so close. But more importantly, he would be something in a husband you haven't had before."

"What is that, Fool?" she asked.

"A good man," I replied.

She sat there, thinking. Slowly, her arms relaxed their grip on the cushion, which slid to the floor.

"I suppose it would suit the Guild's purposes to have me marry him," she said.

"I have no idea," I said. "Perhaps. But I think Scarlet would have approved of him."

"Very well, then," she said. "For the Guild."

"If you like," I said.

"Will you stay on as my new fool?" she asked suddenly.

"No," I said. "But Perrio will. He was one of Scarlet's best pupils. Speaking of which, how did Scarlet manage to afford to send all of them to the Guildhall?"

"An anonymous benefactor," she replied, smiling for the first time.

"I thought as much," I said.

TWENTY

By Chivalries as tiny,
A Blossom, or a Book,
The seeds of smiles are planted—
Which blossom in the dark.

—EMILY DICKINSON

Innsbruck was two days behind us. The baby was sleeping, and Claudia was gazing into the distance as we rode west.

"Was he buried in his motley?" she asked softly.

"He was," I replied. "At the feet of Henry of Champagne."

"What?" she exclaimed. "Good heavens, why?"

"Everyone had heard of the valiant efforts of the dwarf to save his master, and how he had died in the attempt. There was a great clamoring to continue this touching loyalty in the grave, so they were buried together at the Church of the Holy Cross. Or so the story goes."

"How sad," she said.

"Not really," I said. "There was another reason they were buried together. The real reason, in fact. Each day, Isabelle would come to the church, sit by the gravesite, and weep. The whole kingdom spoke of her devotion to her husband. Few knew that the man she wept for every day was Scarlet."

"Oh," she said. "Then I'm glad it was arranged so. How long did you stay on?"

"Not long," I said. "I set up Perrio in the castellum, then sailed back to Cyprus to speak with Lepos. He saw the merit of my idea and agreed to work on Amaury. From there, I went straight back to the Guildhall."

"You left Acre without doing anything about William?" she exclaimed.

"Oh, well, we did do a little something," I said. "Perrio and I waited for him one night when he had been drinking too much. We hit him over the head, then stuck him inside a burlap sack and carried him off to a deserted stable outside of the city. When he woke up, he was bound and blindfolded. Using voices other than our own, we advised him in no uncertain terms that the Queen was well aware of his treachery, and that only her respect for his family prevented her from having him gutted like a fish. We mentioned that that respect was of limited duration. Then we left him there. When he finally escaped, he did what he usually did when confronted with a real threat. He fled."

"I am glad to hear it." she said. "And the sign?"

"The last thing I did before I left Acre was to get that done by a court painter who knew Scarlet. He caught his likeness well, I thought. Not the servant, but the master fool. When I got back to the Guildhall, I went straight to the tavern, which used to be called the Dancing Pig, and bought everyone a round. Then I gave the sign to the barkeep and told him that the drinks had come from Scarlet, and that the Guild wanted to change the tavern name in his honor. No one had been very fond of the Dancing Pig anyway, so the change was welcome. Ever since then, Scarlet has been watching over the rest of us. And whenever I run into one of his pupils, he or she drinks on my coin."

She leaned over to the mule and pulled the sign out of the saddle bag. She looked at the merry face of the dwarf, then put it back.

"I would have liked to have met him," she said. "I'm glad that we reclaimed the sign."

"Thank you, Duchess," I said.

"But I think that you were too harsh on Isabelle," she said.

"I thought I was too easy," I said.

"She was trapped," said Claudia. "Everyone told her to marry Henry. Even Scarlet, and I'm sure that must have torn at him as much as anything when he discovered the truth. To say that she should have committed the act rather than let Scarlet do it is easy, but not everyone has what it takes to kill someone. Not everyone is like you and me."

"True, but . . ."

"Scarlet taught her to be a fool like himself," she said. "How could he then expect her to turn against those teachings and kill Henry? But if he lived on, she would have gone mad, or even died of heartsickness. Scarlet did what he had to do, what he always did. He took care of her."

"And in doing so, left her to take care of herself."

"It was about time that she did so, I think," said Claudia. "And you and Perrio were there to help her through it. Maybe seeing how capable Perrio had become gave Scarlet the will to leave Isabelle, knowing that another fool could take his place by her side. Is Perrio still there?"

"He is indeed," I said. "He was a good choice for her, for he knew the truth and she couldn't charm him. She waited a full year after Henry's death, a proper mourning this time, while Ralph Falconberg dogged her footsteps, hoping. Then she reached out to Amaury, and they wed. Amaury negotiated a truce with Al-Adil that has continued to this day, Lepos joined Perrio, and the royal children run through Acre like children should, unaware that they have all been committed to each other for life. Isabelle has had two more daughters with Amaury, I hear."

"And is she happy?" wondered Claudia.

"That never gets mentioned in the reports," I said.

Claudia looked down at our sleeping daughter.

"Will Portia be a fool?" she asked abruptly.

"I suppose so," I said. "I really haven't thought about it."

"Will she learn to kill, as we have?" asked Claudia.

"What else can she do?" I said. "You left the nobility to join the Guild. You can't go back again just to make her a lady."

"No," she said. "But there must be another way. I don't want her to be a killer. I don't want her to be a fool."

"Not all fools kill," I said. "Some merely entertain and send reports back to the Guild."

"But she's our daughter," said Claudia. "If we let her become a fool, you know that she will be just like us. I want a better life for her than that."

"Shall we find her a nice stolid shopkeeper to marry someday?"

"Stop it," she said. "All that I am saying is that I fully expect our child to be remarkable. I want her to have a life equal to her abilities."

"We'll think of something, Duchess," I assured her. "In the meanwhile . . ."

"Look," she said suddenly, pointing ahead.

In the distance, as the sun began to set, a band of pilgrims was setting up camp by the side of the road, singing as they did so.

The singing was extraordinarily good.

The people nearest to us as we approached looked us over carefully, then one of them suddenly shouted, "Theo!"

"Theo! It's Theo, and his wife," some others called, and soon we were swarmed by fools without motley. Many faces I recognized, but even more hopefully, many I did not, for they were young and new. The novitiates had stuck with the Guild despite the current state of emergency, and many of them looked at us with awe as the older ones quickly whispered our story to them.

Brother Dennis, the Guild ostler, came striding through the pack to lift me off Zeus and squeeze me until I cracked.

"By David's lyre, you made it," he laughed. "And you and Zeus managed not to kill each other. Hello, old friend."

"Hello to you," I replied, but then I saw that he was greeting my horse.

Brother Timothy, Father Gerald's second in command and the Guild juggling instructor, came up, an uncharacteristic grin on his weathered face.

"Theo, Claudia, welcome home," he said. He held his arms out to Claudia and took the baby from her, then helped her off her horse. "I hope you have some money left," he muttered to me. "It's a costly journey when we travel as mere mortals and can't earn our way."

"We have some," I said. "Where's Father Gerald?"

"That wagon over there," he said. "I'll take you."

Brother Dennis took our horses and a team of children carried our bags behind us as we went to greet the oldest man any of us had ever known. He sat on the rear of a wagon, reclining against sacks of flour, bundled in an old brown blanket, staring blankly into space. But his hearing was still sharp, for he turned in our direction immediately when we neared him.

"Who has arrived, Brother Timothy?" he called.

"An old friend," replied Timothy. "Come and greet him."

Father Gerald slipped carefully off the wagon and tottered in my direction.

"Speak, Fool, that I may recognize you," he commanded.

"Hello, Father," I said.

"Theo?" he said, his face creasing into a thousand smiles. He stepped toward me and hugged me hard. "Praise the First Fool, Our Savior! You have returned safely."

"I promised that I would," I said. "And you promised that you would be alive when I got back."

"Then thank God that we are both men of honor," he laughed. "Is this your wife?"

"Hello, Father," said Claudia, a bit nervously.

"My dear, welcome home," he said fervently, taking her hands in his. "We have not settled into our haven yet, but when we do, we shall give you a proper welcome to the Guild. And where is this baby that I heard about?"

"Here she is, Father," said Brother Timothy.

"Let me hold her," said Father Gerald. He took Portia carefully, then gently ran his fingers across her face. "Ah, she's a good one," he said softly. "A child of Theophilos in the world at last. A great event, in my opinion."

"Thank you, Father," said Claudia as he handed her back.

"Well, Theo, we're living in strange days," said Father Gerald. "But they always are, aren't they? We'll have the Guild going again in no time."

"I am sure of it, Father," I said. "I volunteer to help build the new tavern."

He laughed, then turned somber.

"That reminds me," he said. "I have to apologize to you. The one thing we forgot in our haste to evacuate was that sign you brought back from Acre. I know how much . . . what, what is it?"

The older fools were chuckling as I held my finger to my lips and the sign over my head.

Father Gerald could still glare even though blind, but they just laughed harder.

"You've got the sign, haven't you?" he said accusingly.

"I have, Father."

He shook his head.

"You're as hotheaded as you ever were," he said. "One would think that having a wife would temper you."

"As a matter of fact, I helped him get it," said Claudia.

"Oh, my," said Father Gerald, shaking his head in dismay. "You've found the perfect mate, lad. What mischief will this baby get into when it learns to walk?"

"Supper is on," called someone, and we walked together to the cooking fires.

"Excuse me, Father?" piped up one of the younger novitiates. "Why is that sign so important?"

"Well, I don't know that I am the proper one to tell that story," replied Father Gerald. "Theo is the one who knows it best."

I glanced over at Claudia, who was seated on a blanket, nursing Portia. She smiled up at me and nodded her head.

"It's a long story," I said.

"We have a ways to go before we reach the haven," said Father Gerald. "You might as well."

"Tell it! Please!" cried the children.

"All right," I said. "It was in the summer of 1191, after the recapture of Acre by the Crusaders, that I first met a dwarf called Scarlet. It was a day filled with screams. . . ."

HISTORICAL NOTE

History, n. An account mostly false, of events mostly unimportant, which are brought about by rulers mostly knaves, and soldiers mostly fools.

—AMBROSE BIERCE, *THE DEVIL'S DICTIONARY*

Until the discovery and translation of this manuscript, the latest in a series of chronicles preserved at an abbey in western Ireland, the full tale of Queen Isabelle of Jerusalem and Scarlet the Dwarf had never been revealed. Isabelle, in the various histories of the Third Crusade both contemporaneous and modern, had been relegated to a position and a series of marriages to secure that position, with nothing about her actual character except that she was both beautiful and *gente*, a description attributed to Henry of Champagne, perhaps spuriously.

It is worth noting that these histories have been written by men, with more attention paid to events than to personalities, and more to the personalities of men than to those of women. One must therefore take the following comments of Runciman with a grain of salt: "Alone of the ladies of the Royal House of Jerusalem she is a shadowy figure of whose personality nothing has survived. Her marriage and her very existence were of high importance. Had she held political ambitions she could have been a power in the land; but she let herself be passed from husband to husband without consideration of her personal wishes. We know that she was beautiful; but we must conclude that she was feckless and weak." Given her age and the circumstances surrounding the first two marriages, it is hardly fair to judge her for not asserting any ambitions. In fact, the very lack of assertion may have been a valid choice. Her reported behavior after Conrad's death certainly demonstrated her political savvy and grasp of a potentially desperate situation, and her subsequent decision to marry Henry helped to consolidate the bickering forces of the diminishing Crusade and secure the peace treaty with Saladin. Her behavior after Henry's death seems exemplary, and her marriage to Amaury appears to have been her choice, rather than a "passing on," especially given the local pressure to take Ralph Falconberg as her husband instead.

The only previous historical reference found to Scarlet was in *The Chronicle of Ernoul and the Continuations of William of Tyre*, one of the contemporaneous—or at least near contemporaneous—accounts of the era. He is mentioned solely in connection with the death of Henry of Champagne, and even here the sources are confusing. There are three differing accounts of the event, found in what have been designated as the C, D, and E manuscripts of the chronicle. In one, Henry falls through an unbarred window while meeting a delegation of Pisans, Scarlet clinging to him. Both are killed. In a second, Henry leans on the bars while reviewing his troops. The bars give way, he falls, and Scarlet throws himself after him in grief. Had the dwarf not done so, Henry might have survived, but Scarlet landed on him. In the third, Scarlet was his valet and was holding Henry's towel when the latter fell through an unbarred window, dragging the dwarf with him. In this version, Scarlet survived. Ironically, Henry had previously ordered that the window have bars installed, concerned as he was that children played near it.

The motives for the killing of Conrad of Montferrat have long been a mystery. The historians of the time generally blamed the Assassins, but modern historians tend to doubt that theory. Conrad was known to be opposed to Richard and was therefore more likely to be favored by the locals. The killers had been in Tyre long before the seizure of

Sinan's ships, and the timing of the killing, just two days after Conrad's election to the throne by the council of barons, suggests strongly that the two events were related, as has now been confirmed by Theophilos's account.

We also learn from this that Theophilos was one of the sources for *L'Estoire de Guerre Saint*, the poetic recounting of Richard's travels by the jongleur Ambroise. This also seems to be in turn the source of the *Itinerarium Pereginorum et Gesta Regis Ricardi*, the Latin prose translation. Ambroise's account is noticeable for its near deification of King Richard, a feeling clearly not shared by Theophilos.

The troubadour Blondel pops up in the stories of Richard's capture by the German Emperor while returning from the Holy Land. According to legend, Blondel located the missing king by serenading the castle in which he was imprisoned. Richard responded by singing the next verse, and Blondel helped negotiate his ransom. Richard, of course, died a few years later from a crossbow bolt.

The truce negotiated by Amaury lasted, with the occasional minor interruption, for several years. Amaury ruled Cyprus and Jerusalem wisely, by all accounts, setting up a written constitution in Cyprus that consolidated the power of the monarchy. Of the arranged marriages of the children of Amaury and Isabelle, only one came to fruition due to the early deaths of two of Amaury's boys. However, that marriage, between the eventual King Henry I of Cyprus and Alice of Champagne, led to the Lusignan dynasty that was to last in Cyprus for over two centuries, longer in fact than the existence of the European rule in the Holy Land.

Amaury survived one assassination attempt, suspected to be the work of Ralph Falconberg. Ralph escaped responsibility once again, but prudently decided to leave for Tripoli. Hugh Falconberg was last seen heading for Constantinople to seek his fortune after it fell to the armies of the Fourth Crusade, and William seems to have vanished.

Amaury did not last as long as the truce he had arranged. He died in 1205, and Isabelle reportedly died soon after. The crown of Jerusalem passed to Marie of Montferrat, the daughter of Conrad and Isabelle.

She was thirteen years old.